SPECIAL MESSAGE TO READERS

This book is published under the auspices of

THE ULVERSCROFT FOUNDATION

(registered charity No. 264873 UK)

Established in 1972 to provide funds for research, diagnosis and treatment of eye diseases. Examples of contributions made are: —

A Children's Assessment Unit at Moorfield's Hospital, London.

•

Twin operating theatres at the Western Ophthalmic Hospital, London.

•

A Chair of Ophthalmology at the Royal Australian College of Ophthalmologists.

•

The Ulverscroft Children's Eye Unit at the Great Ormond Street Hospital For Sick Children, London.

You can help further the work of the Foundation by making a donation or leaving a legacy. Every contribution, no matter how small, is received with gratitude. Please write for details to:

THE ULVERSCROFT FOUNDATION,
The Green, Bradgate Road, Anstey,
Leicester LE7 7FU, England.
Telephone: (0116) 236 4325

In Australia write to:
THE ULVERSCROFT FOUNDATION,
c/o The Royal Australian and New Zealand College of Ophthalmologists,
94-98 Chalmers Street, Surry Hills,
N.S.W. 2010, Australia

Norman Russell was born in Lancashire but has lived most of his life in Liverpool. After graduating from Jesus College, Oxford, he served a term in the army in Jamaica and the Bahamas. Returning to study for a Diploma in Education, he was later awarded the degree of Doctor of Philosophy. He now writes full-time.

WEB OF DISCORD

Set in the Victorian era, the sequel to *The Hansa Protocol.* Returning from a court appearance, Detective Inspector Box finds himself investigating the violent death of Sir John Courteline, the great philanthropist. It looks like an act of private revenge, but Box soon uncovers a widespread conspiracy. Pursuing the killer's trail of signature deaths across London and Cornwall, Box's investigation finally leads him to the bleak wilderness of Eastern Prussia, where the scene is set for an awesome final confrontation.

Books by Norman Russell
Published by The House of Ulverscroft:

THE DRIED-UP MAN
THE DARK KINGDOM
THE HANSA PROTOCOL

NORMAN RUSSELL

WEB OF DISCORD

Complete and Unabridged

ULVERSCROFT
Leicester

First published in Great Britain in 2004 by
Robert Hale Limited
London

First Large Print Edition
published 2006
by arrangement with
Robert Hale Limited
London

British Library CIP Data

Russell, Norman
Web of discord.—Large print ed.—
Ulverscroft large print series: adventure & suspense
1. Murder—Investigation—England—London—
History—19th century—Fiction 2. London
(England) —History—19th century—Fiction
3. Detective and mystery stories 4. Large type books
I. Title
823.9′14 [F]

ISBN 1–84617–141–5

Published by
F. A. Thorpe (Publishing)
Anstey, Leicestershire

Set by Words & Graphics Ltd.
Anstey, Leicestershire
Printed and bound in Great Britain by
T. J. International Ltd., Padstow, Cornwall

This book is printed on acid-free paper

Contents

Prologue

Incident at Porthcurno, 25 January 1893

Captain Edgar Adams RN closed his brass telescope with a decisive snap, and thrust it into one of the capacious pockets of his regulation greatcoat. His two companions, well wrapped up against the rigours of the Cornish winter, made as if to retrace their steps up the steep path from the sheltered sandy beach, but Adams remained impassive, staring out thoughtfully across the choppy, sullen waters of the Atlantic Ocean.

'Well, Mr Pascoe,' he said at length, 'your surmise was correct. It's a Russian vessel right enough, an ocean-going steamer of 1870s vintage, low at the stern, suggesting cable drums in the aft holds. It's a cable layer, or cable repair vessel. And it's got no business to be lurking here, off Porthcurno.'

Captain Edgar Adams was a lithe, energetic man in his early forties, with a firm mouth and bright grey eyes. His black hair was beginning to show a hint of grey at the temples, and his clean-shaven face was bronzed from long exposure to sun and wind. He had addressed his words to a young man whom he judged to be no more than twenty-five. Pascoe was wearing a light-brown tweed overcoat with matching cap, and looked alertly at the world through gold-rimmed pince-nez, secured by a black ribbon.

'No business whatever,' observed the third man, an elderly, bearded gentleman enveloped in a long astrakhan coat. He wore a tall silk hat, and had encased his hands in rather incongruous black woollen gloves. 'It was very enterprising of Pascoe here to telegraph direct to me at Winchester House. Pascoe, as I think you know, is the chief cipher clerk at Porthcurno. Well done, young man! Now, can we please get back to the cable station before we all perish from the cold?'

'By all means, Mr Dangerfield,' said Captain Adams. 'There's nothing more to be learned here.'

It had been snowing for most of the previous week, and the dismal landscape was pocked with unsightly scabs of half-frozen snow. Mr Dangerfield, one of the directors of the Eastern Telegraph Company, hated snow, and had no great love for Cornwall. It was far too remote from his comfortable panelled office in Old Broad Street. People like Adams were used to all kinds of weather, and young fellows like Pascoe could endure anything within reason.

Still, it had been worth the long drag down from London. It had been prudent of him to alert the Foreign Office to the possibility of skulduggery. It was almost inevitable that some mystery-man like this Captain Adams should have turned up from Whitehall to accompany him down to Porthcurno. It would all make an interesting tale to tell old Sir John Pender, the chairman, when he returned to London.

The three men began the upward climb through the stunted vegetation and masses of storm-weathered rock flanking the winding path from the beach. After a while they reached the Eastern Telegraph Company's settlement and cable station at Porthcurno, an impressive pile of buildings rising in what was virtually a wilderness. The company's house flag flew proudly from a pole near a snow-spattered tennis court. Young Mr Pascoe, the chief cipher clerk, unconsciously assumed command, leading the other two men through the high-ceilinged instrument room, where various machines, gleaming in brass and mahogany, clicked and clattered under the charge of a team of other earnest young men. He opened the door of a little inner sanctum, and Captain Adams prepared to hear the so far hidden details of the incident at Porthcurno.

* * *

'I suppose 'incident' is too strong a word to use,' said Mr Dangerfield. He had retained his heavy greatcoat, and stood near the blazing fire, holding his silk hat by its brim. 'But that Russian ship has been lurking four miles off the Cornish coast for three days, and as you observed earlier, it has no business to be near a sensitive area such as this.'

William Pascoe had sat down on an upright Windsor chair, and proceeded to drape himself in long ribbons of paper telegraph tape. He glanced at the director over his gold pince-nez.

'With respect, Mr Dangerfield,' he said, 'it's not the presence of that ship that constitutes the incident; it's what happened to these transmissions that came through from the Scilly Islands cable after that ship had appeared. On the morning of the twenty-fifth, to be exact.'

'Quite so. Well, I'll leave the two of you alone to talk about it. I shall go along to the mess. I fancy a bite to eat after that cold traipse down to the cove. And perhaps a glass of something, if they've got it. Tell Captain

Adams all about those transmissions. I'll see you both later.'

Mr Dangerfield dragged himself away from the blazing fire in the little office, and went out into the instrument room, closing the door behind him. Young Pascoe smiled. Dangerfield wasn't such a bad old stick, all things considered.

'Captain Adams,' said Pascoe, 'the messages relayed through the submarine cable from Scilly are received in cable Morse, which is printed out on these long strips of paper. This particular batch of signals was sent from the cable station on the isle of St Mary's. They're business communications from Abraham & Company, the marine victuallers on Tresco.'

Pascoe picked up the long paper streamer, and passed it slowly through his fingers. Adams noted the printed Morse characters, signs that needed a skilled reader to interpret. He watched as Pascoe paused at a stage where half the long streamer was lying in a rough curl at the side of his chair. This young fellow evidently excelled at his work, which accounted for his senior position at Porthcurno.

'It was at this point, Captain Adams,' Pascoe was saying, 'that the business messages suddenly stopped. Eleven forty-seven on the morning of Wednesday, the twenty-fifth of January — just a week ago. For nearly half an hour the engines disgorged gibberish. Then, as suddenly as it had started, the gibberish ended, and the business messages resumed.'

Pascoe reached across to the table behind his chair, and picked up a cloth-bound notebook, which he handed to Adams.

'I translated all the messages for that morning into straight English, and wrote them down in this book. I've also transliterated the gibberish. I call it that because I don't understand it. Wiser heads may be more successful.'

Captain Adams looked at the eager young employee of the Eastern Telegraph Company. We could do with a fellow like him on the edges of our concern, he thought. He evidently thinks the way we think. But would he have the skills to survive at the age of twenty-five? Ability needed to be matched by experience.

He said aloud, 'What happens to these messages after you've received them here?'

'They're taken up to Penzance, and relayed by telegraph to London. We have a special arrangement with the Post Office to use their London wire.'

Adams opened the notebook, and began to read. The first part of Pascoe's transcription recorded detailed requests for information from various London ships' chandlers and mercantile grocers. These ended after nine pages, and Pascoe had written in bold handwriting, 'The gibberish starts here.'

Adams started to read silently, and then aloud, his voice becoming more confident as he progressed.

'You've transliterated the Morse very cleverly, Mr Pascoe,' he said, 'so cleverly, in fact, that I can recognize the words as Russian. So from — what time did you say? — eleven forty-seven, on the twenty-fifth last, someone managed to stop the signals from St Mary's, and replace them with this outpouring of Russian — '

'Splicing!' cried Pascoe excitedly. 'That Russian ship out there will have the necessary gear to lift the cable, and make a splice to a transmitting apparatus of their own! It must have been a kind of test, because after a while the business messages resumed.'

Captain Adams had flicked through the remaining pages of the notebook, and saw where Pascoe had written, '12.12 p.m. St Mary's station signals resumed.' There followed a faithful rendering of Messrs Abraham & Company's requests for ship's provisions.

'A test? You may well be right, Mr Pascoe.

But a test of what? That is the question.'

'What did the Russian message say?' asked Pascoe impatiently. 'Is there any clue there?'

Captain Adams smiled, and shook his head.

'Not at the moment, Mr Pascoe. This screed of Russian is nothing more or less than a long quotation from a novel by Nikolai Gogol. It's called *Dead Souls*.'

'There you are, then, sir! It was a test — a test to see if their illicit splice had worked. *Dead Souls*? That sounds very sinister. Is it a gloomy sort of book?'

'As a matter of fact, Mr Pascoe, it's a very funny book, if you understand the Russian sense of humour.'

That statement, he thought, was true enough, and it was a fair answer to the excellent young man's question. But it was only true on the surface. He had seen things on this visit that it would not have been prudent to mention to these good folk at Porthcurno. That ship . . . It would not stay long, now, of that he was sure. They would have learnt very quickly that he was down there in Cornwall. But if ever he saw it again, he'd know it well enough, and not just as a sinister shape anchored near the horizon. For he had often pored over the shipbuilder's original plans of the *Lermontov*, so that he could now picture it as a familiar berth, where he could walk sure-footed on the mess deck, in the cabins, in the hot, thudding engine room, and in the great cold spaces of the cable tanks in the hold. It was part of his vocation to know such things.

And the message, that block of Russian text from Gogol, what did that portend? Well, taken in conjunction with the splicing, and with several other things he'd noticed, it meant devilry. He would leave Porthcurno that very day. No time was to be lost.

⋆ ⋆ ⋆

An elderly porter clad in the livery of the Great Western Railway held open the door of a carriage, and Captain Adams climbed into the long train that would convey him the 300 miles and more from Penzance to London. The porter had led him to that particular carriage, so that Adams was not surprised to find that the compartment was already occupied. He knew the mild, sandy-haired man who sat there, a copy of *The Times* spread out across his knees. The man smiled at him almost apologetically.

'Well, Adams,' he said, 'what did you think of it all?'

'I think there's something very sinister

afoot,' said Adams. 'Dangerfield and Pascoe took me down to the cove at Porthcurno, and I had a good look at the ship. It was the old screw steamer *Lermontov*, which was fitted out as a cable-ship eight or more years ago. I know it well. It was used as an interceptor vessel by the Imperial Russian Marine. After that — '

'Did you tell the Porthcurno people that it was the *Lermontov*?'

'Well, no; but I was happy to confirm their guess that it was a Russian ship. Incidentally, Dangerfield is staying on at the cable station for a few days, which is why he's not with me now. Just as well, I suppose. He'd have wanted to travel back to London with me.'

'The *Lermontov*? Well, well. He was a poet, you know. *Lermontov*, I mean. It's not a genuine Russian name. He was descended from a Scotsman called George Learmonth. Anything else?'

Captain Adams smiled. His companion had evidently been looking up various names in an encyclopaedia. That fact told him that the sandy-haired man had already known the identity of the mysterious ship. That, of course, came as no surprise.

'Anything else, you ask? Yes, there was. At such-and-such a time on Wednesday, the twenty-fifth of this month, the people on the

Lermontov lifted the Scilly Islands cable, spliced into it, and delivered a stream of Russian, which was read at the Porthcurno cable station as cable Morse. It consisted of a string of paragraphs from Gogol's *Dead Souls*.'

The sandy-haired man drew the skirts of his heavy serge cloak about his knees. He uttered a stifled sound, which might have been a sigh, or a sardonic laugh, cut off in mid-utterance.

'Well, Adams,' he said, 'I agree with you that this may prove to be a very sinister business. There's a richly Slavonic flavour about all this that I very much fear means mischief. That business of *Dead Souls* . . . . Very suggestive, don't you think?'

'I do. Either the crew of the *Lermontov* are of a literary turn of mind, or — well, you can imagine the alternative. It was a rehearsal, but for what? It's time for me to disappear from the quarter-deck, and take my luck in a hammock once again. It was a rehearsal — but it was more than that. The only way to find out what it means is for me to run with the pack.'

'I assume you'll let Admiral Holland know? As head of Naval Intelligence he'll want to know where you've gone.'

'Oh, yes, I'll let him know. But for the near

future, I'm entirely at your service.'

'I wish you well,' said his companion. 'Meanwhile, I'll keep my ears open for interesting rumours.'

'You have many ears, haven't you?'

'I have. And many eyes, too. I wish you God speed, Captain Adams.'

A couple of minutes later the train glided out of Penzance Station.

* * *

Early the following morning, the Russian cable-ship upped anchor, and steamed rapidly away from the Cornish coast. Young William Pascoe stood on the headland, watching it as it sailed towards the horizon. He wondered what dangers it had brought in its wake when it had first anchored offshore. To the outsider, the quiet sandy beach at Porthcurno would seem to be little more than a picturesque home for the mournfully crying sea-birds wheeling above the rocky headland. But beneath the sand of the shore lay buried the great network of cables that made Porthcurno the nerve centre of the Empire. Destroy them, and Britain would become suddenly blind and deaf to the doings of the great world beyond its shores. Captain Adams, no doubt, would set various chains of action into motion. But was there anything that he, William Pascoe, could do? Yes, but he would have to be careful and discreet. Russia, he thought ruefully, once roused to anger, would make a formidable adversary. Yes, it would be more prudent to watch and wait — but prudence was something for older men to exercise. A young man was entitled to take risks.

1

Death of the Poor Man's Friend

Detective Inspector Arnold Box shifted his position on the hard pine bench, and wished that he was back in his dilapidated but cosy office in King James's Rents. Police courts always depressed him. They invariably smelt of stale gas, beer and sweat, and the human detritus that filled them formed an exhibition of banal petty crime and drunkenness that never varied. You saw the same kind of weak or brutish faces, and heard the same ugly voices, whining excuses or croaking defiance, whether it was in Marlborough Street, or King's Cross Road, or here, in dismal Tooley Street, on the Surrey side, across the river from Tower Pier.

Box had heard about old Mr Locke, the sitting magistrate. He regarded Tooley Street Police Court as his private fiefdom, relishing his power to discipline and subdue his regular transgressors, at the same time giving the impression that he felt a sense of obligation towards them for providing him with such an interesting way of passing the time. He was a long-faced man, dressed in funereal black. His sparse grey hair was brushed well back from his domed forehead.

Mr Locke had already dismissed three old soaks with a caution, and had turned his attention to an enormous woman clad in a black dress and matching shawl, who stood between two policemen, her brawny arms folded across her chest.

'It says here, Bertha,' observed Mr Locke, 'that you broke several panes of glass in the Eagle public house in St Matthew's Lane, felled the landlord with one blow, and assaulted the police constable who was called to restrain you. Is all that true?'

'It is indeed, Your Honour. You should have seen that landlord hit the floor! Supposed to be the stronger sex, they say; I'm not so sure about that!'

Mr Locke sighed. He fiddled about with some papers on the bench, and then addressed the doughty woman prisoner.

'It strikes me, Bertha,' said Mr Locke, 'that you've gone too far this time. We can't have this type of thing going on. You'll go to prison for three weeks.'

The hefty woman laughed, and glanced round the court, nodding in friendly fashion to some of her neighbours, who rather nervously nodded back.

'Thank you, Your Honour,' said Bertha. 'I could do that standing on my head!'

'Well, perhaps you'd like another three weeks, so that you can do them standing on your feet. Take her away. Next!'

The magistrate's rough audience gave him a rousing cheer, but went quiet when he threatened to turn them all out into the street. The now subdued Bertha was hustled away down the steps beneath the dock.

My man will be next, thought Box. Yes, here he was, stooping and bleary-eyed, with an impassive young constable standing beside him. Poor old John! The court sergeant, an elderly man wearing a tight serge uniform and sporting a patriarchal beard, handed Mr Locke a sheet of paper, which he peered at over his gold wire spectacles.

'John Joseph Martin? Not one of our regulars, I notice. Dear me, you seem to have excelled yourself last night, according to this charge sheet. You became obstreperous — that's what it says here — in the Kentish Man public house in Redcross Street. You were ejected, and proceeded to smash the frosted glass window of the establishment, which I'm told is worth one pound two shillings and sixpence. Is all that true?'

'Yes, sir. I don't rightly know how it happened. Maybe I fell into it. It wasn't done deliberate. I was drunk, you see — '

'Yes, I *do* see. Only too well. It's the drink, my man, that's brought you here in disgrace before me this fine March morning. I don't know what's happening to this country. We seem to be drowning our wits in a sea of liquor. It was a bad night for windows last night, but I expect the glaziers will be happy enough this morning. Now, fortunately, someone's come down to speak for you. Somebody who knew you in better days. Detective Inspector Box, would you care to approach the bench?'

Box was pleased with the effect that his appearance made on the motley crowd sitting on the public benches. It wasn't every day that they saw a Scotland Yarder, a slim man of thirty-five with a neatly clipped moustache, a man who wore a tightly buttoned fawn greatcoat, and sported a curly-brimmed brown bowler hat, tipped forward over his brow in the approved fashion. He always tried to be smart and well turned out. He wasn't vain, of course. Nobody would call him that. And height wasn't everything.

Poor old John Martin . . . He'd worked for nearly thirty years in the stables of the Mounted Branch before retiring. He'd been a decent, dependable man, but a heavy drinker. It was very clear now that he was rapidly losing any self-esteem that might have been left to him. In a year, perhaps two, he would be dead.

When Box had finished his plea for leniency, Mr Locke pronounced judgment.

'It's always sad on these occasions,' he said, 'to have to contemplate a custodial sentence, especially when the defendant is a man of advanced years — seventy-two, in the case of John Joseph Martin. However, the Queen's Peace must be upheld. In your case, Martin, because of the good character given to you by this Scotland Yard officer, I am going to bind you over to keep the peace in the sum of five pounds, to be produced here, within the week. But if this kind of thing happens again, then I'm afraid you'll be locked up. You're free to go. Next!'

* * *

In the cell passage below the court, a seaman sat hunched forward on the dank stone bench, waiting to be called before the magistrate. The broken-down old drunkard who had been sitting on his left, had just stumbled up the steps to the dock. Poor old man! the seaman thought. He'd whispered to him that his name was John Martin, and that he'd once worked for the police. His clothes had been those of the respectable working class, and he'd made some attempt to patch and mend the old, worn garments. He'd reeked of drink, like the rest of them in this dismal hole.

The seaman knew that he'd be next up the stairs. Well, there were only two courses of action open to him. He'd created that row on the previous night solely in order to get himself arrested. If he was fined, and Oldfield was there in the court, then Oldfield would pay the fine and whisk him away to safety. If Oldfield wasn't there, then he'd say he had no money, which was true: he'd posted his pay to Oldfield on the previous night, so that he'd have only a few sovereigns in his pockets when he'd set out to get himself arrested. With no money to pay a fine, the magistrate would lock him up for a few days. Either way, he'd be safe, and within the week someone would be sent to collect him, and take him away.

The enemy had followed him all the way from Königsberg and along the Baltic coast. He thought that he'd thrown them off in Hamburg, but knew that they were still tailing him when he reached Bremen. They would have seen him when he got a berth on the *Berlin Star* at Bremerhaven. No doubt they would have seen him paid off at

Chandler's Wharf, here in good old London. What he had learnt during his month-long investigation beggared belief. It was essential that he now kept himself alive to tell the tale.

That poor old man, John Martin . . . When he got home, he'd find a couple of sovereigns in his pocket — and something else, besides. Would he have the wit to draw a few simple conclusions once he was sober? Could he read? At that moment the seaman's name was called, and the constable took him by the sleeve. He mounted the steps to the dock.

⋆ ⋆ ⋆

Arnold Box was about to follow John Martin out of the court when the next trouble-maker was brought up from the cells. Something about the man caused Box to sit down again. This, surely, was not yet another specimen of the usual police court riff-raff? The prisoner, a lithe, upright man in his early forties, wore the uniform of a merchant seaman. His face was bronzed from long exposure to the elements, but there was nothing about his firm mouth and bright eyes to suggest either a drunk or a reprobate. What could this man have done to land himself in Tooley Street?

'Malcolm Enright, mariner, aged forty-one.' Old Mr Locke paused for what seemed an age, scrutinizing the impassive figure standing before him. 'I must say, Enright, that I'm surprised to see someone of your evidently respectable antecedents in a place like this. It says here that you broke a chair in the Prince Alfred Arms, Unicorn Place — remind me, will you, Sergeant? Unicorn Place.'

'It's just at the end of the street here, sir, near Vine Lane, by the new bridge.'

'Oh, yes. Well, Enright, you've spent the night in our cells, so you've had time to sober up and consider your position. You're still in uniform, I see. You were celebrating a discharge, I take it. What ship were you serving on?'

Box saw how Enright moistened his lips and darted a glance around the court before replying. He's expecting someone, he thought, and that 'someone' hasn't turned up.

'My ship was the *Berlin Star*, cargo steamer, out of Bremerhaven. I was paid off at Chandler's Wharf, and celebrated with a few beers. Maybe they didn't agree with me — '

'Maybe not. In fact, definitely not! And this chair — you didn't break it over someone's head, did you?'

The seaman permitted himself a slight smile. Box watched him, noting the lurking anxiety behind his apparently firm gaze. There was something decidedly odd about this man. Old Mr Locke was right. Enright didn't fit in to Tooley Street.

'No, sir. I didn't hit anyone with the chair. I fell down on it, staggering, like, and it broke. They tried to take the money to pay for it from my pocket. The landlord, and his barman. I knocked their heads together, and threw them out into the street.'

There was a ripple of laughter from the court. Mr Locke turned aside to conceal a smile.

'Quiet! Very well. Now, this kind of thing can't be tolerated, but as this is your first appearance before us, I'm inclined to let you off with a fine. And you're to pay for that chair. You're fined five pounds. Next!'

Box saw the alarm leap up in Enright's eyes. He glanced desperately around the court again.

'I haven't got five pounds — '

'What? Well, in that case, you'll have to serve four days in the cells — *Now* what's the matter?'

The swing door had been hastily pushed open, and a stout man in a black suit bustled into the court. His round face was covered in perspiration. He struggled towards the bench, puffing and panting. Box saw the sailor's shoulders relax with what was clearly relief.

'Your Honour,' gasped the stout man, 'I apologize for my lateness. I intended to be here at the commencement of proceedings, but the traffic on the bridge was horrendous — '

'Who are you?' demanded Mr Locke testily. 'Are you a witness in this case? Have you got a name?'

'Gabriel Oldfield, sir. Chemist and druggist. I heard last night that my poor friend Malcolm Enright had got himself into trouble, and hastened here to provide him with a character. But the traffic on the bridge — '

'Yes, yes. You keep telling me about it. I don't know what you expect me to do. I'm not an engineer. Perhaps next time — if there is a next time — the new Tower Bridge will be open at last, and you can come across on that. Now, your friend Enright has just been fined five pounds, which he says he hasn't got. If he doesn't come up with the money, he'll be sent in the wagon to Southwark Bridewell. It's all the same to me.'

Oldfield was already tugging a bulging wallet from an inside coat pocket. It seemed to be jammed in the silk lining.

'Heave!' cried someone on the public benches. 'Mind the moths!' added someone else, to a shout of laughter.

'Oh, shut up, will you?' cried Locke. 'Any more of that, and I'll clear the court. Now, Oldfield, are you going to pay Enright's fine or not?'

'Yes, sir. I have it here. I'll pay it right away.'

'Very well. Pay it to the court clerk in the office outside. Enright, you're dismissed. Next!'

* * *

Box hailed a cab in Duke Street Hill, and told the cabbie to put him down near the offices of the *Daily Telegraph* in Fleet Street. It was only half past eleven, and he wasn't due back at King James's Rents until two, so there'd be plenty of time for a lunch of bread and cheese in his snug rooms in Cardinal Court, one of a maze of little squares squashed into a rough triangle between Fleet Street and Fetter Lane. The cabbie turned into Borough High Street, and so on to London Bridge.

That man in the court had been right. Traffic on the bridge was nearly at a stand-still, jam-packed with freight-wagons, carts and omnibuses. They'd dug up the road in King William Street to lay a new gas main, and that didn't improve matters . . .

When he had a moment, he'd call on poor John Martin, and see how things were with him. He had a room of his own over a public house near Bermondsey Leather Market. Meanwhile, he'd organize a whip-round among the folk in Whitehall Place to pay his five-pound fine.

The cab broke out of the knot of traffic, crossed Upper Thames Street, and made its way briskly into Cannon Street. It was a bright day, but the sun refused to come out, and was lurking somewhere behind the banks of fitful cloud. Maybe it would rain later.

That sailor man's tale didn't ring true. He wasn't your typical brawler. And he wasn't your typical merchant seaman. He looked like an engineer, though his merchant navy uniform had carried no special insignia. And his friend the chemist . . . They seemed an oddly assorted pair. Malcolm Enright, and — what was the chemist's name? He couldn't remember. Still, it was none of his business. Old Mr Locke had sorted it out.

As the cab passed in front of the Mansion House he glanced to his left, where he could glimpse the narrow opening of Garlick Hill, and recalled that it was in a secluded square leading off this street that he had first encountered his new sergeant, Jack Knollys. He recalled the shattered display cases in

Damian Shulbrede's dim jeweller's shop, and the dramatic rescue that Sergeant Knollys had made there.

It was as they began to skirt St Paul's Churchyard that Box suddenly became aware of the purposeful crowd hurrying along Carter Lane. Arnold Box knew all about crowds. This one was not bent on mischief. Its members, for the most part respectable City clerks, messengers and telegraph boys, were joined by grim-faced workmen and a growing number of street traders, all converging on a narrow slit between the tall buildings of Carter Lane. Box rapped with his knuckles on the ceiling of the cab, and the cabbie opened the flap in the roof.

'Yes, sir?'

'Cabbie, I'm Detective Inspector Box of Scotland Yard. Can you find out where all those people are going? They seem to be pouring down Verity Street.'

The cabbie's face disappeared from the open hatch, and Box heard him call out to one of the hurrying men on the pavement.

'What's amiss, mate? Where are you all going?'

'It's Sir John Courteline. He's been killed. Murdered.'

'Did you hear that, sir? Sir John Courteline

— who'd want to harm a hair of his head, for God's sake?'

'I don't know, cabbie,' Box replied. He forgot all about having a quiet lunch in Cardinal Court. 'I don't know,' he repeated, 'but I'd like to find out. Can you get this cab down Verity Street and into Edgerton Square?'

The driver closed the roof flap, and began to manoeuvre his cab along the narrow lane called Verity Street. The vehicle moved forward through a seething mass of angry men, their faces contorted with rage and grief. It was a grief that Box shared. Sir John Courteline, millionaire financier, was known as The Poor Man's Friend. Hundreds of projects for the relief of England's poor were wholly financed by him. Thousands literally owed their lives to him. He had funded trade schools, free hospitals, work projects. Five years earlier, he had been knighted for his services to the poor. And now he was dead — murdered, if these angry, frantic men were right.

The cabbie stopped his vehicle against the railings of the central garden in Edgerton Square, an elegant, secluded rectangle of tall, eighteenth-century houses with bow windows and wrought-iron balconies. Box could see the front door of Sir John Courteline's house gaping wide open, though the near hysterical crowd thronging the pavement made no attempt to trespass beyond the whitened doorstep, where two stalwart constables were stationed.

Box scribbled a note on a piece of paper, and handed it to the driver, together with two half crowns.

'Cabbie,' he said, 'be sure to deliver this note to the duty sergeant at 2 King James's Rents. You know where it is, don't you? Across the cobbles from Whitehall Place, on the other side of Aberdeen Lane.'

Box left the cab, and pushed his way through the crowd. Someone shouted angrily, 'Who'd want to shoot Sir John Courteline, for God's sake? What's happening to this country?' There was a groan of assent, accompanied by a surge of bodies towards the open door of the house, through which Box could glimpse the rich appointments and gleaming gas-lanterns in the hallway. Box elbowed his way through the crowd, and hurried up the steps. Luckily, both constables had saluted him in recognition, so he had no need to waste time in idle chat on the pavement.

As soon as he stepped into the hall, he heard the screaming. It was a woman, hidden somewhere in the house, giving vent to wave after wave of hopeless, abandoned lamentation. Box stood transfixed. He could sense grief in the sound, but something else, a kind of horrified despair. After a few moments the sound subsided, and terminated in a single chilling cry of anguish.

Box took hold of the heavy bolts behind the front door, and slammed it shut. The hall reverberated to the angry crash, bringing a uniformed sergeant out from a sort of glazed sentrybox beneath the stairs. The man saluted, and Box raised his hat in reply. Evidently the sergeant recognized him, which was just as well.

'Who have you got here, Sergeant?' he asked.

'Inspector Graham, sir, from 'C' Division. We haven't sent to the Yard yet — '

'I was just passing, Sergeant. Tell Mr Graham that I'm here, will you?'

As Box's eyes adjusted to the gloom of the hallway, he realized that a group of frightened domestic staff stood huddled together near the great mahogany staircase. They, too, had been transfixed by the screams of the unseen woman. They seemed to be shrinking in horror from an ugly, heavy pistol lying on the hall floor. At that moment the sergeant returned. He followed Box's gaze, and said, 'It was thrown down by the assailant, sir, as he ran from the house. Mr Mervyn, the butler there, saw the man coming out of the study.'

The butler stepped forward as though he had been summoned to tell his story, but Box shook his head and held up his hand.

'Not now, if you please, Mr Mervyn. Will you please send your staff about their duties. I'll speak to you later.'

As the butler shepherded the frightened servants down a dim passageway leading from the hall, Box drew the sergeant into the glass sentry-box beneath the stairs.

'Sergeant,' he said, 'who was doing the screaming when I came through the front door just now? It sounded like the torments of the damned.'

'That was Lady Courteline, sir. Very upset, she was, which is not surprising, really. She's a Russian lady, Mr Box, and I believe they're regular corkers in the screaming line.'

'Are they, now? Well, I'll remember that morsel of wisdom. When did this attack take place?'

'It was no more than twenty minutes ago, sir. About ten to twelve, by all accounts. Here's Inspector Graham now.'

A door to the right of the hall had suddenly opened, and a stout, whimsical-looking man stepped out to greet Box. He spoke with a kind of suppressed chuckle, as though humour was his natural bent. He wore a smart but comfortable uniform, and carried his pill-box hat in his hand.

'Sergeant Miller,' he said, 'go through and take brief statements from the servants. Leave the butler till later. Come in, Mr Box.'

The two men entered a comfortable panelled room in which a cheery fire was burning in an ornate grate. Inspector Graham closed the door.

'Miller says that you were just passing,' he said. 'Well, either that was an act of Providence, or a very curious concatenation of circumstances. Will you associate yourself with this case, Mr Box? It'll have to be a Yard job, in any case.'

' "Concatenation"?' said Box, shaking his head in mock disbelief. 'Honestly, Joe, I don't know where you get these long words from. What does it mean?'

'It means a chain of circumstances, Arnold, as your nanny should have told you. But this is a bad, bad business. It reminds me of that poor young man you and I found shot in Thomas Lane Mews last January. There he is, Inspector, by the fireplace.'

Sir John Courteline lay on his back, his surprised eyes still open, his waxed beard jutting grotesquely upward. There was a bad wound in the chest, and the carpet was heavily stained with blood. The dead man was dressed in striped trousers and a frock coat. His sober waistcoat was buttoned over a white silk liner. By placing his ear close to the dead man's chest, Box could hear the quiet ticking of a watch in its fob pocket.

Sir John Courteline's right arm was flung outward. Inspector Graham pointed to a thin cigar lying near the nerveless fingers. It was still smouldering, and had begun to burn the carpet.

'The assailant must have just flung himself into the room, and shot him,' said Graham. 'As you can see, it was a totally unexpected assault.'

'Did you recognize the make of weapon, Joe? A .38 Colt. All the villains of the nation seem to have them, now. Our assailant rushes in, shoots his victim, rushes out again, and flings the weapon away — I wonder . . . I'll talk to the butler, now. He's our best lead at the moment.'

Graham had crossed to the window which looked out on to Edgerton Square. He pulled the net curtain aside.

'That crowd's still milling around out there,' he said. 'There'll be trouble today, Arnold, mark my words. Sir John Courteline was The Poor Man's Friend. Before the night's out, The Poor Man will be out for blood. I'll fetch the butler.'

When the shaken Mervyn came into the study, Box pointed to a chair which he had placed so that the butler's back was turned to the dead body of his master. Box sat down beside him. His sense of outrage at Courteline's death was still strong, but his professional instincts were gradually taking control.

'Now, Mr Mervyn,' he said, 'I'd like you to sit there quietly, and tell me what you saw of the man who shot your master. I don't want you to tell me what he did, just what he looked like.'

Mervyn, he judged, was nearer seventy than sixty. He had a smooth, gentle face, framed by white mutton-chop whiskers. Box thought that he had probably been in service all his working life.

'Well, sir, the man was about thirty years of age, with close-cropped gingery hair. He had a fleshy sort of neck — a roll of fat bulging over his collar. I'd just come out from the kitchen passage. He threw the gun down on the hall floor. You could smell the gunpowder . . . He turned and glanced at me as he reached the front door. I'd run down the passage, you see, when I heard the shot. There was something odd about his face.'

Box said nothing. Instead, he slowly drew the index finger of his right hand across his right cheekbone. The butler's old eyes lightened with surprise.

'Yes, sir! Where you're pointing on your own face this villain had a crimson scar, or sore. Perhaps it was a birthmark?'

'Well, Mr Mervyn, we'll see. You've been of great help. And how is Lady Courteline? Does she have anyone with her?' As he spoke, Box gently escorted the butler to the study door.

'Lady Courteline is a little better, now, sir. Miss Olga is with her, and Dr Grace. Oh, dear! What terrible times we live in!'

When Mervyn had gone, Box turned to Inspector Graham.

'It was Killer Kitely, Joe. I thought it might be. He does that, you know. Runs in and shoots and runs out again. It was Killer who shot the Master of the Patents Office last February. We know he did it, though we can't prove it. It looks as though we've got him this time, though. Just as well, I suppose. As you said just now, the mobs will be out for vengeance over Courteline's death. Kitely will be the appeasing sacrifice.'

He glanced sombrely at the inert figure lying in front of the blazing fire.

It's an assassination. Kitely's been hired to

do the job — but who by?'

' 'By whom'.'

'What? Yes, that's what I said. We may know who did it, but we've got to find who it was who hired Kitely, and why — hello! What's this?'

Box knelt down beside the body. A piece of blood-soaked cardboard lay under the fingers of the outstretched hand. Perhaps Sir John Courteline had been looking at something when his assassin struck?

'Have I missed something?' asked Graham.

'You'd have found it, Joe. It's just that I've noticed it first.'

Gently, Inspector Box removed the card. It proved to be an ordinary printed visiting card, bearing the name Dr N.I. Karenin. Box turned the card over. The other side was not stained, and the neat printed letters could be seen quite clearly. But they were in a script that Box could not recognize. There was no address given on either side, just the name in neatly embossed characters. Whoever Dr N.I. Karenin was, his visiting card had presumably been the last thing that the murdered philanthropist had read.

'I'll take this with me, if I may, Joe,' said Box. 'I'm going now to report to my superintendent at the Rents. Then I'm going after Kitely. After this escapade, he'll go to earth, and I know exactly where to find him. Before the day's out, Joe, I'll have our friend Kitely under lock and key. And then the mob will have their sacrifice.'

2

A Cable from Petrovosk

It was nearing two o'clock when Arnold Box emerged into Carter Lane, and jumped on to the rear stair of a passing omnibus which would take him down to the Embankment. There were one or two passengers sitting uncomfortably on the back-to-back knife-board seats. The sky above St Paul's had turned a menacing greenish-black, and he could smell the pent-up rain in the waiting air.

As they passed the Temple Gardens the heavens opened, and within seconds the open top deck of the omnibus was awash. The few passengers turned up their collars and tried to shrink themselves into their coats. It was not yet three o'clock, but the Embankment was suddenly plunged into gloom.

As they approached the Whitehall end of the Embankment, Inspector Box saw the magnificent building of New Scotland Yard rising in all its glory of red brick and Portland stone above the trees. Its many windows shone with the special sharp glow of electric light. It had been opened two years earlier, in 1891, and the Metropolitan Police had moved there, lock, stock and barrel, taking Sir Edward Bradford, the Chief Commissioner, and his 15,000 officers, with them. He had 598 inspectors, and Arnold Box was proud to be one of them.

Not everyone, though, had made the move from the old to the new Scotland Yard. A goodly number had been left behind, marooned in a dilapidated, mildewed collection of soot-blackened old houses just fifty yards on from Whitehall Place. Box swung himself down the slippery stairs of the omnibus, and wove his way through a tangle of mean lanes that took him into the cobbled enclave of King James's Rents.

As Box ran up the wet steps of Number 2, he saw that the irregularly shaped entrance hall was thronged with uniformed policemen, a motley collection of men of varying girth and size, some in wet cloaks over their thick serge uniforms. Box uttered a little cry of satisfaction. Old Growler had evidently decided to assemble a posse.

'Are you waiting for me, gentlemen?' he asked, in his loud but pleasing London tones. He knew that Superintendent Mackharness would place these men at his disposal if he asked. 'You'll have heard the news. I've just this minute got back from Sir John Courteline's house. Would you all go through to the drill hall? I'll be with you as soon as I can. Hello, Sergeant Porter. I didn't know you were here at the Rents. Is that Sergeant Ruskin at the back? I'll be with you in minutes, seconds. Just go behind the stairs to the drill hall.'

Box stood with his hand on one of the swing doors of his office, watching the couple of dozen officers as they clattered over the bare boards of the passage behind the stairs. In a few moments' time he'd brief them as to his plan of campaign. There was a lot to be done, and timing was the crucial thing. If he moved too quickly, Kitely would give them the slip; move too slowly, and he'd disappear for good. Killer Kitely was a slippery customer.

As Box entered his office his sergeant, Jack Knollys, turned round from the mirror that rose above the fireplace, where a cheerful fire was burning. The mirror was plastered with visiting cards and various pasted messages, but Box knew that his sergeant had not been looking at them. He'd been ruefully examining his face, across which a livid scar ran from below the right eye to the left corner of his mouth. Poor lad, he'd always be sensitive about that scar, particularly now that he was courting Vanessa Drake.

'You've heard the news, Jack?' said Box. 'I'll cut a long story short, and tell you that this murder was done by a villain called Killer Kitely. I'm giving him a little time to run back to his lair, and then I'm going after him. He's got a kind of den in a row of houses in East Dock Street, down at Shoreditch, not so far from St George's in the East. Do you know those parts, Sergeant?'

'No, sir. Being a Croydon man by birth and breeding, I'm not really well up on all these exotic places on this side of the river.'

Sergeant Knollys was a giant of a man, with close-cropped yellow hair. His voice was unexpectedly quiet, and what Box called 'educated', with a hint of mocking humour behind it.

'There's nothing very exotic about Shadwell, Sergeant,' said Box. 'But Sergeant Porter's in the drill hall, and he hails from Shoreditch, and knows his way around. He's coming with us to bring Kitely in. So you'd better get your hat and coat — '

There was the sound of a chair being pushed back in the room above, and the rackety gas mantle trembled and spluttered as a heavy tread shook the soot-stained ceiling. Box sprang to the door, and was standing in the vestibule when an elderly, thickset man in a frock coat appeared on the landing at the top of the steep stairs. Evidently, Superintendent Mackharness had been on the look-out for him at the upstairs window of his office, and had seen him hurrying across the square.

'Box,' he said, in a powerful, well-enunciated voice, 'come up here, if you please. I shan't keep you more than a few minutes.'

Box hurried up the stairs and entered the gloomy, mildewed office of Superintendent Mackharness.

* * *

'I received your note, Box. Sit there in that chair, will you? This is a devilish business. Why Courteline, of all people? There's already a flurry of activity at the Home Office, so I'm told. And Lord Salisbury was seen slipping into the Foreign Office earlier on. Deep waters, Box, mark my words! Incidentally, how did you manage to get so quickly to the scene of the crime?'

Mackharness had seated himself at his carved oak desk, upon which reposed a number of slim cardboard folders. Well over sixty, with a yellowish face lightened by well-tended muttonchop whiskers, the senior officer of King James's Rents regarded Box with bright, black eyes, in which there lurked a kind of defensive wariness.

'Well, sir,' said Box, 'I was returning from a visit to Tooley Street Police Court, and I just happened on the Courteline business by chance. You could say it was a concatenation of circumstances.'

'Concatenation?' Mackharness repeated the word with evident distaste.

'Yes, sir. It means a chain of circumstances — '

'Yes, yes, Inspector, I know what it means,' Mackharness interrupted testily. 'I'm not exactly deficient in my knowledge of the English language. I'm just startled to hear *you* using such a word, that's all. But never mind all that. You'd better tell me what happened when you got to Courteline's house in Edgerton Square.'

While Box talked, Mackharness listened intently, all the time drumming on the desk with the heavy, spatulate fingers of his right hand.

'This visiting card — did you bring it away with you?'

Box produced the bloodstained card from his jacket pocket, and handed it to his superior. Mackharness held it at arm's length, turning it over once, and then back again. He gave it back to Box, and sat back in his chair.

‘Dr N. I. Karenin,’ he said. ‘I don’t recall the name. You’ll look him up in the directories, I expect, but somehow I don’t think you’ll find him, Box. Did you see those foreign characters on the reverse? They simply repeat the fellow’s name, but in the Russian alphabet.’

‘How did you know that, sir? About the Russian alphabet?’

Mackharness began a frown, which he suddenly turned into a condescending smile.

‘You have evidently forgotten, Inspector Box, that long, long ago — longer ago than I care to remember — I served as an officer in the Crimean War. It was useful to know something of the Russian language, and the peculiar alphabet that they use to set it down in writing. I served under Raglan, you know. Most of us knew a bit of Russian — not just us, but Johnny Turk as well.’

‘And it just spells out the same name, sir?’

‘Yes. I’m inclined to think that card was actually printed in Russia, though I can’t be sure. Incidentally, the initials N.I. almost certainly stand for Nikolai Ivanovich.’

‘How did you — ’

‘Don’t dare ask me, do you hear? I just know, that’s all. Now . . . Do you want to follow up this case officially? There’ll be a lot of publicity, as you’ll appreciate. There’ll be all kinds of protests and marches from the humbler sort of person, Box. It's the unions who put them up to it. And the anarchists. But never mind all that. What are you going to do? What do you want *me* to do?'

'Sir, I know who did this murder, and I know where he's hiding out. I see you've already mustered a body of officers downstairs. With their help, sir, I'll flush our murderer out before nightfall.'

'Well done, Box! Use those officers as you wish. And you say that you've identified the perpetrator of this foul outrage?'

'Yes, sir. It was Killer Kitely. I don't know whether you recall the name — '

'Ahem! Kitely, you say? Well, get after him, will you? Take Sergeant Knollys with you. Oh, *Kitely*? Joseph Kitely, aged thirty-eight, five feet seven, murderer and assassin. A slippery customer, Box. Make sure you don't lose him!'

* * *

Sir Charles Napier, Her Majesty's Permanent Under-Secretary of State for Foreign Affairs, sat back in his chair and observed his distinguished guest. By rights, he thought, he should be sitting here at this ornate desk, not me! But there, politics was a peculiar game, and Lord Salisbury, the former Prime Minister, who had so recently presided over the partition of Africa while acting as his own Foreign Secretary, was now the Leader of Queen Victoria's Loyal Opposition.

'I can't see Mr Gladstone taking exception to my coming here, Napier,' said Lord Salisbury. 'I've not much patience with his democratic notions, but he knows that well enough. I think he trusts me to do the best I can for Britain, whether in or out of office. He's called an emergency meeting with the Home Secretary for later this afternoon over this damnable business of Sir John Courteline's murder. London's up in arms. Meanwhile, you and I can have a discreet chat, without treading on anyone's toes. So tell me more about Afghanistan. I thought I'd resolved that business once and for all in '85.'

Lord Salisbury, a very tall, heavily built man, bald but bearded, had rather gingerly lowered himself into an upright chair on entering Napier's first-floor room in the Foreign Office. He regarded the under-secretary with melancholy eyes set deep under beetling brows. His eyes never quite focused, because he was extremely short sighted; it was said that vanity forbade his wearing spectacles in public.

'Well, sir,' said Napier, 'you'll appreciate

that the Amir, Abd-ur-Rahman, remains loyal to the British Government, and is content that we direct his foreign policy — '

'I appreciate that the Amir is a shrewd man, Napier, who has the knack of playing his cards right, if rather too close to his chest for comfort. If Russia's contemplating mischief in the area, it's just possible that Abd-ur-Rahman may pretend to be deaf. But go on, Napier, I'm setting the cart before the horse.'

'I've received intelligence from one of our people in Baluchistan, a man called Abu Daria, that Russia had been covertly arming some of the northern Afghan tribes. That in itself is alarming, but another of our agents, a man who works for the railway in Petrovosk, on the shore of the Caspian Sea, tells us that a company of ostensibly civilian engineers — Russians, I mean — have been seen in the vicinity of Meshed.'

Lord Salisbury sat up in his chair, and looked at Napier with renewed interest. He stroked his luxuriant beard thoughtfully.

'Ah! Meshed. Now I can see a picture emerging . . . I suppose these informants of yours are trustworthy? Could anyone have tampered with their despatches?'

'They both communicated by cable, sir. Abu Daria linked up with the other man,

Piotr Casimir, at Petrovosk, and they sent a joint cable from the telegraph office there.'

'Hm . . . Well, Meshed is one of the Russians' classic lines of advance towards India, so if there's anything in what your couriers have told you, then the Tsar and his advisers may be contemplating another attempt to overturn the Raj. In which case, Napier, I should say that His Imperial Majesty has taken leave of his senses. Since last year he's turned his attentions to China. He's borrowing French money to build a trans-Siberian railway. But Meshed . . . Well, it makes one think.'

'What would you advise, sir? Obviously, I will be ruled by whatever Lord Rosebery, the present Foreign Secretary, recommends, but I do have a certain standing in the matter of foreign affairs.'

'Well, you and I have worked closely for a good few years, Napier, and by the look of things in the country at the moment, we may find ourselves in harness again before very long. Mr Gladstone' — Salisbury permitted himself a rather mischievous smile — 'Mr Gladstone is throwing all his energy into this Home Rule for Ireland business, and for a man in his eighties he's putting up a remarkable show. But the country's not with him, and that will see him out of office in a year's time. And this business of Courteline today will unsettle the voting masses. I don't hold any kind of brief for so-called 'public opinion', but Gladstone does, and he'll bow to the inevitable when it happens.'

'And about Afghanistan, sir?'

'Oh, yes. Sorry, Napier, I was looking a bit too eagerly beyond the present. I don't like the sound of this at all. Not one bit. As you know, I'm a diplomat where foreign relations are concerned, and my motto is 'There's always a pass through the mountains'. You can always escape bloodshed and conflict if you're clever enough. Sir Abraham Goldsmith is giving one of his receptions for the Diplomatic Corps at his house in Arlington Street this Friday evening. He's angling for a peerage, you know, and won't mind if you suggest another name for his guest list. Get him to invite Captain Andropov, the Russian military attaché, and have a civil word with him over a glass or two of claret. And it might be an idea to chat with someone more or less civilized from the German Embassy. They'll be just as interested as us, you know. The balance of power must be upheld at all costs.'

The great aristocrat lumbered to his feet. His bald head shone in the bright March light streaming through the windows from St James's Park. He began to pull on a pair of stout leather gloves, but suddenly stopped, and looked speculatively at Napier.

'Was there nothing going forward in the Baltic? This Meshed business could be a sign that Russia's on the move in an old and unwelcome direction, but in that case, I'd expect all parts of that great body politic to move at once.'

'I've heard nothing untoward so far, sir. Nothing in the way of troop movements, at least. But we have a man in Vilna who reported only last week that the Russian Government has been setting up some kind of secret establishment in the pine forest near the coastline of their province of Lithuania. Some kind of experimental weapons station, he says.'

'Ah! Interesting. And who do you suppose would feel threatened by that, Napier?'

'The German Empire, sir. The land they call Lithuania is perilously close to the East Prussian wilderness around Königsberg. All the more reason, I suppose, to hope that Goldsmith has invited some of our better class of Prussian to Arlington Street. Meanwhile, I'll ensure that we continue to keep a wary eye on these places.'

'Do so. You'll be accounted wise. The Caspian and the Baltic — both more or less inland seas, both firmly in the skirts of Holy

Russia, which has been cautiously slithering down the Baltic coast for years — there are sinister possibilities in both areas. We live in interesting times, Napier.'

'We do, sir. Thank you very much for calling on me. I'll follow your advice, and ask Sir Abraham Goldsmith to invite Captain Andropov to that exotic house of his in Arlington Street. For a merchant banker, I believe he's very accommodating.'

'He is — so make sure that *you* are invited, as well! Get the Russians into a corner, where they can't wriggle away from a bit of clever questioning. But don't angle an invitation for *me*, if you please — I'm going down to Hatfield for a week or two, and there, Napier, I intend to stay. Meanwhile, the best of luck to you!'

When Lord Salisbury had gone, Sir Charles Napier stood at one of the windows of his spacious office, looking down on to St James's Park. Only a few weeks had passed since a most hideous conspiracy, centred in Germany, had been exposed, and its proponents utterly crushed. Now, it would seem, it was the turn of the great Empire of Russia to muddy the waters. Any move by Russia into Afghanistan could only be aimed at violation of the Indian borders. Salisbury had counselled caution, but he knew as well as Napier that any attack on India from that quarter would lead to war.

Those agents — 'correspondents', as they called themselves — were very difficult to control or contact. They were independent operators, well paid, but with a genuine regard for Britain. Both Abu Daria and Piotr Casimir had sent their reports via telegraph from Petrovosk. What about the man in Vilna, Jacob Kroll? He, too, had sent a telegraphic message. It had been relayed from Vilna via Königsberg.

Cables . . . A magical web of global communication, one of the glories of the nineteenth century! But that great electrical wonder, apparently, had its dangerous weaknesses. Earlier that year he had been visited by a man called Dangerfield, one of the directors of the Eastern Telegraph Company, who had suspected that all was not well with the cables coming into Britain at Porthcurno, on the Cornish coast.

Napier moved uneasily. Was it any longer a prudent thing to trust to cabled messages? They came in the anonymity of code, so that one couldn't say, for instance, 'Ah! Abu Daria's handwriting gets no better!' It would as well to check by other means that the three agents remained free from harm.

* * *

Killer Kitely crouched beside the window in the unfurnished room and listened to the shouts and curses of the mob in the narrow street outside. What light there was glinted on the shards of glass on the bare wooden floor. One piece of brick had drawn blood just below his left eye.

Curse it! Curse them! Why had he turned round when that cringing skivvy of a butler had appeared on the scene? They'd got that cocky little jackanapes Box on the trail, and he was there, outside, in East Dock Street with a pack of bobbies and a gin-sodden mob from the alehouses and the rows of flea-ridden brick cottages.

What was that? A vibrant groan from outside in the street — *crash*! They were trying to break the front door down. Well, it was a very special front door, lined with sheets of iron. He'd quit this cursed place as soon as he was ready. It had been worth it. A hundred pounds in gold, the gaffer had given him.

Someone was shouting. Shouting through a megaphone. What was he saying?

'Kitely! This is Detective Inspector Box of Scotland Yard. Come out, with your hands above your head. We'll give you five minutes only!'

What's that? A cheer? A cheer for Box from those half-starved, consumptive labourers and dockers? What had that busy little bantam ever done for them, or for their thin wives and barefoot children? But they were all after his blood, curse them, just because he'd blasted their favourite toff to kingdom come. Well, before he made himself scarce, perhaps they'd like a dose of the same medicine . . .

Box, standing with Sergeant Knollys among a knot of uniformed policeman on the opposite side of East Dock Street, looked critically at the blank windows of the mean house where Killer Kitely lay hidden. This row of houses down near Shadwell Basin contained Joseph Kitely's lair. Box had ringed the whole side of the street with police, so that all normal exits were covered. But there was more to this warren of derelict houses than met the eye. He turned to a stolid, bearded man of thirty or so who was standing motionless beside him, surveying Kitely's lair through field-glasses.

'I don't like the feel of this, Sergeant Porter,' said Box. 'Kitely's taking too much time to come out. He's up to something. I know all about these houses. They're joined by tunnels through the cellars, and they go right down to the docks. I want you to go now, Sergeant, to Old Field Court. There are gratings there, in the area of number six. Take Sergeant Knollys here with you. See if you can find Sergeant Ruskin — he's here, somewhere — and tell him to go with four constables to Connaught Lane, just past Samuelson's warehouses. There's a tunnel entrance there. Kitely might emerge through either of those exits.'

Sergeant Porter saluted, and he and Knollys disappeared down an alley. There was no point in waiting any longer, thought Box. It was time to storm Kitely's citadel. He put the megaphone to his lips.

'Joseph Kitely — '

His words were immediately drowned by a deafening report that echoed along the narrow street. A bright flash of flame lit up one of the shattered ground-floor windows of the besieged house. At the same time one of the bystanders screamed and spun grotesquely off the pavement into the carriageway. Kitely had fired into the crowd from his lair.

In the beleaguered house, Killer Kitely crawled across the floor of the bare room and out into the passage. Best to leave the double-barrelled shotgun behind him. He stood up, and tiptoed through the dust and debris into the dim rear quarters of the house. There was a strong smell of escaping gas, and a menacing hissing sound coming from the back scullery. Time to go.

In a dark corner of the pantry was a trap door, under which a ladder led down to a tunnel that would take him into the area of a house in Old Field Court. Box and his clodhoppers would be left laying siege to an empty house. Curse this gas! They'd hear him coughing. He seized the handle of the trap door, and pulled.

The trap door remained firmly shut. Kitely rattled the handle in fury, and felt the rigid resistance of bolts that had been shot closed under the trap. Someone had cut off his way of escape. Had the police got down there, too? Coughing and wheezing, Killer Kitely stumbled into the dark kitchen. There would be a hatchet there —

Kitely saw the hissing slow-match when it was too late to prevent it igniting the marine flare to which it had been attached.

* * *

Outside in East Dock Street it had started to rain. The crowd was now screaming with rage. A further volley of bricks and stones showered into the empty house, and the clatter of uprooted cobbles turned to thunder as they rolled down the steep slate roof.

Thank goodness that Mackharness had assembled such a large force of men to accompany him on his mission! It was time to curb the enthusiasm of the mob, and Old Growler's men could do that task admirably. He'd make one last attempt to make Kitely see sense. He cupped his hands, and shouted across the street.

'Joseph Kitely — '

As though in reply, the house in East Dock Street erupted in a ball of orange flame. Two men on the roof shrieked, and slithered down into the road. The crowd cried out in alarm and pushed desperately back away from the inferno. The windows of the house became six bright orange rectangles darting out wicked tongues of flame.

Box heard footsteps behind him, and saw that Knollys had returned. Both men were silent for a moment, watching the burning house. A number of policemen, their serge uniforms smoking, emerged from the alley beside the houses, dragging a burning bundle between them. The crowd, which had fallen silent, began to disperse.

'Sir,' said Sergeant Knollys, 'you were right about Connaught Lane. Sergeant Ruskin found the tunnel opening you mentioned. It's got a battered iron gate covering it. He and his men had staked it out. I was present when the gate was pushed open from inside. A man's face peered out for a moment — a pale, cadaverous face it was — and then drew back into the tunnel. I thought you'd want to come back and take a look, sir.'

'I do, Sergeant Knollys, because whoever it was, it wasn't our friend Kitely. Let's start walking. I'll be very interested to see who comes out of that tunnel.'

As Box and Knollys walked away from East Dock Street, some of the policemen upended a rainwater butt on to the wet pavement, and doused the smouldering remains of Killer Kitely.

* * *

It was now late in the afternoon, and the March sky was darkening. Box and Knollys threaded their way through a maze of bleak, wet streets rising in huddled squalor from the bustling docks bordering the Thames.

As they turned the corner from Green's Basin, the stocky, bearded figure of Sergeant Porter appeared beside them as though by magic. He checked them with a warning hand, and jerked his head towards Connaught Lane. They shrank back against the blank wall of a warehouse and looked out across the half-demolished site towards the concealed tunnel entrance. There was nobody in sight.

'Sergeant Ruskin's done well,' Box whispered.

'He has, sir. There's six of them there, all watching that tunnel. They — look, sir!'

The battered iron gate closing the tunnel had been cautiously pushed aside, and a figure was emerging. It was a man in a long black overcoat, with a peaked cap pulled well down over his eyes. It was an incongruous sight to see anyone emerging from what Box knew to be a disused ventilation shaft belonging to a long-replaced deep sewer.

'Nimble enough, but not in the first flush of youth,' muttered Box. 'Five foot ten or thereabouts. I wonder who he is? Are you trained in surveillance, Sergeant Porter? If you're not, tell me honestly.'

'I am trained, sir. I can tail that cove with the best of them.'

'Very well. He's moving off down the lane towards the river. Split from me now, Sergeant, but don't lose sight of Sergeant Knollys and me. Remember the golden rules: no footfall, no shadows, move only when your quarry's just out of sight.'

The man walked swiftly through the lanes and alleys of the docklands, bearing steadily downhill towards the river. After ten minutes or so, pursuers and pursued emerged on to the dockside. The sky above the river had grown surly and threatening, and a few gas lanterns were flaring along the quays, where several cargo ships were moored.

'St Thomas's Stairs,' Box muttered. 'What's he up to? Is he going to cross the river? Come on, we'll lose him if we're not careful!'

Box broke cover, and the two sergeants followed him. The river was alive with ships and boats of all kinds. Winking mast lights crossed and recrossed each other in the growing gloom. Their quarry had disappeared under a cast-iron arch, and was clattering down a flight of steps. Evidently the man suddenly realized that he was being pursued, for he all but jumped into a steam launch that had evidently been waiting with steam up for his arrival.

Box stood on the end of the pier, watching the launch as it moved rapidly into mid-stream, where it was lost among the maze of shipping. It was now raining heavily, but Box seemed not to notice. Sergeant Porter shaded his eyes with his hand, and tried to follow the progress of the launch.

'No identity marks, sir,' he said. 'It was a grimy little craft, but a swift one for all that. Well, we've lost him. I don't suppose we'll ever know who he was.'

'Maybe not, Sergeant Porter,' said Box, 'but at least we can assume that he was involved in that gruesome funeral pyre back at East Dock Street. I reckon he was the man who hired Kitely, and then made sure that he couldn't escape from his lair. So we know something about our cadaverous friend. Perhaps a bit of gentle probing in certain quarters will reveal a bit more. Time will tell.'

3

Why Lady Courteline Screamed

The gas lamps were glowing in Edgerton Square when Box called at Sir John Courteline's house early that evening. As he stepped over the threshold, he fancied that the hallway still echoed to the screams of the frantic widow, although in reality it was enveloped in a brooding calm.

Lady Courteline received Box in her private sitting-room on the first floor. She lay on a sofa drawn up to the fireplace, where a low fire was burning. An open door in the room led into a kind of miniature study, where, Box had been informed, the family's physician was waiting in case he was needed.

'No, Mr Box,' Lady Courteline was saying, 'I was not present when my husband was shot. It was, I think, just before twelve o'clock — some minutes before — and I was here upstairs, talking to my daughter Olga. My husband was downstairs in his study. He said he was going to smoke a cigar.'

Box looked gravely at the handsome, dark-haired woman reclining on the sofa. Her quiet voice held the faintest hint of a foreign accent. Whatever her earlier emotional state, she had regained her natural poise, and her delivery, though low, was firm in tone. But she looked like a woman completely crushed by sorrow, and the dark shadows beneath her haunted eyes told Box of almost unendurable pain.

'Was Sir John about to go out, Lady Courteline? Although he'd not yet put on a topcoat, he seemed dressed for a foray out of doors.'

'Yes, he was on his way out to one of his numerous daily engagements. It was his habit to smoke a cigar in the study before leaving. He smoked those thin, dark little things that don't last for hours — what do you call them?'

'Cheroots.'

'Yes, that's right. My husband, Mr Box, was a public figure: I may say, a national figure. He had enormous philanthropic interests, and was fiercely concerned for the welfare of the poor, as these demonstrations outside his house today will have shown you. As to the manner of his death, I am at a loss to account for it. I cannot help you in the least. Sir John was universally esteemed.'

'Do you by any chance know, ma'am, where your husband was going today?'

'What? No. I've no idea. My husband is frequently away from the house in the afternoons. At one time, years ago, he'd tell me where he was going, but with the passing of the years we both felt that it was a useless courtesy. If there were any grand evening engagements, then, of course, I would accompany him. But these daytime things — no.'

The widowed woman seemed to lose sight of Box for a moment. He could see her anxious eyes fill with vacancy as her mind moved away somewhere far from Edgerton Square. Box felt suddenly uneasy. If Sir John Courteline had been due at a public function somewhere that afternoon, why had no one connected with that function responded to his very public death?

'I will have been left very comfortably off,' said Lady Courteline, 'and Olga, too. Perhaps I shall return to Odessa . . . ' She was speaking to herself, in her inner world, not to Box. She caught sight of him waiting attentively for her to speak, and burst back into the present with a start. She looked at Box for a moment as though she could not recognize him.

'My husband, Mr Box,' she said, 'belonged to many clubs and societies — debating clubs, dining clubs, coteries of like-minded men who would meet together for mutual congratulation and bonhomie. Like all men, he revelled in secret societies and exclusive gatherings. Sir John rather liked being inscrutable over these activities of his, and we pretended to be overawed. He was very much in the world, was my husband.'

Lady Courteline suddenly sat up on the sofa. She bit her lip in vexation. Box saw a guarded expression come to her face, and her voice, which had started to rise imperiously, subsided to what he imagined was its usual refined, quiet tone.

'I think that is all I can tell you, Inspector Box. You may wish to talk with my daughter Olga, who is downstairs. It remains for me to thank you, from the bottom of my heart, for your success in running to earth the foul assassin of my dear husband.'

There was an unmistakable tone of dismissal. Box rose from his chair. At the door he turned, and asked one final question.

'Lady Courteline, did you or your husband ever know a Dr Nikolai Ivanovich Karenin?'

Lady Courteline's body convulsed, and she collapsed on to the sofa, crying out, as though in pain, 'Karenin? No! I recollect no such name!' The physician appeared immediately from the adjoining room. He took the widow's hand in his, and shook his head as a sign to Box that his interview should go no further. Box stepped out on to the landing, and the doctor firmly closed the door of Lady Courteline's room.

* * *

As Box came down the stairs, a fair-haired young woman emerged into the hall from a room near the front door of the house. She was wearing a simple black evening dress, and had thrown a light cashmere shawl across her shoulders. She looked at Box with what seemed like hauteur, but he recognized it as a special kind of nervous shyness that some girls betrayed when confronted by authority.

'You will be Inspector Box,' said the young woman. 'I am Olga Courteline. Come into the morning-room, please. I should like to talk to you.'

They entered a small, candle-lit room, where Olga motioned Box to sit beside a round mahogany table near the fireplace. Although she had called it the morning-room, Box thought that it was probably a kind of household office. Olga Courteline sat opposite him at the table.

'Inspector Box,' said Olga, 'you have just come from seeing my mother. She will have told you what happened today, but she is in a very emotional state, and I thought a few words from me would give you a more accurate view of events.'

A cool customer, thought Box, fully in control of herself. Whatever her private feelings, this young lady was expert at concealing them. He took a notebook from his pocket. Olga Courteline wouldn't quail at the sight of him taking a few shorthand notes.

'What happened, Mr Box, was this. Mother and I heard the sound of a shot downstairs. It was unbelievably loud, like a great clap of thunder. People were shouting and running. Mother and I sat transfixed with fear. I said: 'Something has happened to Father'. Mother said nothing. She just sat quite still and frozen.'

'But in the end, I believe, she went downstairs?' asked Box gently.

'She did. 'Let me see him', Mother said. I tried to dissuade her, but she insisted. I yielded to her entreaty, and that, I may say, was a great mistake. Mervyn and I helped her downstairs and into the study. Mother knelt by Father's body, and touched his neck. She looked at her fingers — I think she expected to see blood on them, but there was none.'

For the first time, the girl's voice faltered. Conjuring up the morning's horrors was beginning to have its effect.

'What happened next, Miss Courteline?' asked Box. 'Your evidence is very valuable to me.'

'Mother saw the cigar smouldering on the carpet near Father's hand. 'It's still lit', she said, and then she touched his hand. Suddenly, she started to scream. We should not have brought her down there. She screamed without ceasing. I half dragged her into the domestic quarters of the house where the cook and I attempted to calm her. It was useless. She screamed until she collapsed.'

Box was quiet for a moment. He was wondering why this girl had decided to talk freely about her father's murder, and her mother's reaction to it. Most people did not volunteer that kind of information. They waited to be asked. Olga seemed to sense what was passing through his mind.

'I'm telling you all this, Mr Box, because I know that Mother will have spoken dismissively of my father. She'd got into the habit of ridiculing his liking for clubs and coteries, and all the rest of it. But as you can see from her reaction to his murder, she loved him dearly. That isn't hard to understand. My father was a great benefactor of mankind. In time, perhaps, he will be seen as a saint. So don't set too much store on Mother's slighting remarks. They are merely a mask for a lifetime of devotion.'

When Box left the room, Mervyn was waiting to open the front door. Box took the bloodstained visiting card from his pocket, and handed it to the butler.

'Do you recollect this calling-card being left at the house today, Mervyn?' he asked.

The butler viewed it with evident distaste, turning it over to look at the Russian characters on its reverse. He handed it back to Box.

'No, indeed, sir,' he said. 'No such card was left here today.' Mervyn hesitated for a little before adding, 'It was very clever of you, sir, if I may say so, to identify the assassin so quickly, and then bring him to book.'

'It's very kind of you to say so, Mr Mervyn,' said Box. 'But I've still got to find who it was who hired Killer Kitely to do the murder. I'm only halfway there, you see, and maybe this calling-card will take me a bit further along the path.'

He accepted his hat and gloves from Mervyn, and stepped out into Edgerton Square.

* * *

It was quite dark when Box got back to King James's Rents. Sergeant Knollys was sitting at the long table, writing carefully in a notebook. He looked up from his task as Box pushed open the swing doors and came into the warm office. He sank down in his chair with a sigh, and threw his hat and gloves on the table.

'I've been to see Lady Courteline,' he said. 'She tells an interesting tale, Sergeant, but there's something about her manner that I can't quite fathom. I met her daughter, too. But never mind them for the moment. How did you get on at East Dock Street?'

'Well, sir, there's not much left of that side of the street where Kitely's hideout was, but they'd set up gas flares in the ruins, and — well, guess who was there, sitting on top of a pile of wet debris?'

'Not Mr Mack? Surely they wouldn't send a Home Office explosives expert to a place like that?'

'Mr Mack it was, sir. Maybe someone high up told the Home Office to show some interest over Sir John Courteline's murder. There he was, in the ruins of Kitely's house, with his umbrella up, and smoking that clay pipe of his. He was holding a length of gas-pipe.'

'What did he say?'

'He said it was a very nice piece of work, simple and effective. The gas-pipe had been severed with a hacksaw. He'd found that, too, and told me the name of the tool shop where it must have been bought.'

Box laughed. The past year had brought him into close contact with the old expert from the Home Office Explosives Inspectorate, and there had grown up between him and Box a mutual regard. Mr Mack was no stranger to King James's Rents.

'But there was more to it than that, sir,' Knollys continued. 'He told me that he'd found the remains of a marine flare, and part of the metal mechanism used to hold a slow-match. Our murderous friend had arranged for Killer Kitely to be blown to pieces.'

Arnold Box lit a thin cigar, flicked the wax vesta into the grate, and smoked in silence for a while. Knollys was content to wait. He listened to the coal settling in the grate, and the gas mantle spluttering and hissing.

'Our murderous friend,' said Box at length. 'Perhaps he was the man whose name is printed on that card: Dr N. I. Karenin.'

'We can't be sure about that, sir.'

'No; but there's such a thing as being too cautious, Sergeant. That card . . . I thought at first that Sir John Courteline had been holding it when he was shot, but I've changed my mind about that. I've just spoken to

Mervyn, the butler, and he was positive that no such card had been handed in at the house today.'

'You said that the card was lying near his hand?'

'Yes, but not *in* his hand, Sergeant. He wasn't clutching it. I rather think that it was Killer Kitely who placed that card there after he shot his victim. This Dr Karenin told him to do it, as much as to say, 'Here's my master's calling card. Please accept a bullet through the heart, with his compliments'. It's just a thought.'

'It sounds as though there's politics involved somewhere, sir.'

'Perhaps; but that's none of our business, Sergeant. Dr Karenin's name isn't in any of the medical registers, by the way, which doesn't surprise me. Nobody I've asked seems to have heard of him.'

Box sighed, stretched his arms, and stood up. He retrieved his curly-brimmed bowler from the table, and settled it carefully on his head, using the mirror to check that he's got the tilt just right. He picked up his gloves.

'I'm going home, Sergeant,' he said. 'It's half past eight, and I've been running around since eight this morning. I'm going to my digs in Cardinal Court, where Mrs Peach has promised me a plate of steak and kidney pie, to be washed down with a pint of porter. I'm leaving you here to hold the fort. Remember, the teeming millions are seething all around you, and much sin and wickedness is being plotted by countless villains. Keep your weather eye open.'

Sergeant Knollys laughed, and turned back to his work. Box hovered near the swing door for a moment, then came back to the table.

'I'm going out to Finchley tomorrow, Jack, to have tea with Louise — Miss Whittaker. I'm going to tell her all about Lady Courteline. There was something about her reaction to her husband's murder that I can't quite fathom. And there were things her daughter Olga said that puzzle me a bit. I want to hear a female slant on the matter. It's time for me to have a word with Louise.'

* * *

Detective Inspector Box stood on the narrow strip of lawn in the long, brick-walled garden of Miss Louise Whittaker's semi-detached house in Finchley. He had been sent out of the neat modern villa to smoke one of his slim cigars in the chill light of the March afternoon.

Ethel, Miss Whittaker's little maid, demure in cap and apron, appeared at the back door.

‘Tea’s served, Mr Box. Missus says to come in when you’re ready.’

Arnold Box threw the butt of his cigar behind a convenient bush, and walked into the house.

‘Well, Ethel,’ said Box, ‘you’re very solemn today! Usually the very sight of me sends you into a fit of the giggles.’

Ethel smiled, and gave him a small curtsy.

‘That’s on account of you being so funny, sir, coming to pay court to Missus, and pretending to be fierce. But I’ve heard all about what you did yesterday, sir, about poor Sir John Courteline, I mean, so I’m knowing my place. Miss Whittaker’s in the study, sir.’

Box had first met Miss Whittaker when she had appeared as an expert witness in a celebrated fraud case. Since that meeting, he had called on the woman scholar and college lecturer many times. They had taken tea together, and, chaperoned by Miss Whittaker’s young friend Vanessa Drake, they had been to the theatre. Box would have blushingly denied Ethel’s assertion that he was ‘paying court to Missus’, but he had more than once told the lady scholar bluntly that he liked her very much, and she had not objected.

Ethel conducted him to the large front room of the house, where he was received by his hostess, a very beautiful, raven-haired young woman. She had been sitting at a large table in the bay window, working on a manuscript, but she rose when Box came in, and sat down opposite him at a small table near the fireplace, where an ample afternoon tea had been set out.

'I hope you enjoyed your cigar, Mr Box,' said Louise Whittaker. 'Let me pour you some tea.'

Box admired the lace tablecloth, the thin, patterned china, the silver teapot, the inviting sandwiches and cakes on their stand. He also admired Miss Whittaker's grey silk dress, with its demure white cuffs and collar. It was nice to sit back quietly, and watch her pouring out the tea.

'What are you working on today, Miss Whittaker?' he asked. 'Your table in the window there seems more piled up with books than usual.'

'I'm engaged on something rather different from my usual linguistic studies,' she replied, glancing at the many reference works and papers arrayed on her table. 'I'm writing an introduction to the collected works of Mary Shelley. Have you heard of her? She was Shelley's second wife.'

'Shelley? He was the poet, wasn't he? 'Daffodils', I seem to remember.'

'Mary Shelley, Mr Box, was a woman who dared to see herself as an equal of her genius of a husband, and of her philosopher father. And so her imaginative powers were liberated, and she gave us that strange creation-tale *Frankenstein*. But I suspect that you have not come here today to hear about Mary Shelley.'

'No, Miss Whittaker. I've come partly because I want to tell you about a woman who's engaging my attention at the moment. I refer to Lady Courteline, widow of our great benefactor of the poor, Sir John Courteline.'

'Ah, yes! The papers today are full of the case. They say some very flattering things about you, Mr Box.'

Box was not really a vain man, but he rather enjoyed the look of respect that came into his friend's eyes. He tended to forget that he was himself something of a public figure.

'I almost literally walked into the case, Miss Whittaker, and as soon as I crossed the threshold of his house I knew who'd murdered him . . . '

As Box told Louise about his visit to Sir John Courteline's house, she sat quite still, cradling her teacup in her hands, and looking thoughtfully at the flickering flames in the grate. When he had finished his tale, she treated him to a brilliant smile. He realized that she was sharing his professional triumph.

By tacit consent, they turned their attention to the business of afternoon tea. After Louise had poured them both a second cup of tea, Box resumed the thread of his narrative.

'It's the attitude of Lady Courteline that's puzzling me,' he said. 'There's something wrong there, and I can't put my finger on it. When I talked to her yesterday, she was obviously distraught — yes, that's the word. She'd screamed and screamed, her daughter told me, and I heard the sound of her grief myself, when I first went to the house.'

'Distraught? Do you mean that when you called on her yesterday she was still screaming?'

'Well, no, miss, she was calm and collected then, but her face was — was ravaged with grief. That sounds over-dramatic, I dare say, but I can't express it any other way. She was ravaged.'

Louise Whittaker put her cup down gently on the tray, and sat back in her chair.

Did she say anything, Mr Box? Or did she just sit there, looking ravaged?'

Dash it all, why did her look of mild amusement so unnerve him? What with her, and little Ethel, coming into her house was like entering the lion's den.

'She began to talk to me about her husband. About Sir John Courteline. She told me about his work, his committees, his charities. 'My husband this, my husband that'. Then she said he belonged to clubs and societies, and she became very sarcastic, if that's the word I mean. She said that he was really just a big boy who liked belonging to gangs. She said he liked being inscrutable, and that they pretended to be overawed.'

'They? Whom did she mean by that?'

'Well, I think she meant herself and her daughter. Do you see, Miss Whittaker, she was angry, scornful — just like you are, when you're having a go at men! Angry. But at the same time she was ravaged with grief. Her face showed that. I can't square the two things at the moment.'

Louise Whittaker looked into the flames of the cheerful fire. There was a slight frown on her face, an expression of thoughtful puzzlement.

'Do you mean that she spoke of him as though he was a public figure? As though she was someone looking in from the outside?'

'Yes, that's exactly it! She was angry that he had gone and got himself shot. She was relieved that she would be left well off. And yet — there were black shadows under her eyes, and she was as pale as death. She was ill, sick with grief — '

'Are you sure of that, Mr Box? Sick with grief? Sometimes, you know, when two things are supposed to be linked, and one of them won't fit properly, then it's possible that they're not linked at all. You say that Lady Courteline was sick, and you have the evidence of your senses to confirm that. But sick from what cause? Grief? Or fear?'

'Fear . . . I'd not considered that. But fear of what, miss? Not of Killer Kitely, because she never saw him. She didn't know about him.'

Louise shifted her gaze from the fire, and looked directly at Box.

'I wasn't thinking of that kind of fear. I meant fear *for* something — or someone. Those screams — they invite a question that may seem too obvious to ask: *Why* did Lady Courteline scream and scream?'

'Because her husband had just been murdered.'

'Are you sure of that? I mean, did she scream because her husband had been murdered, or did she scream after she had been told something? In whose presence did she scream?'

This was more like it! Louise was about to explore a particular female slant on the case.

Box drew a cloth-bound black notebook from his pocket, and leafed through its pages.

'Lady Courteline was in her sitting-room talking to her daughter Olga. They heard the shot, and sat transfixed with fear — '

Louise held up her hand to stop him.

'A moment, Mr Box. Who was it who talked about being transfixed?'

'The daughter, Miss Olga Courteline. I saw her briefly yesterday, and took shorthand notes of what she said. Let me read you her exact words. 'Mother and I heard the sound of a shot downstairs. It was unbelievably loud, like a great clap of thunder. People were shouting and running. Mother and I sat transfixed with fear. I said: 'Something has happened to Father'. Mother said nothing. She just sat quite still and frozen'.'

Louise sighed with what was evidently satisfaction. She stood up, and leaned on the corner of the mantelpiece. It was a habit of hers that Box had noted; it indicated that she was sole mistress of this particular hearth and home.

'You see, Mr Box,' she said, 'that was the reaction I would have expected. Frozen fear. She knew in her heart that her daughter was right. Something had happened to her husband, and so she waited, petrified, for confirmation. It's the next bit that's vital.

What happened then?'

'The butler, who had seen the assassin, ran up the stairs and broke the news of his master's death.'

'How did he know that Sir John Courteline was dead?'

'He had rushed into the study and seen his master lying on the hearth rug. He knelt down and ascertained that he was dead, and then conveyed that news to his mistress.'

'And what did she do?'

'According to her daughter, she said, 'Let me see him'. The daughter tried to dissuade her, but she insisted. It turned out to be a mistake. She was helped downstairs and into the study, where she in turn knelt down by the body. Again, let me read you Miss Olga's exact words. 'Mother knelt by Father's body, and touched his neck. She looked at her fingers — I think she expected to see blood on them, but there was none. Mother saw the cigar smouldering on the carpet near Father's hand. 'It's still lit', she said, and then she touched his hand. Suddenly, she started to scream. We should not have brought her down there. She screamed without ceasing. I half dragged her into the domestic quarters of the house where the cook and I attempted to calm her. It was useless. She screamed until she collapsed'.'

Box's studiously neutral tones failed to mask the horror of the daughter's narration. Miss Whittaker picked up a blue glass candlestick, examined it, and returned it to the mantelpiece. They both listened to the ticking of a little china clock, and to the coal settling in the grate.

'Well?' Louise Whittaker demanded.

'What do you mean, miss?'

Louise shook her head in half-amused vexation.

'Oh, Mr Box, you know perfectly well what I'm asking. What was it that Lady Courteline *saw* that made her scream? And don't say that it was her husband's body, because it wasn't!'

'She didn't see anything special, Miss Whittaker. She saw her husband, and she saw his lighted cigar. And — There was another piece of physical evidence present, but it couldn't have meant anything to her.'

'Ah! I think we're getting somewhere at last. What was this piece of evidence?'

'It was a calling-card by the dead man's hand. I believe it was placed there by the assassin himself on behalf of the man who hired him. On it was printed the name 'Dr N. I. Karenin'. When I questioned Lady Courteline myself yesterday, I asked her if she knew the name. She became very agitated — she was under great stress, of course

— and denied any knowledge of a Dr Karenin.'

Miss Whittaker's face flushed crimson. She stamped her foot in vexation.

'And you believed her! You believed her because she is a lady of title, and the widow of a public idol. So, as far as you were concerned, what she said was true. But that was why she screamed. It was seeing the card that made her scream in anguish. Of course she was upset that her husband had been murdered, but her hysteria, her sick fear, arose because she saw and read that card.'

'So you think that she knew this man Karenin?'

'Of course she knew him! Or knew him in the past. And, more to the point, Mr Box, she *feared for him*. Karenin is a Russian name. Lady Courteline is Russian by birth. A little delving into your titled lady's history, Mr Box, might bear some interesting fruit. Let me give you a piece of advice: don't allow yourself to be bullied by women's wiles. Find out why Lady Courteline is shielding the man who brought about the murder of her husband.'

Miss Whittaker rang the bell to summon Ethel. It was time for her to return to work.

'Thank you, miss,' said Arnold Box stiffly, 'for a very pleasant repast. Very nice indeed.

And thanks for your help.' He sighed, and added in a low voice, 'Miss Whittaker — Louise — I'm sorry to have made you angry. I seem to have a knack for doing that. But in fact, all I ever want is for you to be happy, miss.'

Louise Whittaker took Box's hand, leaned forward, and swiftly kissed his cheek.

'As Ethel often remarks, Mr Box,' she said, 'you're ever so funny! I'm not angry with *you*, Arnold Box. I'm angry with *her*, for involving you in whatever devious game she's playing. You're always welcome here: you should know that, by now. True friends don't always need to observe the social niceties. Go after this Karenin. I must get back to Mary Shelley.'

When Box had gone, Louise sat at her table in the bay window, watching little Ethel bustling about, removing the tea things. Forgetful of the author of *Frankenstein*, her thoughts dwelt on Arnold Box. What a lively, honest, decent man he was, despite his infuriating assumption of male superiority. That perkiness of his was a mask for a natural diffidence, an endearing modesty that made him at times underestimate his own very great talents. How thankful she was, though, that he was not an intellectual sort of man! She saw enough of those in her professional life. Arnold Box was refreshingly different.

* * *

As Box crossed the cobbles towards 2 King James's Rents in the early evening, an elderly man with a straggling white moustache approached him from the turning into Aberdeen Lane.

'My name's Fred Wilson, sir,' said the man. 'I'm a messenger for the Prudential Assurance Office in Holborn Bars. You'll be Detective Inspector Box, I expect?'

The man had a rough but kindly voice. He peered at Box with rheumy, pale-blue eyes.

'The very same, Mr Wilson,' said Box. 'And what can I do for you?'

'Nothing for me in particular, Mr Box,' Wilson replied. 'But it would greatly oblige a friend of mine if you'd go up into St Edward's Churchyard tomorrow morning, at eleven o'clock.'

'St Edward's Churchyard? I suppose I mustn't ask who this friend of yours is?'

'Better not, sir. St Edward's Churchyard, just beyond Goldsmiths' Court, on the turn into Coleman Street.'

Before Box could reply, the elderly messenger had touched his hat and walked rapidly away in the direction of Whitehall Place.

4

Diplomatic Incident

At eleven o'clock the next morning, Inspector Box climbed up the four worn steps into the churchyard of St Edward's, Coleman Street. A faded old man, with a campaign medal pinned to his rusty old coat, saluted him with a tug at his forelock, and locked the churchyard gates behind him. Oh, well, thought Box, time to enter the lion's den.

The churchyard was no bigger than a modest suburban garden. It contained a few tottering tombs, a good deal of gravel, and a stone shelter built against the soot-blackened north wall of an unremarkable eighteenth-century church. To right and left rose the blank walls of commercial buildings. The old man with the medal, apparently preoccupied with his own thoughts, limped across the graveyard, and disappeared through a small door into the church.

Sitting in the stone shelter was a slight, sandy-haired man with a mild, clean-shaven face. He was wearing a long overcoat with an astrakhan collar, and his tall silk hat and ebony walking-cane reposed on the bench beside him. He treated Box to an almost apologetic smile.

'Good morning, Mr Box,' he said. He managed to invest the simple greeting with a tone of sardonic weariness.

'Good morning, Colonel Kershaw. So it's like that, is it?'

'Yes, Box. It's like that. At least, I think it is. Will you smoke a cigar with me?'

'I will, sir.'

Box sat down beside Kershaw on the stone bench and looked at his companion. Lieutenant-Colonel Sir Adrian Kershaw RA was rumoured to be one of the powers behind the throne. Box was one of a small number of people, who, through personal experience, knew that the rumour was true. Colonel Kershaw was a man feared by his enemies. It was, perhaps, more illustrative of his powers to know that he was feared, too, by his friends.

Colonel Kershaw took a stout cigar case from his pocket, opened it, and offered it to Box. Three slim cigars reposed in the case, and beside them a rolled-up spill of paper secured by a loop of twine. Kershaw's pale-blue eyes caught Box's for a moment. Box took a cigar, and also the spill of paper, which he slipped into his overcoat pocket.

The two men lit their cigars, and smoked in silence for a minute or two. Then Kershaw spoke.

'I'm glad you came, Box,' he said. 'Evidently old Wilson hasn't lost his talents to persuade. I didn't think we'd meet again so soon after that Hansa Protocol business, but there it is. Let me first congratulate you on your brilliant solution of the Courteline case. Very commendable.'

Kershaw smiled, and drew thoughtfully on his cigar. Box regarded him quizzically. Something tantalizingly abstruse lay behind the colonel's words.

'But I didn't solve it, Colonel Kershaw. I laid hands on the villain who fired the shot, and holed him up in his den. Somebody else — somebody quite unknown to me — blew Killer Kitely to Kingdom Come.'

'Well, yes,' said Kershaw. 'I suppose that's true, as far as it goes.'

'And there's another mystery, sir, that I haven't solved. Sir John Courteline was dressed and ready to go out somewhere at the time of his murder, but no one seems to know where he was going. More to the point, no one has come forward to say that Sir John failed to keep an appointment.'

'Well, you see, Mr Box,' said Kershaw, narrowing his eyes against the invasive smoke of his cigar, 'people don't like being involved unnecessarily with the Law. I don't myself. But Courteline's whereabouts on that fatal day — fatal for *him*, you know — brings me very conveniently, to my business with you today.

'Earlier this year, in the company of a man called Captain Edgar Adams RN, I went down to Cornwall, to a place called Porthcurno, the little spot where some of the major submarine telegraph cables come up out of the ocean and on to the British mainland. And there, Mr Box, Adams and I detected the stirring of yet another international hell's brew — '

'Not the Germans again?'

'No, not the Germans. From all appearances, it's the Russians this time. From what we saw at Porthcurno, Captain Adams and I deduced that Russia is about to step out of line, and wreak havoc with the balance of power in Europe and beyond. I've been thinking about Russia for the last two months, and so has our friend Sir Charles Napier at the Foreign Office. Captain Adams, by the way, belongs to Naval Intelligence. He was lent to me by Admiral Holland, on the understanding that he was to be given as free a range as possible.'

Box felt the characteristic surge of

excitement that always occurred whenever this subtle and rather sinister man crossed his path. They had worked closely together in the past, but Kershaw was not his official superior. He always asked Box to assist him, and had made it perfectly clear that he was free to decline. It was this freedom of association that added to the thrill of working with Kershaw.

'And this brings me now, Box,' said Kershaw, 'to the mystery of Sir John Courteline. You ask where he was going on the day of his murder. The answer is, that he was going to see *me*. Courteline was one of my secret servants.'

The secret servants . . . Kershaw always referred to people like Fred Wilson and the old man who had secured the church-yard gate as his 'nobodies'. Their great value lay in their social anonymity. The secret servants, though, were salaried agents of Secret Intelligence, men and women who knew that their lives could be in danger when they went out to do Kershaw's mysterious bidding. And the murdered Sir John Courteline had been one of them.

'Sir John Courteline was of particular value to you, sir?'

'Yes. He was my hidden eye on Russia. Mine, not the Foreign Office's. He knew all kinds of people in Moscow and St Petersburg, high and low, good and bad. Courteline had all but retired from secret intelligence work, but if anything particularly odd seemed to be afoot in Russia, Courteline would come to see me. But I don't know why he wanted to see me on this occasion. He never lived to tell me.'

Kershaw made a little sound, which might have been a laugh, or a stifled sigh.

'And this Captain Edgar Adams, sir: what's become of him?'

Kershaw shifted uneasily on the bench. He frowned with what Box thought at first was annoyance. He swiftly realized that the frown was one of anxiety.

'I don't know. I last saw Captain Adams in London, after we'd returned from Cornwall. He's an officer in the Royal Navy, but decided that he'd follow a certain line of exploration by turning himself into a merchant seaman. This was in January. He set out on his travels almost immediately, and returned to London only a few days ago. But I've not been able to speak to him yet, because he's been dogged by a very determined enemy.'

'So you reckon he's gone to ground in London somewhere?'

'I do. I'm convinced that he's found out

certain things that will confirm a theory I have about the state of Europe at the moment. I can't act decisively until I've talked to Adams face to face . . . I'm sorry that I can't be more forthcoming. I think you'll know that it's not for lack of trust in you, either as a man or a colleague.'

'And what do you want me to do, sir?'

'I want you to do something that at first sight seems to have nothing to do with what I've just told you. But appearances, as you well know, Box, are frequently deceptive. This evening, Sir Charles Napier is attending a reception for members of the Diplomatic Corps at Sir Abraham Goldsmith's house in Arlington Street, just off Piccadilly. I was wondering whether you could contrive to station yourself somewhere in the vicinity? It's just that I feel something dramatic is going to happen at the reception tonight, and I'd value your presence there, if you're agreeable. You might like to bear a particular name in mind: Captain Igor Andropov. Just bear it in mind, you know.'

'Andropov. Very well, sir. And will you be there, Colonel Kershaw?'

Kershaw smiled, and threw away the butt of his cigar.

'I will, Box. I've not been formally invited, but I'll be there, none the less. Will you agree to — to hover in the vicinity?'

'I will, sir. And now, if I may, I'd like to show you a visiting-card that I took from near the dead body of Sir John Courteline. I believe that it was deliberately left beside him by his murderer. It may mean something to you.'

Box took the bloodstained visiting-card from his pocket, and handed it to Kershaw, who looked thoughtfully at the side containing the Russian characters.

'Dr N.I. Karenin,' he muttered. 'Nikolai Ivanovich, most likely. Hm . . . '

'Then you know who this man is?' asked Box, eagerly.

Kershaw sighed, and slipped the card into an inside pocket of his great-coat.

'I'm not Little Jack Horner, you know, Box. I don't just put my thumb into a nice big pie, and pull out a juicy plum, saying, 'Oh, what a good boy am I'. Karenin? No, I don't know anyone of that name. As for the Nikolai and the Ivanovich, it's just that Russian names have a certain predictability — and monotony. But if you'll let me take the card away with me, I'll find someone at the reception tonight who'll steer you in the right direction.'

Colonel Kershaw stood up, and treated Box to a kindly smile. He picked up his silk hat and his ebony cane. At the same time, the old man with the medal appeared from the church, carrying a bunch of keys.

Box thought to himself: he's playing the innocent, but he'll have to get up early to deceive me. He's drawing me into something, but he's not going to tell me what it is yet. Well, so be it. Wily old fox! It was time to make arrangements for hovering in the vicinity of Arlington Street, just off Piccadilly.

* * *

'Inspector Box! What brings you down this particular alley this evening?'

'Well, well. Fiske of the *Graphic*. I could well ask you the same question. And the intrepid Mr Carter, of the *Sketch*. How are you, gents? As for why I'm here, it's to get a cup of hot coffee. It's chilly tonight, even for early March.'

Arnold Box looked at the two reporters, who were leaning against a wall near to a rather flimsy coffee stall, where a taciturn, nondescript sort of man displayed a steaming urn and a pile of chipped mugs. Billy Fiske was the *Graphic*'s chief political reporter, an impressive figure, much given to flapping overcoats and old-fashioned high-crowned hats. He sported a fiercely intimidating black moustache. Ted Carter, a frog-faced man with a hacking cough, and a navy-blue muffler tied round his throat, was Court and Society Correspondent for the *Sketch*.

Box threw a penny down on the counter, and received a steaming mug of coffee. He wondered why there should be a coffee stall so near to Sir Abraham Goldsmith's imposing residence. He also wondered what Billy Fiske was doing there.

'I'm here to report the social goings-on for our avid readers, Mr Box,' said Fiske. 'Another brilliant levee for the glittering ornaments of the upper echelons of our society. The coaches have been coming and going for the last half hour. Gentlemen in sashes, and ladies in ball gowns, some with tiaras (but most without) have ascended the steps outside the brilliantly lighted mansion of the celebrated merchant banker, Sir Abraham Goldsmith.'

'Strewth! You don't actually write like that, do you, Billy? I've never bothered to read your stuff'

Fiske of the *Graphic* laughed, and gulped down some of his coffee.

'No, Mr Box, that's not my style. I'm imitating poor Ted here — Ted, if you cough any louder, you'll cough your fat head off.'

The frog-faced man managed a smile. He

rubbed his mittened hands together, and stamped his feet. Box realized how very cold it was in the alley, and wondered why these two eminent reporters had chosen to freeze there together. Still, their presence simplified the business of hovering.

'Mr Box,' said Ted Carter of the *Sketch*, between coughs, 'ignore this overbearing ignoramus. I pen my reports in a dignified and elegant style, worthy to rank with the best in *The Times*. I've made a note of all the most eminent persons who've arrived so far. The German Ambassador and his suite came on foot from Prussia House. His Excellency the Russian Ambassador, accompanied by Princess Orlova, arrived just minutes ago. The French party — well, they'll come deliberately late, so as to spite the Prussians.'

'Any sign of Captain Igor Andropov?' asked Box.

Mr Fiske cursed roundly as he splashed hot coffee down his coat.

'Andropov?' he growled. 'He's the military attaché, isn't he? He may be here, for all I know.'

Box smiled, and said nothing. A palpable hit, as someone or other once said. So that's what had brought Billy Fiske, chief political reporter, to this social gathering of big bugs! Box glanced at the self-effacing stall holder, and saw that he, too, was smiling, as though at some secret joke that he was not allowed to share.

* * *

The sumptuous reception salon of Sir Abraham Goldsmith's residence was filled with a glittering throng of ladies and gentlemen, invited ostensibly for a pleasant evening's fraternization beneath the glowing chandeliers, which held clusters of elegant white candles, and the white and gilt stucco ceilings. The candle-light, reflected from many prisms and brilliants, caught the jewelled necklaces of the ladies, and filled the great room with the deeply rich scintilla of many diamonds.

In a pillared gallery high above the salon, Sir Charles Napier looked down on the chattering crowd of guests. Liveried footmen wove expertly through them, offering glasses of claret. The Germans, he noted, had made a conscious effort to mingle with the other nationalities. The French cultural attaché had been buttonholed by that old bore von Metz, and the German Ambassador himself was evidently being very pleasant to Mr Austen Chamberlain.

And the Russians? They were gathered

around their ambassador, Prince Orloff, like sheep around their shepherd. Orloff seemed to be on the defensive. He looked, as always, very stiff and proud in evening dress. He was wearing the sash and star of the Order of St Stanislaus. Beside him was Count Kropotkin, Head of Mission, with his beautiful countess, and a number of junior attachés, all duly deferential. The ambassador's wife, Princess Orlova, had attracted a minor coterie of ladies from the other nationalities, and had retired with them to a side room.

And where, thought Napier, was his particular *bête noir*? Ah! There he was. Slightly behind the main Russian group, and frowning like a spoilt brat, was the Russian military attaché, Captain Igor Andropov.

A voice behind Napier, a voice belonging to a man half-hidden by an archway framed by tall palms, suddenly spoke. Napier continued to look down on the brilliant throng.

'Did you send young Andropov a Note this morning?' asked the voice. 'If you did, then that would explain his brow of thunder. That, and the fact that he's clearly drunk. He looks more like an apoplectic pig than ever.'

'I don't recollect your name appearing on the guest list, Colonel Kershaw,' said Napier. 'But of course I knew you'd get in some way or other. Yes, I sent him a formal Note. It was Salisbury's idea in the first place. I think he contemplated something like a mild complaint, but I had a word with the Foreign Secretary before he left for Scotland this afternoon, and he thought a Note would be more to the point. But come out from behind those palms, Kershaw, and sit down here. I received bad news from Brian Fitzgerald this afternoon. I want to tell you about it.'

Kershaw did as he was bid. Fitzgerald, he knew, was the supervisor of Foreign Office correspondents in Northern Europe. A genial cloth-merchant by trade, he had been based in Riga for many years.

'I heard from Fitzgerald today that two of my people, Abu Daria and Piotr Casimir, were found murdered, tied back to back and shot through the head. Their bodies were in a timberstore at Petrovosk. And my agent Jacob Kroll — you remember Kroll? — was pulled dead from the river at Riga. He'd evidently been attacked by thugs, and his body flung into the Dvina. Those three men have been murdered for revealing what they knew about Russia's aggressive intentions towards India, and their secret machinations in the forests of Lithuania.'

'Perhaps. Or maybe they were murdered in case they revealed what they *didn't* know.

Dead men tell no tales either way.'

In the salon below, a pianist seated himself at a great rosewood piano, and began to play. His music was designed to complement the conversation — tuneful, and sweetly harmonic. The noise of conversation began to rise, and the footmen appeared with further supplies of claret.

'I received no response from Andropov to that Note I sent this morning,' said Napier. 'I think this is the right time for me to go down there and pay my respects to Prince Orloff. Then I'll steer young Andropov into a corner to hear what he has to say.'

'I wish you well,' said Colonel Kershaw. 'Do you want me to come with you?'

Sir Charles Napier laughed, and moved towards the staircase.

'Certainly not! You stay up here, out of the way. After all, I'm hardly venturing into the lion's den — merely the pig's sty.'

Kershaw watched Napier as he descended the staircase into the salon. He had known Charles Napier since boyhood. They had had their differences, but since the affair of the Hansa Protocol earlier that year, each had revised his estimate of the other. Elegant and beautifully spoken, Napier was a born diplomat, a fluent linguist, and a skilful weaver of the many subtle threads of politics.

He wore his clothes well, and tonight his white shirt front was adorned with the insignia of a Knight Bachelor.

Colonel Kershaw thought of the blood-stained card that Box had given him earlier that day. He had shown it to M. Scriabin, head of security at the Russian Embassy. Scriabin had pulled a wry face, and told him that this Karenin had been gaoled for a breach of state security in the '70s, and that he had been released from prison the previous year. He had told him, too, the name of a man living in London who could tell him all about Dr Karenin and his history. He would contrive to let Box know that.

There was Napier now, weaving his way through the throng. Now he was bowing to Prince Orloff, who was returning the compliment with a vengeance. His attendant suite bowed their heads briefly. And now he was talking to young Captain Andropov . . .

What was this? A sudden, violent movement from the Russian attaché, and he had flung the contents of his claret glass in Napier's face. Several women screamed, the pianist stopped in mid-phrase, and conversation froze. In moments, a number of angry men had closed in on the attaché, pinioned his arms, and dragged him away. He was shouting something in Russian, his face contorted with drunken rage.

Napier was wiping his face with a scarf that someone had passed to him. Even from where he stood in the balcony, Kershaw could see the ugly red claret stain splashed across Napier's dress shirt. He suddenly felt a surge of cold anger, but he did not let that prevent him from noticing that one of the footmen had hastily deposited his tray on a window sill and hurried out into the hall passage. So that was it!

Napier was speaking to the assembled company in French. 'Please, my friends, it is nothing. A young man's foolish misunderstanding. Please continue the *soirée*. In a few minutes' time the grand buffet will be served.' Napier glanced at the pianist, who immediately continued his quiet recital. The conversations were renewed.

Prince Orloff's face was white with shock. He looked beside himself with shame.

'My dear Sir Charles,' he stammered in English, 'you will believe me when I say that I had no notice of this terrible insult. I apologize unreservedly and publicly, on my own behalf, and that of the Imperial Government. That man will be withdrawn to Russia immediately, and disciplined. I am devastated, dishonoured . . . ' The ambassador was wringing his hands in anguish.

‘Come up into the gallery, Your Excellency,’ said Napier. ‘We can talk privately there. Meanwhile, let me assure you that I regard Andropov’s action as a mental aberration. The matter is of no consequence.’

Sir Charles Napier and Prince Orloff made their way through the guests towards the stairs. Napier acknowledged the many murmured expressions of sympathy that were offered to him in several languages. The Russian Ambassador maintained a stiff posture and determined silence until they had reached the seclusion of the gallery, where they sat down at a table.

‘This afternoon, Sir Charles,’ said Prince Orloff, ‘Andropov came to me and showed me the Note that you had sent him. It suggested that the Russian Imperial Government had authorized incursions into Afghanistan, perhaps with a view to attacking India. I am happy to assure you that these suggestions are unfounded.’

‘I am delighted to hear it, Your Excellency. Your assurance is, of course, entirely sufficient. Thank you for clarifying the situation for me.’

‘Your Note to Andropov further suggested that Russian engineers were working on unspecified projects in the vicinity of Meshed. Again, I am happy to assure you that this is not the case. Your informants were mistaken.'

'Again, Prince Orloff, I must thank you for your kindness in making things clear. They were simply enquiries, as I'm sure you'll understand. Captain Andropov evidently misread my intentions. Having those points clarified assures me, not for the first time, that relations between our government and yours are conducted on a basis of frankness and mutual regard.'

Prince Orloff smiled, and inclined his head. Then his eyes rested on Napier's stained shirt front. Once again, the old aristocrat blushed with shame and anger.

'Do you believe me when I say that I was not privy to that fellow's outrageous assault? I can't fathom the reason for it. He is supposed to be a diplomat — but he will be one no longer. He will be returned to his regiment, if they will have him — but who is this? Ah! Colonel Sir Adrian Kershaw. Please join us, Colonel. I have been apologizing to Napier here for that man's conduct.'

Colonel Kershaw glanced briefly at Napier, and then sat down beside the ambassador.

'My dear Prince Orloff,' said Kershaw, 'as you know, I am the kind of person who finds out things. Now here is something about Captain Igor Andropov that you may not know. Young as he is, that man has been heavily in debt for years — ruinously in debt. Very soon, he may lose the small estate that has given him the necessary entrée into Russian public life.'

'You astound me! Are you sure of this, Colonel Kershaw?'

'I am, Your Excellency. Andropov was bribed by a certain faction to create a diplomatic incident here, tonight. That faction had previously ensured that there would be sufficient bad blood between Britain and Russia for something like this to occur. Andropov is no Russian patriot. He is a hired turncoat. So, as I'm sure Sir Charles Napier has told you, there is no diplomatic breach between you and us. Russia's honour has never been in question.'

The ambassador stood up, and shook both men vigorously by the hand.

'Gentlemen,' he said, 'the matter is closed. I will go down to join my suite. And then, perhaps, we can all assemble for the grand buffet!'

The two Englishmen watched the old Russian aristocrat as he descended the stairs. Sir Charles Napier looked at Kershaw with a mixture of awe and amused vexation.

'You monstrous creature, Kershaw! So you knew all the time that this incident was going to take place. You knew Andropov would be here, and you didn't think it necessary to warn me. Really!'

'Well, you see, I didn't know what exact form the incident was going to take. Trust a fellow like Andropov to waste a very decent Médoc! Incidentally, I think Mrs Beeton has a recipe somewhere, called, 'To Remove Claret Stains from a Boiled Shirt'. I'll look it out for you. By the way, did you notice one of the footmen rushing out as soon as the wine-throwing took place? He's gone to alert the Press, who are lurking in the alley beside this house. Somebody tipped them off about all this, and paid that footman to relay the news. It'll be in all the papers tomorrow, and no matter what you and old Orloff say to each other, the papers will blow the matter up out of all proportion. The so-called 'incident' was contrived solely for that purpose.'

Napier stood in thought for a moment, looking down on the crowd of guests.

'You may well be right, though my intelligence seems to confirm that Russia really is making these incursions in Afghanistan and beyond. Prince Orloff is secretly furious beneath that veneer of diplomatic sweet reasonableness. He's convinced that we're seeking an opportunity to quarrel. He didn't believe my reassurances just now, and, of course, I didn't believe his protestations of innocence.'

'Well, Charles,' said Kershaw, 'perhaps we'll speak further about all this. Incidentally, it's not only the gentlemen of the Press who are shivering out there in the cold; Detective Inspector Box is there, as well. I rather think that our friend the footman will have met his match in that alley.'

⋆ ⋆ ⋆

Box waited in the shadows of the cold alley until the footman, incongruous in his blue and silver livery and powdered wig, had poured out his excited account of the incident to the waiting reporters. Fiske of the *Graphic*, and Carter of the *Sketch*, grinning broadly, had beaten a hasty retreat. Both men, Box knew, needed only the bare bones of a story: their great journalistic skills would provide the necessary meat.

As soon as the gleeful reporters had gone, Box emerged from the shadows, and seized the startled footman by the collar.

'I just want a little verbal statement from you, my friend,' said Box, showing the man his warrant card. 'So let's have no bluster, and no clever tales. Who tipped you off about this little game?'

The footman, a young fellow of twenty or so, licked his lips nervously, and glanced at the entrance to the alley, which the taciturn coffee seller had carefully blocked by pulling his stall across the entrance.

'So help me God, guvnor, I don't know who the man was. He approached me yesterday, as I was exercising Lady Goldsmith's dogs in the park. He gave me five pounds in sovereigns, and said that if anything peculiar happened in our house tonight, I was to come out here and tell a man called Fiske what had happened. I didn't mean no harm, guvnor — '

'I never said you did. What was he like, this man? I don't suppose he gave you his name and address, did he, and a nice little photograph of himself in a leather-covered frame?'

'No, sir. He didn't do anything like that. He was a tall man, with very black hair. Pale as a ghost — corpse pale, he was. He spoke English, but with a foreign accent, like a lot of the gentlemen do who come to our house. I won't lose my place, will I, guvnor?'

'No, you won't. You've not broken the law, but you might take a few lessons in loyalty to your employer, my lad. You might have compromised him, and damaged his reputation as a banker, and all for five pounds. Go on, hop it.'

When the footman had scuttled away, Box turned to the stallholder.

'I suppose you're another of the colonel's private regiment?' he asked. 'He thinks of everything, doesn't he?'

The man smiled. He had cleared the stall of its urn and pile of cups, which he had stowed in a cupboard beneath the counter, and had begun to drag the whole thing out into Arlington Street.

'He thinks of most things, Inspector Box,' he said. 'You'll usually find me working in a little lane off Leicester Square, but I came here tonight to oblige the Colonel. If the gentlemen of the Press were turning up, they'd need somewhere to plant themselves comfortably. Thinks of everything, the colonel does.'

5

Voices from the Sea

The cable ship *Lermontov* had lain at anchor for most of the dark hours of Friday night, half a mile off the Cornish coast. As Saturday dawned, and the sun rose, its light was quickly smothered in the drifting mists of grey rain falling widely across the sea. It was just possible for a sharp ear to detect the sound of the engines that worked the cable-lifting gear. A pall of black smoke hung over the vessel.

In a sheltered fissure high on the cliff top William Pascoe, chief cipher clerk, well wrapped up against the rigours of the cold morning, stared out to sea through powerful binoculars. Yes, it was as he thought. The mysterious vessel had returned to its haunt, and this time he was able to make out its name and provenance, painted on the stern in Latin characters: *Lermontov, Odessa*. They were busy splicing into one of the cables. Soon, no doubt, they'd send a message for him and his colleagues at Porthcurno to pick up and relay to London.

The rain began to clear, and the low banks of cloud glowed with a diffuse sunlight. Far off, near the horizon, a smudge of smoke appeared. That, thought Pascoe wryly, will be the naval frigate that someone in London had decided to send across from Plymouth, to keep an eye on things. Activity on the *Lermontov* ceased, and Pascoe heard the rasping of its anchor-chain. The ship remained stationary, but Pascoe knew that before the frigate had come fully into view, the Russian ship would begin to move away, probably in the general direction of the French coast.

★ ★ ★

In the snug inner office leading off the main transmission room at Porthcurno cable station, a comfortable, fair-haired man in his forties puffed away at his morning pipe, and scanned the early editions of the newspapers. They were full of the drunken Russian attaché's attack on Sir Charles Napier — and making heavy weather of it, by the look of things.

'A grave assault on the dignity of the English race,' the *Morning Post* declared. 'Russia may be quite certain,' it went on to say, 'that Her Majesty's Government will demand full reparation.' Well, maybe.

What did *The Times* have to say? 'It may be time for Britain to reappraise her alliances. For too long, it seems, we have made Prussia the bogey-man with which to affright ourselves. Has the time come to believe the Kaiser's protestations of friendship? Has the time come to understand the deep concerns of the Berlin government, and to see that fear of Russia is a legitimate cause for concern?' Strong stuff!

The fair-haired man put the paper down, and walked out into the transmission room. William Pascoe had come hurrying in from his early-morning jaunt. Thank goodness he'd left his bicycle outside! Here he was, making no attempt to remove his damp pea jacket, looking as though he was bursting with news. It was only seven o'clock, and the six night operators were still on duty, sitting at their busy machines.

'Ah! So you're back from your jaunt at last, William!' said the fair-haired man. 'It's been frantic here for the last hour. Very heavy traffic from Alexandria, which seems to be carrying a lot of the Malta stuff this morning. Heavy going, for a Saturday! But it's all commercial, and we're slackening off, now, thank goodness. The day men will be down in half an hour.'

'Has there been anything from nearer home in the last twenty minutes or so, Bob? I saw that ship down there again this morning. It was splicing into one or other of the cables — '

'You and your mystery ships! As a matter of fact, a message had started to come in as you arrived. It's coming through now, on Number 5, over there, the old Kelvin-Muirhead machine. Perhaps it's the message you're hoping for.'

Bob Jones moved away to talk to one of the other operators, and William Pascoe sat down in front of Number 5 engine, a gleaming Kelvin Siphon Recorder. His experienced fingers made a few quick adjustments to the terminals and to the speed of the electro-magnetic engine. Then he caught the moving paper tape between his hands as it rolled off the spool, reading the peaks and dips recorded by the elderly machine, and mentally translating them into letters.

The message was in English, and directed from the cable station at Carcavelos in Spain to the military section of the Russian Embassy in London. 'Have ascertained,' it ran, 'that the German cargo steamer *Berlin Star*, out of Bremerhaven, is in reality a contraband runner, smuggling arms from Britain to dissidents in Russia. Let all necessary action be taken.' What could it mean? Was it a hoax? Perhaps, but the letters concluding the message were undoubtedly the signal code for the receiving telegraph office at the Russian Embassy. Here was Bob Jones again.

'Any luck, William?' said his colleague, good-humouredly. Bob Jones was an easy man to work with. Although much older than Pascoe, he didn't seem to begrudge the younger man his seniority.

'Yes, Bob, I'm quite certain that this message was relayed here from a splice, made just an hour ago by that rogue cable ship, the *Lermontov*. I'll write it down in plain English, and send it enclosed in a letter to Mr Dangerfield at Winchester House. Perhaps he'll pass it on to that clever chap who was down here in January — Captain Adams. And I think I'll go down to my friend Hugh Trevannion at St Columb's Manor on Monday. I'd value his advice.'

Young Pascoe turned the knurled brass knobs that stopped the mechanisms rotating, and the Kelvin-Muirhead Recorder fell silent.

The rush of calls on the cable station had subsided, and Jones had strolled over to the blazing fire.

'Incidentally,' he said, 'if secret messages can be so easily breached by splicing the cables, then the government should consider using direct-voice communications through the Post Office's electric telephone lines. That new line from London to Paris has been wildly successful.'

'Oh, yes,' said Pascoe, smiling, 'a very great success — at eight shillings for three minutes! It's only used by the Stock Exchange to talk to the gentlemen of the Paris bourse. The government would never sanction using the electric telephone for serious work, ingenious as it is.'

'Well, I'll give you a little piece of fatherly advice. Forget all this cloak-and-dagger business. Your job — *our* job — is to forward incoming messages to their destinations. If we do that, we'll all keep out of trouble. I'm off, now. Time for a bit of shut-eye.'

William Pascoe went into the inner office, and rummaged among the pile of newspapers. He'd leave the heavy ones to Bob and the others. Where was the *Graphic*? There'd be a leader by William Fiske, the great political correspondent. Yes, here it was.

> *We ask ourselves this morning, what Lord Salisbury would have done. Readers will know the answer to that rhetorical question. He would have sent the whole menagerie of snarling bears*

and their lackeys packing, bag and baggage, to St Petersburg. We wait to see what the present administration will do. Their Liberal principles may caution them to use the kid-glove; the temper of the British people this morning will tell them, unequivocally, to shake the naked fist of retaliation. Prince Orloff and his minions will contrive to produce excuses for the hideous insult to Sir Charles Napier. Let the lion's fearsome roar drown the uncertain growls of the bear.

Marvellous! It was good to know that not everybody in the capital believed in hiding their heads in the sand.

⋆ ⋆ ⋆

Squire Trevannion glanced out of the long medieval window of the living-room at his ancient Cornish manor of St Columb's. How far off London seemed! For himself, he would be content to remain here, within the confines of his walled cliff-top estate, until he died. But the old, stable world was shrinking fast. The railways, and the web of telegraphic cables and humming wires, had reduced the vast realm of Britain to a comparatively small and manageable island.

Here was young Pascoe now, pushing open the gate in the dry-stone wall that gave entrance to St Columb's from the cliff path. He'd sent a note over on Sunday, saying he wanted to call and ask for advice. Best go to the door and greet him. Would he mind these old, patched tweeds? Pascoe always dressed smartly — too smartly, to some folk's way of thinking. One day, if he wasn't careful, he'd forget that he was a Penzance man, born and bred.

'Now, I wonder,' said Trevannion, as he ushered his visitor over the threshold and into the long, low parlour, 'what brings you this far out from Porthcurno today? I'm sure it's not merely for the pleasure of my conversation.'

'As I said in my note, Hugh, I've come to ask you a favour. It's nothing very much, just permission to use your cliff path down to Spanish Beach. You see, somebody told me recently that a boatload of men came ashore one January night from that Russian cable ship — '

Hugh Trevannion sprang to his feet. His face, normally wooden and impassive, was flushed with anger.

'For goodness' sake, Pascoe,' he cried, 'can't you leave that wretched business alone? Damn it, man, it's six weeks since those odd messages came through your machines. Leave it, I say. You're a clever fellow, I've no doubt, but there are cleverer people in London who'll ferret out the meaning of it all.'

'I'm sorry to annoy you so much, Hugh — '

'I'm not really annoyed with you, William. It's just that as I get older, I get grumpier! By all means go down my private path to Spanish Beach. I expect you want to talk to the folk at the inn. They're the people who've been putting these rumours about. I wish you'd give it up. But there, young men don't really like to accept advice from folk of my age, even though they ask for it. Get down to Spanish Beach. I know you won't rest until you've heard what the folk at the inn have to say.'

⋆ ⋆ ⋆

As Hugh Trevannion stood at one of the windows, watching Pascoe as he hurried across the sparse grass towards the cliff, a voice behind him said softly, 'Curiosity, so you English aver, killed the cat.'

Trevannion turned from the window to look at the man who had been his secret guest since mid-February. A tall man, whose bony wrists protruded from the sleeves of his black jacket, a man with strong, sinuous hands, from the fingers of which some nails were missing. Familiarity with the man brought these things to the forefront of Hugh's attention, but on first acquaintance, it was the face that had held him fascinated.

It was a face of almost ghostly pallor, chalk-white. The features were regular, and the man was clean-shaven, so that when you saw beyond the pallor you realized that he must have been very handsome in his youth. He was nearer fifty than forty, but his hair was of a deep bluish black. His eyes, of a startlingly pale blue, had the unsettled gaze of a fanatic.

Hugh Trevannion felt a surge of excitement. He forgot about Pascoe, as he met the disturbingly unfocused gaze of the corpse-pale man. Had the moment arrived when the manor, and its lands, were to be truly his own again? Dr Karenin had come into his life at a desperate juncture, when total ruin had threatened him, not financial ruin alone, but mental disintegration, for he had begun to hear the voice of his dead sister Meg talking and singing about the house. Karenin had brought him solvency and security. All he had to do was say nothing, and think nothing.

'That is what you English say, is it not? 'Curiosity killed the cat'. Well, that young man should have heeded your warning. Spanish Beach is a decidedly unhealthy place at this time of year.'

'Are you ready, now, Dr Karenin, to conclude the business?' asked Trevannion in a trembling voice. 'You promised that today would be the day — Monday, the thirteenth of March.'

'I did, Mr Trevannion, and you'll find that I am true to my word. Let us go up to my room, and conclude the business there.'

An old twisted staircase took them to the second storey, where Trevannion's guest occupied a large room overlooking the wild, boulder-strewn approach to the edge of the cliff. The man sat down at a roll-top desk, and carefully sorted some papers into order. Trevannion sat in tense watchfulness on an upright chair.

This had once been his sister Meg's room. It still contained her vanity-table, and the double doors of the tall wardrobe concealed her clothes. Meg had died of pleurisy during the fierce Cornish winter of '85. Sometimes Hugh fancied that she was still moving quietly about the ancient house.

When his guest picked up a time-worn document bearing a number of wax seals dangling from faded tapes, Trevannion cried out in satisfaction, and stretched out his hand. Dr Karenin clung on to the document, and quelled his host with a single glance from his pale-blue, restless eyes.

'Wait!' His tone was peremptory, almost threatening. Even as he spat out the single word of warning, Trevannion wondered at his excellent command of English.

'Wait! Yes, my friend, this is the original title deed of St Columb's Manor, which lay safe for centuries with your family and its lawyers, and then began its ignominious travels, as you were obliged to mortgage your birthright to grasping strangers. Well, I have it, now, and in a moment or two I'll affix my signature to a deed of relinquishment that will make this title deed yours once again. But you must give me your verbal assurance that you will honour your side of the bargain.'

'My side?'

'Yes, Mr Trevannion, *your* side of it. In a few moments' time you will be a true property owner once again, an English milord, living on his own ancestral acres. How romantic it sounds! But unlike other English landed gentry, you, my friend, are bound to *me*.'

Dr Karenin picked something up from the desk, and held it up to the light.

'What would you say this thing was, Mr Trevannion? Long and thin, like a needle, and capped with a little diamanté globe? How elegant it is!'

'That? Why, it's a hatpin. There are a great many of them in that little box. They belonged to my late sister, Miss Margaret Trevannion.'

'Miss Margaret . . . Well, she had good taste in hatpins! Sister of the Lord of the Manor, she resides in glory with the saints. Amen. But you, my friend, are still living, and bound to *me*.'

Dr Nikolai Ivanovich Karenin slowly turned his pale-blue eyes and fixed them on his host. He had placed the hatpin down carefully on the desk.

'You have observed me, no doubt?' he asked. 'You have noticed my pale complexion? That is what they call prison pallor. It is the result of twenty-five years in a Russian prison! The paleness etches itself on the skin, so that if you were to live the rest of your life in the tropics, you would be branded with the leprous white mark of the convict.'

Dr Karenin seemed lost in his own vivid musings. He hugged the title deed of the manor closely to his chest. Then he suddenly began to laugh, his shoulders heaving with a strangely terrifying mirth. Hugh Trevannion waited.

'We Russians, Mr Trevannion,' said Karenin at length, 'we Russians do everything by extremes. So a man who's rotted in gaol for a lifetime comes out looking like a leper . . . Oh, yes! We Russians are terrible creatures. And that is the kind of man to whom you are bound, Hugh Trevannion — that, and worse. I have more work to do, work that will bring me flying back to this sanctuary of yours. I have restored to you your estate. In return, you must always give me sanctuary, either here, or elsewhere. Is that a bargain?'

'It is. You need not doubt my word. Now, will you sign the transfer?'

Without warning, Karenin suddenly lunged towards Trevannion, and encircled his throat with a sinuous, bony hand. Trevannion shrieked with fear.

'Whatever happens, my friend,' the corpse-white Karenin whispered, 'you ask no questions, venture no opinions. That curious cat — the young man from Porthcurno — who knows what will happen to him? Do not presume to ask. And to avoid you asking any curious questions, Mr Trevannion, I'll let you share some little secrets.

'You recall what happened to Sir John Courteline? Well, Courteline was my enemy, and, with the hired help of a murderous thug, I sent him to perdition. Later, I left a device in the killer's wretched hovel which blew him to pieces. There, you now share one of my deadly secrets. If you ever contemplate becoming a danger to me by talking too much, then, my friend, your life will not be worth a day's purchase.'

Karenin suddenly laughed again, and relinquished the title deed of St Columb's Manor to Trevannion. He turned back to the desk, dipped a pen in an inkwell, and taking a handwritten note from the sheaf of papers, he signed it with a flourish. When he spoke again, it was in a pleasant, businesslike tone, accompanied with something approaching a smile.

'There you are, my friend,' he said, 'the deed of relinquishment, duly signed. The manor of St Columb is truly yours once more.'

* * *

The next day, Hugh Trevannion left St Columb's Manor early, and took a hired trap to the busy town of Truro, where he deposited the precious title deeds with his lawyer. The business done, he turned into a nearby coffee shop, where the day's papers were available for customers to read. He selected the *Exeter Express* from the rack, and laid it flat on the table. The front page, usually covered in lines of advertisements, had produced a black headline, A RUSSIAN ATROCITY. The story beneath it cried out for his attention.

> *Tuesday, 14 March. We have learned from our London correspondent that at two o'clock this morning the German cargo steamer Berlin Star, out of Bremerhaven, was fired upon by an unidentified Russian ship, in the open seas twelve miles south of Heligoland. The unprovoked attack, which occurred in a dense fog, was witnessed by the British freighter* Camberley, *Captain James Jerome, Master, who has made an immediate deposition to the German authorities, and to the British Consul in Hamburg.*
>
> Later. *It has been reported from our correspondent in Hamburg that the* Berlin Star *caught fire immediately, and sank at twelve minutes to three this morning, with the loss of the master and all twelve crew. A statement issued by the Russian Ambassador to the Court of St James's, Prince Gregory Orloff, vehemently denies any Russian involvement in this unprovoked atrocity.*

Trevannion put the newspaper aside, and sipped his coffee. It was grave news, but under the new dispensation ushered in by Dr Karenin, it was none of his business. Let the great world go its own way — his world lay on the edge of the cliffs at St Columb's Manor. Say nothing, think nothing. That must now be his saving creed.

* * *

Hugh Trevannion returned to St Columb's in the mid-afternoon, but instead of pushing open the gate in the dry-stone wall, he walked along the narrow road that would take him to the cliff edge. It was a blustery day, with angry grey clouds scudding across the sky. Once arrived at the edge of the cliff, he looked down the giddy slope to Spanish Beach, 200 feet below.

The spume-crested waves flung themselves against the rocks, broke up into violent spray, and retreated, only to revisit the inhospitable shore with renewed violence. Below him, Hugh could see wind-blown plants and gnarled bushes growing perilously from the many outcrops. Gulls wheeled and screamed across the uneasy sky.

Something shifted in the foaming channels between the rocks, something that seemed to be endowed with a kind of erratic life, lunging forward with the inrush of the waves, and retreating when the waters retreated. But it was in reality a dead thing, broken and lifeless, the body of a young man, floating on its back, its white face staring sightlessly up towards the cliff-top from which it had been flung. Soon, it would be swept out to sea, to be yielded up, no doubt, days later, on a strand further along the Cornish coast. From the top of the cliff, Hugh Trevannion looked down in stunned terror at the bobbing white face of his dead friend William Pascoe, and listened in dread to the phantom mourning dirge begun somewhere in his head by his dead sister Meg.

* * *

Sir Charles Napier, seated at his ornate desk, read William Pascoe's message aloud, for the benefit of the man sitting opposite him. The message had been brought earlier that day by a courier from Mr Dangerfield, of the Eastern Telegraph Company.

''Have ascertained that the German cargo steamer *Berlin Star*, out of Bremerhaven, is in reality a contraband runner, smuggling arms from Britain to dissidents in Russia. Let all necessary action be taken'. What do you think of that, Herr Fischer?'

It was to be one of those German mornings, thought Napier, occasions usually characterized by the cautious sharing of routine information in an atmosphere of frigid *politesse*. He had asked Herr Fischer, the German commercial attaché, to call at the Foreign Office that day, but a second visitor had arrived unannounced, bringing with him the usual fulsome apologies. He was in the anteroom now, reading the morning's papers.

'It's mischievous nonsense, Sir Charles,' said Fischer. 'As commercial attaché at the German Embassy, I naturally have records of all vessels of the German mercantile marine, and what they are carrying. I have access to all manifests and bills of lading. The *Berlin Star* is one of the vessels of the Hofmann Line, a very reputable company.'

'The *Berlin Star* was in the Thames only recently,' Napier observed.

'Quite so, She docked at Chandler's Wharf on Tuesday, 7 March. She was carrying general merchandise, as you can readily ascertain, I've no doubt. I'm inclined to see the message as a hoax, especially as it implies that Britain is covertly arming the Russian anarchists, which is nonsense, of course. But it is very good of you, Sir Charles, to call me in like this. I can assure you that His

Excellency the German Ambassador is most grateful.'

Napier looked across the document that Dangerfield had sent him at the dapper man with the bristling moustache and eye glass sitting opposite him. The man's appreciation of his gesture was only too patently genuine. In this matter of the Russian cable, he was convinced that Germany was an innocent and aggrieved party.

'I've got a very decent '69 brandy here, Herr Fischer,' said Napier, rising from his desk. 'I hope it's not too early for you to imbibe?'

'Not at all, Sir Charles. How very kind! And may I, without impertinence, convey my commiserations to you on the recent outrage perpetrated against you? It was a cause of deep pain to many of us at Prussia House.'

And he means it, thought Napier, as he busied himself at a wine table in a dim corner of the room. They all mean it! What was happening to the old diplomatic certainties? Prussians were designed by nature to be forever flying at Britons' throats — but not now. Did the Germans know things about Russia that they were not yet willing to share?

As he poured their drinks from a crystal decanter, he glanced briefly out of the window at St James's Park, where banks of daffodils were glowing among the lawns. Spring was well on the way. Would 1893 be a year free from international tensions? He smiled sardonically, and turned to his guest.

'There you are, Herr Fischer: *Gesundheit*!'

'*Gesundheit, Herr Ritter*! Ah! A fine brandy, this!'

'So you intend to treat that cable as a hoax?' asked Napier. 'I wonder why it was despatched in English? That's very odd. Still, if it contains any kind of truth — I mean a genuine threat to an unarmed German merchant steamer — then I place myself, and my government, at your disposal.'

'It can only be a hoax, Sir Charles. But I'll mention it to His Excellency. Perhaps the Hofmann Line can be alerted to the possibility of unpleasantness. These are strange and stirring times, Sir Charles. We must wait and see what happens — if anything.'

Some minutes later, Herr Fischer left the room, and Napier rang a small hand-bell on his desk. Almost immediately, the double doors of the chamber were thrown open, and the duty secretary announced Colonel von Hagen, military attaché to the German Embassy.

Colonel von Hagen was wearing morning coat and pinstriped trousers, but he looked as though he would have been more comfortable in the field-grey uniform of the Prussian Hussars, to which he belonged. He was clutching a highly polished briefcase, and Napier wondered idly whether it was his valet's daily task to buff up the briefcase at the same time as the colonel's boots. Von Hagen clicked his heels and bowed. Napier motioned vaguely to the chair that Herr Fischer had only just vacated.

'Sir Charles,' said von Hagen in heavily accented English, 'I will come to the point immediately. It could never be said that I strove to see the English point of view. I see only the needs and demands of Germany, its Kaiser, and its folk.'

'Oh, quite,' said Sir Charles Napier, settling himself in the comfortable chair behind his desk. This was more like it! He was at home with these arrogant Junkers, and knew how to play their game.

'Nevertheless, recent developments in Europe have been so peculiar, that I have determined to talk to you in your capacity as head of the Foreign Office intelligence service. You have, no doubt, heard of the Russian weapons project in the forests of Lithuania?'

'I have, Colonel. I am also aware that any such developments in that area of the Baltic coast could be construed as a potential threat to the integrity of Prussian Germany. I can advise you that that is also the view of Her Majesty's Government.'

'Good. I am pleased to hear you say so. The Russian secret project has been under way for the last eighteen months. Many people are under the impression that they are developing a new kind of land-vehicle for aggressive use against Germany. Some have wondered whether it could not be a new kind of boat — possibly an under-sea boat. But no. It is more sinister than that. Our German Intelligence is brilliant in its methods, and they have found out the truth.'

Von Hagen began to struggle with the leather straps of his briefcase. Napier watched him. Here was yet another modern German with a bristling waxed moustache, and a glinting monocle. Did they never have short sight in *both* eyes?

'Ah! Here. This is what our intrepid agents have discovered. The Russians, Sir Charles, are constructing not a land vehicle, not an under-sea boat, but a great ship of the air, a monstrous dirigible.' He struck the papers that he had taken from his briefcase with the back of his hand. 'They have seen it, tethered in a great shed deep in the woods of Lithuania. They estimate it to be two hundred and sixty feet in length, and eight tons in weight. Our experts in Berlin have computed that this aerial ship will reach a speed of ten knots.'

'But Colonel von Hagen, what can be the possible use of such a grotesque contraption? What is it for?'

'Ah! I forget; you are not a military man. This monstrous ship will be equipped with special hand-shells, or bombs, which can be dropped at will from the air on to the innocent people on the ground, What is to stop them? What field-piece can fire up into the air? This aerial vessel is but the prototype of more to come. The Russians will have the potential to destroy our cities, kill our innocent civilians by the thousand — and that is why I bring you this set of plans today. The time for traditional animosity between England and Germany is over. We must share intelligence, Sir Charles, if we are to survive this new and terrible aggression.'

The German military attaché gathered up his papers, and handed them to Napier. For the second time that morning Sir Charles saw the workings of a quite genuine anger which was not directed against him or his country. The Germans were very clearly shocked and unsettled by recent events. Even if the Russian cables were hoaxes, it was very clear that the German authorities had no idea of their provenance.

'These documents, Herr *Oberst*,' Napier said, 'will remain a close secret between our two organizations. I will undertake to share with you any reports that we receive from our own agents in the Baltic area. Our two countries have a joint interest in preventing any further Russian creeping down the Baltic shores.'

Colonel von Hagen stood up, and bowed stiffly. He seemed to be striving to say something — something which normally he would not have dreamed of saying. Finally, he brought himself to utter a formal, stilted little speech.

'You will, I hope, accept my commiserations on the insult offered you recently by the drunken oaf Andropov. Such a thing is quite unacceptable in polite society. These Russians are pigs!'

6

The Hatpin Man

Arnold Box hurried across the cobbles and up the worn steps of 2 King James's Rents. A clock somewhere in Whitehall struck nine. As he stepped into the entrance hall, he saw the blackboard and easel standing by the stairs, and groaned. Charlie, the night helper, had written the word 'Assignments' in large curly chalk letters on the board, and had embellished his work with a wavy line beneath the word.

Most days, detectives would come in to work and resume the thread of cases where they'd left off, or wait to be summoned upstairs when requests came in for specialist help. 'Assignments' meant that Superintendent Mackharness had been inundated with emergency requests since he'd arrived that Monday morning. All pending work would be suspended while Box and the others investigated the cases that their superintendent assigned to them. Box hurried up the stone stairs.

Mr Mackharness had evidently been

working himself up into a passion. His desk was covered with slim buff files and a number of hastily opened letters. His trim white side-whiskers stood out in contrast to his irascible red face. He rummaged through the files, picked one up, and fixed Box with a baleful glance.

'Ah! There you are. I thought you weren't coming in this morning. I've been here since half-past six. They were queuing up here for attention. There's been an assault on a Russian diplomat, which will cause the usual political fuss and flurry. There's a suspicious death at Highgate, a body found bound on the tracks just outside Paddington Station, a drowning in the Regent's Canal, this business out at Falcon Street — but you don't want to hear all this. Why should *you* be bothered?'

'Sir — '

'We're stretched to breaking-point,' Mackharness continued, ignoring Box's attempt to speak. 'I've had to send out Wilson and Campbell, and I've begged two more inspectors from Kinghorn Street. The sergeants are all out, too, including your Sergeant Knollys, so you'll not have *him* to hold your hand when you go now — immediately, you understand? — to Falcon Street.'

Superintendent Mackharness thrust a cardboard file into Box's hand, and began a renewed search through the various objects on his desk. One of his hallmarks was extreme tidiness. It was obvious that the senior officer of King James's Rents was having a very bad Monday morning.

'Sir,' Box ventured in as mild a tone as he could muster, 'what am I to *do* in Falcon Street?'

'Do? I thought I'd told you. These constant interruptions of yours break my train of thought. Go down to Falcon Street, and talk to a Sergeant Griffiths of City. He'll show you the body of a man found dead in shop premises at number 14. Gabriel Oldfield, chemist and druggist. Found dead in 'bizarre circumstances' according to this Sergeant Griffiths. Go and look into it. If it's cut and dried from our point of view, give it back to City. Otherwise retain it — What are you peering at, Box? Aren't you interested in what I'm saying?'

While the various diatribes were in progress, Box had been attempting to make out some of the many objects reposing on Mackharness's mantelpiece. He counted the bobbles on the moth-eaten green velvet over-mantel, he examined the dried ferns in pots, and the framed photograph of a stern woman whom he knew to be Mrs Mackharness. Further along, there was a medal of sorts in a little glazed frame. One of these days he would find out what that medal was.

'I'm not peering, sir. I expect it's a trick of the light.'

'Very well. Now, when you get back from Falcon Street, I want you to make preparations to go down to Cornwall, to a place called Truro, and call upon an Inspector Tregennis. I've heard of him, and I think he's a very capable officer. A young man was pushed to his death off a cliff down there, at a place called Porthcurno.

'Porthcurno?'

'Yes, yes. It's in Cornwall. It looked like an accident, but Tregennis is not satisfied. It's all in this report. Here, take it away with you, and read it. Now, there's a stopping-train from Paddington at four-fifteen this afternoon, or you can go tomorrow by the ten-twenty. Sergeant Knollys will be back by one o'clock this afternoon, so he can go with you. That's all, I think. Dismiss.'

* * *

Inspector Box looked down on the body of Gabriel Oldfield, chemist and druggist, and saw why the sergeant had used the word 'bizarre' to describe his fate. He lay on his back, his open eyes seemingly fixed on the ceiling of the simply furnished bedroom above his shop in Falcon Street, a bustling thoroughfare near St Martin's-le-Grand. The sheet, neatly turned down, came up to his neck. His mouth was slightly open, but the face betrayed no kind of surprise. The morning sunlight that streamed through the bedroom window glittered and glanced from the large diamanté head of a woman's hatpin thrust through the counterpane.

Box turned away from the bed, and addressed Sergeant Griffiths, a young, clean-shaven man, who stood rather awkwardly near the door, cradling in his arm the distinctive crested helmet worn by the City of London Police.

'Your inspector did right to call the Yard in over this business, Sergeant,' he said. 'We know something about your Mr Oldfield, including the possibility that he had someone staying here with him — someone who isn't here now.'

'He *did* have a gentleman staying with him, sir. I've glimpsed him once or twice. As a matter of fact, I passed the time of day with him just a couple of nights ago. A naval man, I'd say, in his forties, five foot ten or so. Very well spoken. If you come up to the attic floor, sir, I'll show you the little room where that naval gentleman may have slept.'

The room occupied a space under the roof at the back of the premises. It was very simply furnished with a truckle bed, neatly made up with pillows and blankets. A narrow, grimy window, which looked down on the row of back yards behind the shops, stood wide open, its curtains flapping in the roof-top breeze.

'Your man evidently camped, rather than lived, here, Sergeant. He slept in his clothes, as like as not, waiting for something to happen. Enright, his name was. Malcolm Enright.'

Box gazed out from the wide-open window across the uneven roofs. The great dome of St Paul's Cathedral looked intimidating in its apparent nearness.

'There's a row of newly broken tiles over there on the right, Sergeant, which suggests that Malcolm Enright left the premises through this window. Presumably, he was able to clamber down a drainpipe and into one of the alleys behind these houses.'

'Do you think this man Enright was the murderer, sir?'

'No, Sergeant. Malcolm Enright isn't our mysterious hatpin man. As a matter of fact, I've a pretty shrewd idea who he really is, but that's not exactly a police business. Whoever went through that window did so in order to *escape*, even though it was dark. I say 'dark' because I think the murder took place in the small hours. Enright was desperate to escape, and took the risk of falling.'

The two officers went downstairs and into the shop, where the wooden shutters still remained in place. Through the gloom they could see the three tall ornamental bottles of coloured water, the trade sign of a chemist, standing in the shop window. There was a strong balsamic odour in the air.

'There's nothing taken or disturbed, sir,' said Sergeant Griffiths. 'There are twenty-four sovereigns in the till, two cheques totalling four pounds ten, and five pounds thirteen and six in silver and copper.'

Box glanced at some of the items for sale on the neatly stacked shelves. 'What's this, I wonder? Hagel's Pancreatine Emulsion. 'Definitely prolongs life in cases of consumption'. Does it really? Aromatic vinegar — that's a smelly stuff for ladies to dab on their temples. Arrhenius's Universal Relaxant. The mind boggles.'

Inspector Box turned away from the shelves, and sat down on a tall stool near the counter. He glanced at the heavily bolted front door of the premises.

'Sergeant Griffiths,' he said, 'tell me again about the discovery of this murder. You say that you were approached by a boy, out there in the street?'

'Yes, sir. Just after eight-thirty, it was. I was walking back from the magistrate's office in St Paul's Churchyard, when I was accosted by a young lad crying blue murder. It was this Mr Oldfield's shop boy He told me he'd been sitting on the doorstep for half an hour, wondering why his master hadn't opened for business.'

'And then he decided to take a look?'

'He did, sir.' Griffiths turned over a page on his notebook. 'This is what he said to me. 'I went into the shop, and found Mr Oldfield dead, upstairs. He'd been murdered! It's not respectful to do a thing like that. I don't want to go in there again'.'

'Where is this boy, now? And what did he mean by murder not being respectful?'

'I sent him over the road to Mr Palmer's, the photographer. He's a nice old cove, and he promised to look after the boy until he's wanted. The boy's name is Tom Slater. A very respectable boy, well dressed and well cared for. He told me that he was fourteen. I don't know what he meant by murder not being respectful, but boys do say peculiar things these days. It's on account of not listening properly at school.'

'Sergeant, our murderous friend the

Hatpin Man came here on purpose to murder both Mr Oldfield and Malcolm Enright. Enright managed to escape, and no doubt he'll be in touch with the relevant authorities before the week's out.'

'The relevant authorities, sir?'

'Yes. It's a Secret Service affair, you see. I know something about it. That doesn't mean that we don't go after the Hatpin Man, because, of course, we do. But the whole matter needs to be left with Scotland Yard. I'll leave you here, now, to hold the fort, while I go across the road to see this boy Tom Slater. I'm anxious to meet a young fellow who doesn't think that murder's respectful.'

* * *

Mr Palmer bowed Inspector Box into his spacious photographic showroom, which occupied the front upstairs rooms of his shop. There was a smell of polished mahogany in the air, mingled with the aroma of freshly made toast.

'I saw you crossing the road, Inspector,' Mr Palmer was saying, 'and I knew you'd be coming up here. It's a great honour to meet you, I must say. The whole town's talking about your cornering of the blackguard who murdered Sir John Courteline. They say the

Russians were behind that. And now they've sunk a German ship. Frightful! But what can I do to help you?'

Mr Palmer, an elderly man with curly white hair, was wearing, as far as Box could judge, some kind of artist's smock. A red cravat drooped from the floppy collar of his Byronic shirt.

'I've come to speak to Mr Gabriel Oldfield's shop boy, Tom Slater. I believe you're kindly looking after him for the duration.'

'I am. He's through there, beyond the beaded curtain, having a bite to eat. It's not nice for a boy to discover a murder. Poor Oldfield! Whatever harm did he do to anybody? Poor young Slater — he'll be thrown out of work, now.'

Box had crossed to the front windows of the shop, and was looking down across the crowded thoroughfare to the opposite pavement. Both the front door and the opening of a side entry beside the chemist's shop were clearly visible from where he stood.

'Mr Palmer,' he said, 'I wonder whether you saw anything unusual from these windows of yours, late afternoon yesterday, or early evening, say? I see you've a telescope set up here, so I take it that you like to survey the passing scene in Falcon Street from time to time?'

'I do, Inspector, and I frequently take test shots for the new lenses that I acquire for clients. I keep some fine specimens always to hand — Bausch and Lomb, Wrays, and so forth. I took some yesterday, as a matter of fact. Let me see, now, where did I put them after I developed them? Ah! Here they are. These are two bromide prints, which I think will interest you. I did them late last night. This first one shows a gentleman who's been staying with Mr Oldfield for the last week or so. You'll understand that I didn't actually set out to photograph him. I was testing a particular camera, and it so happened that the man was just entering the shop as I uncapped the lens. It's a very good image — instantaneous, you see.'

Box looked at the sharp print of the shop across the road. Although the man opening the door was in profile, and looking down towards the ground, there was no doubt whatever that it was the image of Malcolm Enright, mariner, aged forty-one.

'And this one, Inspector — well, there's a little story attached to it. I was looking out from that window yesterday evening, about seven o'clock, when the man in this second photograph stopped at Mr Oldfield's shop, and looked in the window. I thought he was a remarkable kind of man — from a photographic point of view, that is. A portrait photographer's point of view.'

Box looked at the second print that Palmer handed him. It showed a clean-shaven, middle-aged man in a black suit, just turning away from the shop window.

'I had a fresh plate in that Ross camera you see standing over there in the bay. I caught this mysterious fellow just as he turned away from Mr Oldfield's window. He was a very striking man, very pale, almost like chalk, and with very dark blue-black hair. He glanced up in this direction, and I saw that he had piercing light blue eyes. He had a foreign way of walking, if you know what I mean.'

'A foreign way of walking? I'll bear that in mind, Mr Palmer. You called him a mysterious fellow, sir. What was mysterious about him?'

'Well, Inspector, he pushed open the door of the shop, and went in. I noticed that in particular, because it was late — Mr Oldfield closes at half past seven, and it had just turned seven when the man went into the shop. He'd already put the shutters up.'

'Very interesting, sir. And what happened next?'

'Nothing happened, and that was the odd

thing. The man went into the shop, but he never came out. My windows up here were open, and I fancied I heard Oldfield shooting the bolts on his front door at closing time. But the chalk-pale man never came out.'

'Would you be willing to lend me these two photographs, Mr Palmer? They'd prove very useful to me.'

'Lend them? You can have them! I still have the negatives, you see. But what's that noise in the street?'

The cheerful sound of military music drifted up through the open window from Falcon Street. Mr Palmer leaned out, and peered up the road towards St Martin's-le-Grand.

'It's a German band on the pavement, Mr Box,' he said, 'just on the turn into Colchester Mews. They've been playing to quite decent crowds these last few days, and they've collected a positive mountain of copper! People are sorry for them, I suppose, on account of the German ship that was sunk.'

'Well, yes, Mr Palmer,' said Box, preparing to take his leave, 'but there's nothing more fickle than a crowd of British bystanders. It'd only take one word from above, saying that the Russians were our dearest friends in the world, and your kindhearted copper-throwers would cheerfully tear the German bandsmen to pieces. I'd like to see young Tom Slater now, if I may.'

* * *

Tom Slater looked up curiously as Box entered the room beyond the beaded curtain. The boy was sitting at a cluttered table, with a plate of buttered toast and a cup of tea in front of him. His slender neck was encompassed by a shiny new starched collar, and he was wearing a smart Norfolk jacket and knickerbockers.

'You're Inspector Box, aren't you?' he asked. 'You caught the murderer of Sir John Courteline. Somehow, I thought you'd be taller than you are.'

'Well, I'm sorry to disappoint you, young Slater,' said Inspector Box, 'but you'll have to make do with me as I am. We can't all be giants in this world.'

The boy took a quick bite from his piece of toast while Box extracted a notebook from the pocket of his overcoat. He licked the point of his blacklead, and looked expectantly at the boy. Young Tom anticipated his question.

'Thomas Slater, aged fourteen. Number 7, Beaufort Lane, Monument.'

'Good. Well done. Beaufort Lane, Monument. Now, Thomas Slater, I'm going to ask you a few questions. First of all, tell me how you came to be working for Mr Oldfield.'

'Sir, I used to work for Mr Edison in Paul's Walk. The legal stationers. When Mr Edison retired, he recommended me to Mr Oldfield. That was about a year ago.'

'And did you like Mr Oldfield?'

'Yes, sir. He was a very nice, friendly gentleman. Kind and considerate, he was, though some folk said he was a fusspot. I didn't know what to do this morning. Him and I were both very punctual. I used to knock prompt at eight o'clock, and he'd open the door. Then I'd take the shutters down and we'd be open for business at half past.'

'But not today?'

'No, sir. I sat on the step for a while and then I went round the back. The door was . . . was ajar, so I went in, and up the stairs. And I found . . . I found . . . '

The boy's voice began to tremble, and a tear rolled down his cheek. Box slipped his notebook into his pocket, and sat down at the table.

'Don't think about that, now, Tom. Just tell me why you said those peculiar words to Sergeant Griffiths.'

Tom's face flushed red, and the tears began to flow unheeded.

'What do you mean? I told him the truth.'

'I know you did. There's no need to take on like that. I'm not shouting at you, or accusing you of anything. But you said something very odd, Tom. You said, 'He's been murdered! It's not respectful to do a thing like that'. What did you mean by those words?'

Tom Slater did not answer at once, He continued to eat his toast, and sip his tea, regarding Box with a sulky frown. Box, a keen photographer himself, looked with interest at the various mahogany cameras stacked on shelves around the room. That was a Thornton Pickard over there, and next to it one of those magnificent Negrettti and Zambras . . . Box sighed. Such aristocrats were beyond the pocket of a man who earned twenty-five shillings a week. He suddenly recalled John Martin, the fallen ostler. Martin's fine had been paid earlier in the week by Sergeant Billings from Stables. Poor old John Martin! He'd really have to visit him soon, to see how he was. He lived somewhere near Bermondsey Leather Market. Maybe after the coming jaunt to Cornwall with. Sergeant Knollys . . .

He jumped slightly as Tom's youthful tones suddenly broke the silence. The boy's brow had cleared, and he looked positively cheerful.

'When I went up to Mr Oldfield on the bed, I thought he was asleep, but then I saw the dagger thing sticking up, and the card on his forehead, and I knew he must be dead.'

'A card?' said Box gently.

'Yes. There was a card placed on his forehead. I carefully took the card away. I was terrified in case I touched him . . . I took it away. It wasn't respectful to do a thing like that.'

The toast had all been eaten, and the tea half drunk.

'When you say a card, Tom, do you mean a calling-card?'

There was a slight but definite edge of compulsion to Box's voice. Tom, avoiding his eyes, felt in his pocket, and took out a white card, which he handed to Box.

'It wasn't right,' he said.

It was a simple printed calling-card, bearing the legend: 'Dr N. I. Karenin.'

7

The Strangers at Spanish Beach

'Inspector Box! Fancy meeting you again!'

Fiske of the *Graphic*, displaying a jaunty smile beneath his fierce black moustache, stood on one of the platforms at Paddington Station, looking into the third-class carriage. The great black engine at the front of the stopping-train to Exeter was already making ferocious noises prior to beginning its long journey to the West Country.

'I suppose you just happened to be passing, Billy?' said Box, who had lowered the window on seeing the political reporter weaving his way through the crowd. 'Sergeant Knollys and I are going down to Exeter on business. What's that little wicker-work basket you're carrying? You haven't taken up selling things as a sideline, have you?'

For answer, Billy Fiske passed the basket to Box over the window sill. He pushed his old-fashioned high-crowned hat off his forehead, and stood with his hands in his overcoat pockets, looking nonchalantly down the platform.

'That's a little something by way of refreshment,' he said, 'for you and Sergeant Knollys there to while away the weary hours on the way to Exeter. Or beyond. Just a little courtesy from one gentleman to another.'

Arnold Box put the hamper down on the seat beside him, and looked at the irrepressible but kind-hearted reporter. Somehow, he'd found out that they were on their way to Cornwall. Maybe the walls at King James's Rents had grown too thin for comfort.

'Thank you kindly, Mr Fiske,' he said. 'And while you're here, you can tell me how you came to be in that alley when the row at Sir Abraham Goldsmith's residence blew up.'

Mr Fiske glanced around him before lowering his voice. There were times, as Box knew, when the reporter liked to make a mystery of quite mundane experiences. After all, that was one of the vital skills of his trade.

'I got a note, Mr Box, a note delivered to my desk at the *Graphic*. *Be there*, it said. *Something very exciting in the news line's going to happen*.'

Box contrived to look excited.

'I don't suppose it was delivered by a milky-white cove with blue-black hair and a foreign way of walking, was it?' he asked.

'It may have been, for all I know. The little post-boy received it. Albert, he's called.

Supposed to be fourteen, but looks twelve, and behaves like it. But it was a good tip-off, Mr Box and, thanks to you not kicking up a fuss, I got my story. Did you read it?'

'I never read your stuff on principle, but Sergeant Knollys here read it, and thought it was very good. All about the lion's fearsome roar drowning the uncertain growl of the bear.'

'That's right. I thought it was good myself, though I shouldn't say so. I took little Froggy Carter with me to add social credibility, as it were. He did a very nice account of it all for the *Sketch*. And here's another little morsel of news for you, courtesy of the *Graphic*. Lady Courteline left England early today for Odessa. She's believed to be planning a visit to relatives in Russia.'

'Odessa? Who told you that, Billy?'

'A little bird told me, Mr Box. A little bird with white mutton-chop whiskers.'

'Name of Mervyn, and with a nest in Edgerton Square?'

'That's as may be. Anyway, she's gone to Russia. Maybe she took fright when these nasty incidents began, though she's nothing to fear, poor dear lady, for all that she's a Russian by birth. Incidentally, we've heard on the grapevine that the Russian papers are howling about 'Anglo — German aggression'.

Strewth, Mr Box, can you imagine Anglo — German *anything* after the Hansa Protocol business? And the Berlin papers are going mad with talk about a secret Franco — Russian pact — but hello! It looks as though you're off. Have a nice time in Exeter.'

The engine had worked itself into a frenzy, and a number of porters were sternly ordering people to stand back from the train. A whistle was blown, and a flag unfurled. As the train moved away on its long journey, Mr Fiske mouthed the word 'Porthcurno' at them through the closed window, grinned impudently, and raised his hat in mock salute.

* * *

'I've not had time to think today, Sergeant,' said Box, settling himself glumly into his thinly upholstered seat. 'Old Growler practically threw me out of the Rents this morning. Assignments! He gave me two trains to choose from for this Cornwall jaunt, hoping that I'd choose the Exeter express tomorrow, so that he could sneer at me for being a wet lettuce, and plumping for the easy option. That's why we've caught this one, the four-fifteen stopping-train.'

'Very kind of you to choose for us both,

sir,' said Knollys drily. 'Just about three hundred miles, with interesting stops along the way.'

'I'm not giving him the satisfaction, Sergeant, of smirking at me for choosing the soft option. We'll stay the night somewhere when we get there.'

The long train had drawn out of the station, and was moving in rather stately fashion through the London suburbs. It was a bright afternoon, but a grey haze was creeping across Paddington from the general direction of Maida Vale.

'Sir,' said Knollys, 'this Dr Karenin has turned out to be something more than just a man who came to England in search of private vengeance. He's right at the centre of the Courteline affair, and now, from what you say, he's popped up at Falcon Street — '

'Yes, he has; and that shows that he's still in England, and still intent on some peculiar venture of his own. That's why I've brought that photograph of Hatpin Man with me. The one that Mr Palmer gave me. Colonel Kershaw told me that there'd been some devilry going on at Porthcurno, where this unfortunate man Pascoe worked. Perhaps our friend Karenin had been up to his murderous tricks down there, too.'

'You may be right, sir.'

'This Karenin seems to be the common factor behind the deaths of Courteline and Killer Kitely, and it was Karenin, in his rather nasty guise of the Hatpin Man, who silenced Gabriel Oldfield, presumably for similar reasons. (Maybe Oldfield was one of the Colonel's lesser fry. I don't know.) Then again, it was Karenin who engineered that nasty incident at Sir Abraham Goldsmith's reception. The common factor, that's what he is.'

'You visited an old Russian gentleman, didn't you, sir? A retired art dealer who'd known Karenin in his youth. You told me that Colonel Kershaw had dug him out for you. Did you learn anything from him?'

'His name was Borodin, Sergeant, and he lived in one of those narrow houses in Russell Street, Covent Garden. This Mr Borodin told me a very sad tale, Sergeant — very touching, really. Dr Nikolai Ivanovich Karenin was a struggling young doctor, living in Odessa in the '60s. He fell in love with a beautiful and well-connected young lady called Maria Askasov, who apparently doted on him. At the same time, the young John Courteline was living in Odessa, managing a shipping line for his wealthy father, and he, too, fell for this Maria Askasov.'

'And the girl's parents, no doubt, were fond of money? I can see where this is going to end, sir.'

'Yes, so could I, Sergeant. Dr Karenin was of a revolutionary turn of mind, and threw in his lot with a firebrand called Zinoviev. Karenin and Maria had planned to elope, but on the eve of their flight, Karenin and Zinoviev were seized, and accused of subversion. Karenin was sentenced to twenty-five years in prison. No one knows what happened to Zinoviev. Mr Borodin believes that it was Courteline who betrayed the couple to the authorities. If that was true, it adds a bit of credibility to Karenin's desire for revenge.'

'It does, indeed. And so the young lovers were parted. That's a very sad tale, sir.'

'It is, Sergeant. But life goes on. Within the year Maria Askasov had married the young John Courteline, much to her parents' delight. And she lives now, a lifetime later, as Lady Courteline, in her widow's house in Edgerton Square.'

The train was leaving London behind. Box opened the wickerwork hamper that Fiske of the *Graphic* had given them. It contained a number of savoury-smelling items carefully wrapped in tissue paper, and flanked by four bottles of Style's Burton Ale. Box opened one of the little parcels. The two halves of a Scotch egg, laid side by side, looked up at him reproachfully.

'Here, Jack,' he said, 'have a Scotch egg, and one of these bottles of ale. What else is there? Two beef rolls, A slab of Cheddar cheese. Celery. Some oat cakes. I wonder has he — ? Yes, a bottle opener. So let's partake of afternoon tea.'

'You know, sir,' said Knollys, when he had consumed both halves of the Scotch egg, 'our Dr Karenin seems very adept at murders — not short of a few ideas, as they say. I wonder why he didn't give himself the pleasure of finishing off Sir John Courteline himself?'

Box propped his bottle of ale upright in a corner of the hamper, and absent-mindedly wiped his mouth on his sleeve.

'Well, you see, Sergeant,' he said, 'Karenin didn't want to run the risk of Lady Courteline recognizing him. If she'd stumbled across him in her house in Edgerton Square, she'd have shown that she knew him. Couldn't help herself. 'Karenin!' she'd have cried, and all would have been revealed. Why take the risk when you can hire someone like Killer Kitely to do the work for you?'

Sergeant Knollys regarded his superior

officer with something like affectionate concern. The guvnor isn't thinking straight this afternoon, he thought. His mind's elsewhere.

'Sir, you said just now that Karenin didn't want to run the risk of Lady Courteline recognizing him. Then why did he leave his card? And have you considered the alternative?'

'What do you mean? What alternative?'

'Maybe Karenin hired Killer Kitely because he didn't want to run the risk of Lady Courteline *not* recognizing him.'

'But she did! At least — '

'She never saw him, sir. What she *did* see was a card with Karenin's name written on it. It's not the same thing. Anyone can leave a card. Conjurors produce cards from the most unlikely places.'

The train clattered over a blackened viaduct, and skirted a depressing huddle of terraces surrounding a factory with four high smoke stacks, which poured thick yellow vapour to the skies.

'Sleaford Heath,' said Box. 'This is Seabutt's Chemical Works, where they found Smiler Molesworth buried in quicklime after Thomas John Bridgehouse confessed all to the chaplain at Wandsworth. An illusionist? You're suggesting, aren't you, Sergeant, that our pale-faced assassin is not the man he seems.'

'Something like that, sir. After all, most people in England have never heard of him. What's the point of drawing attention to yourself when your identity means nothing to your audience?'

'You know, Sergeant Knollys,' said Box, and there was a glint of excitement in his eyes, 'you've set me thinking straight again. You say that no one in England's ever heard of Dr Karenin. But there is something that the general public knows about him. They know that he's a *Russian*. It's not *who* he is but *what* he is that he's advertising. It's a Russian who murders decent Englishmen with hatpins; a Russian who arranges the death of one of England's greatest idols. It's a Russian who publicly insults the popular and respected Sir Charles Napier. And then, lo and behold! it's the Russians who sink an innocent German ship, the *Berlin Star*. You've hinted at a conjuror's misdirection, and perhaps that's what it is. When we've done with this Cornwall business, Sergeant, we must pay a call on Colonel Kershaw, and tell him what we think.'

* * *

'I'll be frank with you, Mr Box,' said Inspector Tregennis of the Cornwall Constabulary, 'I saw no call for Scotland Yard to be involved in this case, but the chief constable thought otherwise. One of the directors of the Eastern Telegraph Company was very fond of poor William Pascoe, and started to talk to various high-up folk in London. That's why you're here, I expect. However, you're very welcome, and so are you, Sergeant Knollys.'

Box and Knollys had entered Cornwall in the dark hours of the previous night, crossing the Royal Albert Bridge at Saltash in a savage downpour of rain. They had spent the night in a lodging-house at St German's, and early that morning had caught a slow train which had carried them down the peninsula, and through St Austell to Truro.

Inspector Tregennis, a tall, clean-shaven man with alert blue eyes, had been waiting at the station to greet them. He had taken them on foot to the police station, and into a cramped rear office, where a fire burnt in an old-fashioned blackleaded grate.

'It's just a week today, Mr Box, since poor William Pascoe was killed, and there's been an interesting development since then. It was thought originally that the young man had lost his footing on the cliff path, and plunged to his death, but I've found a witness who swears that Pascoe was deliberately killed. Murdered. I have him here.'

Tregennis left the room briefly, and returned with a hale, weather-beaten old man in the well-worn garments of a gamekeeper. Or perhaps, thought Box, noticing the capacious pockets in the man's coat, a poacher.

'Caleb Strange,' said Tregennis, 'this gentleman is Inspector Box of Scotland Yard. The hefty man standing beside him is Sergeant Knollys. Tell them your story.'

'Well, mister,' said Caleb Strange, 'I reckon Inspector Tregennis there knows me well enough. I'm the man who tends the grounds of Mr Hardesty's place, Penhellion Court, but I've also got permission to lay traps for rabbits and such over the land of Squire Trevannion down at St Columb's. I was out that way last Tuesday, the fourteenth. I was crouching down behind the rocks just above the main road from St Columb's to Penzance, seeing to a trap. I looks up, and see Mr William Pascoe climbing up the steep path from Spanish Beach.'

Caleb Strange seemed disinclined to continue. He sat silently shaking his head, apparently at the wickedness of the world.

'And what happened?' asked Tregennis, sharply.

'Well, I'm telling you, aren't I? Poor young William! For all his fancy machinery at Porthcurno, he was a local lad. Very good family, the Pascoes. His father was a mining engineer, you know. That's where William got his cleverness from. Anyway, he was coming up from Spanish Beach, which is so called because some galleons from the Armada were wrecked there in 1588.'

'Yes, yes, never mind that. You saw Pascoe coming up the cliff path?'

'I did. When he got to the top, he stood on the cliff edge, looking down the slope towards the beach. It's a good climb, that — two hundred feet, I reckon. Then he turned round and looked across at St Columb's Manor, where his friend Mr Trevannion lives — mortal peculiar *he*'s been, too, these last few days.

'Anyway, I'm still crouched there, watching — I'm about a hundred yards further up, towards the main road — and suddenly, I see a man walking slowly across the cliff edge towards young Pascoe. I don't know where the man came from, he just seemed to appear from nowhere. He was a tall man, thin, and clad in black. He wore no hat, but I could see that he had dark hair, and a pale cast of feature. I watched as young Pascoe turned to look at the man, who continued to walk towards him. He may have been smiling, but I'm not sure. It was a long way off, you see.'

'And what happened then?' asked Box.

'In the end, sir, the man came up to William Pascoe, and spoke to him. He laid his left hand on William's arm, and pointed to something down the slope. William turned to follow his gaze — and the man suddenly used both hands to push poor William over the edge.'

'I expect you hid then, didn't you, Caleb?' asked Inspector Tregennis gently. 'No point in joining poor Pascoe down the slope and into the sea.'

'You're right, sir. I was so shocked my legs locked under me, and I stayed there bent to the ground for more than half an hour. I don't know who that man was, sir, but he killed poor William Pascoe. Murdered him. It wasn't an accident. I went home in the end, and thought about it, and then I went and told Mr Hardesty, because he's a magistrate, and knows what's right. And he sent me to you. And there's an end of it.'

Box had extracted from his notecase a copy of the photograph of Hatpin Man that Mr Palmer of Falcon Street had taken from his upstairs front window.

'Could that be the man, Caleb?' he asked.

Caleb Strange looked closely at the picture for a while, and then handed it back.

'It could be, sir. The man in the picture's got a general likeness to my killer. But I can't be sure, and it's no good me saying that I can, just to please you. But yes, it could be him, a murderer, and a foreigner among us.'

'A foreigner?'

'He means a stranger, Mr Box.'

'Yes, sir, a stranger in our midst. But we've had real foreigners down here, Inspector, as you well know. Reckon you should tell Mr Box here about them. Tell him to go down to the beach and talk to that cantankerous devil Sedden, and poor old David Truscott. They'll tell him all about the foreigners what came here.'

When Tregennis had seen the old man out of the police station, he returned and sat down by the fire. He looked speculatively at Box.

'Do you reckon you know who this killer is? You had a photograph — '

'It was just a forlorn hope, Mr Tregennis. There's someone on the loose in London who may be tied up with this business down here. It's early days. What did Caleb mean by saying that this local squire, this Mr Trevannion, was 'mortal peculiar'?'

'Mr Hugh Trevannion's lived alone at St Columb's Manor since his sister died, and the solitary life doesn't suit him. He's become very nervy — very jumpy. The Trevannions are a very old Cornish family, and Squire Hugh's very much respected round these parts.'

'It might be an idea if Sergeant Knollys and I paid him a little visit,' said Box. 'It's just possible that he may be able to throw some light on what William Pascoe's motive was in going down to this Spanish Beach place.'

Inspector Tregennis shifted uneasily. He looked suddenly ill at ease.

'Squire Trevannion's away from the St Columb's Manor at the moment,' he said. 'He's staying with Dr Manders of Penzance as a resident patient for a week or two.'

'What's the matter with him? Is he ill?'

'He's — Oh, what's the use of beating about the bush? He's undergoing a mental crisis. He's seeing things, Mr Box, and hearing things. Ghosts, and suchlike. He fancies that his late sister, Miss Margaret Trevannion, is walking the house, and talking to him. So he's living with Dr Manders for a couple of weeks.'

'Is he going to get over this mental crisis?'

'Yes, he is, according to Dr Manders. He just needs rest, encouraging conversation, and the administration of certain medicines. He knows me well, Inspector, and I've already called upon him. Will you leave Squire Trevannion to me? I can get him to talk, whereas he'd be alarmed at a couple of Scotland Yarders asking him questions.'

Inspector Tregennis smiled. He was relieved to see that his visitors took the remark in good part.

'Let me come over with you to St Columb's, and show you the way down to Spanish Beach. It's a little fishing place, no more than a hamlet. I won't come down with you. It would be as well if you appeared out of the blue as a nice surprise for Andrew Sedden and his cronies.'

* * *

The two detectives carefully negotiated the plunging pathway down through the stunted shrubs, giant ferns and treacherous boulders, emerging after fifteen minutes or so on to a little stone quay where a few fishing boats were moored. Box pointed to a two-storey building rising above a huddle of single-storey stone cottages.

'That'll be the ale-house, I expect. We'll need to interview the landlord. Sedden, that old man called him. And someone called

David Truscott. That was the other name old Caleb Strange mentioned.'

It was gloomy inside the ale-house, which carried a weather-worn sign informing them that it was The Cormorant. The name 'Andrew Sedden' was written over the lintel of the door. There were five or six rough-looking men sitting at a single trestle table, pewter tankards in front of them. The close air smelt of pipe smoke and stale beer.

Andrew Sedden proved to be a sullen, oppressive sort of man, heavily built but running to fat. He was half-shaven, and slovenly dressed in a nondescript moleskin suit. He stood behind a small bar, his arms folded, his eyes hostile.

'William Pascoe?' he said. 'Yes, I knew him. A clever young fellow he was — too clever by half. He nosed around down here, mister, asking silly questions. Well, he'll ask no more questions now.'

'No, he won't ask any more questions, Mr Sedden,' said Box, 'so I'm here to ask them on his behalf. It's my job to ask questions when someone's been murdered.'

'Murdered? Who says so? Pascoe came down that slope from St Columb's once too often, lost his footing, and plunged down on to the rocks. He wouldn't be the first to have departed this life by that route, and I don't suppose he'll be the last.'

It had gone very quiet in the dim room, and all eyes were turned on Box and the surly landlord.

'Inspector Tregennis thinks it's murder, Mr Sedden, and whether you like it or not, he and I are going to get at the truth.'

'Tregennis!' The landlord spat on the floor in disgust. 'Arthur Tregennis has grown too big for his boots. He's never got over having a crooked constable in his force, a man who committed murder right enough. He was caught by another of your kind, a policeman who came down here from Warwick to solve Tregennis's case for him — '

'There's a witness, Sedden.' Sergeant Knollys' powerful voice cut across the landlord's reminiscence. 'A man called Caleb Strange. He saw the killer push William Pascoe over the edge of the cliff. What do you say to that, my friend?'

'Caleb Strange? Why do you listen to that old reprobate? Gamekeeper, he calls himself. He's no true Cornishman. Gipsy trash, more like. Maybe he's looking for someone to cross his palm with silver, mister. I'm telling you, Pascoe met his death by accident. Didn't he, mates?'

There came a mumble of agreement from the assembled drinkers.

'And what about these Russians that Pascoe said were lurking around these parts in January?' asked Box. 'I suppose he imagined those as well, did he?'

'No, of course he didn't imagine them. What's that got to do with it? There was a Russian ship anchored off Porthcurno, which is on the other side of the headland. Some of the crew landed here in their skiff, and laid in provisions. They had a few drinks, too. We often get ships lying off this coast, mister, and we're not given to asking questions about landing-permits and such to a bunch of tars who just want to feel dry land under their feet for an hour or two, and then row back to their ship. Russians, they were. Where's the harm in that?'

A voice came out of the darkness, an old, obstinate voice, quavering, but clearly the voice of a man who was not afraid of the morose landlord's bullying ways.

'I keep telling you, Andrew Sedden, they weren't Russians. And they didn't all go back to their ship.'

'What are you talking about, you old fool?' bellowed the landlord. 'Of course they were Russians. It was a Russian ship, wasn't it? You keep your mouth shut, or find somewhere else to sup your ale.'

Box looked at the man who had spoken out

of the darkness. He was old, probably over eighty, and by the looks of things very poor. His abundant hair was white, and his old eyes very keen.

'Are you Mr Truscott?' asked Box. 'I've heard about you. So they weren't Russians, you say?'

'You hold your noise, Truscott — ' the landlord began. He was quelled by a sudden move from Sergeant Knollys, who seized the front of his greasy shirt in a single great fist, and twisted it round into a kind of knot. Sedden's loud voice died away to a squeak.

'You hold your noise, too, Sedden,' said Knollys in a pleasant, friendly tone. 'My governor there wants to ask Mr Truscott a question.'

'If they weren't Russians, Mr Truscott,' asked Box, 'what were they? These men who came off the ship.'

'I don't rightly know what they were, sir,' said the old man, 'but they weren't Russians. I served in the Crimea, all through that war, and got to know the sound of Russian well. And the sound of Turkish, too. Those men from the ship sat round in here, mumbling away in their own language, and I sat where you see me now. It wasn't Russian, I tell you. And when they went back down to the quay, there was one of them missing. I saw him slip away, as sure as I see you now.'

There was a deathly hush as Box produced his photograph of Hatpin Man, and put it into Truscott's hand.

'Was that the man?'

'Yes, sir. That's him. But he never spoke while he was in this room. Pale as death, he was, and silent as the grave.'

8

Home is the Sailor

Superintendent Mackharness sat with his big square hands folded on the table in front of him, listening to Arnold Box's account of his investigations in Falcon Street and Cornwall. The fire in the dim mildewed office was burning smokily, and a sickly daylight filtered its way through the sooty windows facing across the cobbles to Whitehall Place.

Mackharness thought: I was too short-tempered with him the other day. Mildred says I'm becoming 'testy'. Maybe she's right. I must stop snarling at him the way I do. It's not his fault that he gets me on edge.

Box finished his account of his investigation in Cornwall, and waited for his superior to comment. His eyes strayed, as always, to the cluttered mantelpiece, with its moth-eaten fringe of bobbled green velvet The picture, the sea-shell, the glass paper weight, the medal . . . One day, he'd find out about that medal. He saw Mackharness watching him, and dropped his eyes.

'Now, Box,' said Mackharness, 'let me

make a few comments about these recent cases. You've clearly established that there's a common factor in these murders — the Courteline murder, in which I include the silencing of Joseph Kitely, the murder of Gabriel Oldfield, and the killing of this young man William Pascoe. That common factor is the man N.I. Karenin, a Russian national. His activities have contributed directly to the present unrest in London and elsewhere. Do you agree with me?'

'Yes, sir. And I'm convinced that Karenin is not a lone wolf, bent only on some kind of private vengeance — '

'Clearly not, Box. Quite right. Well done. This is a conspiracy, and Karenin is only the visible element of that conspiracy. We need to delve, and we need assistance from other quarters to do that. Nevertheless, this Karenin must not be left at large. So I'll procure warrants for his arrest during the course of today. Mark my words, Box, this business is all tied up with the sinking of that unarmed German merchant ship, and with the ugly incident involving Sir Charles Napier.'

Box saw Mackharness flush with anger. Mention of Russians to the superintendent was like waving a red rag before a bull. Mackharness suddenly changed the subject.

'What about Inspector Tregennis, at Truro, Box? Can he be left alone with his part of the business, or does he need further help from us?'

'I had a long talk with Inspector Tregennis, sir, before Sergeant Knollys and I caught the train back to London. I think he can manage very well by himself, at least for the moment. He agrees that this Squire Trevannion needs to be investigated, particularly as he's had a guest staying with him since February, a mysterious character who nobody ever meets.'

'Could it be Karenin?'

'It could be, sir. Inspector Tregennis means to keep a close eye on him, and on his little estate of St Columb's.'

'Good, good. Well, Tregennis knows where to find us if he wants further help. Meanwhile, we need to keep our eyes peeled for further Russian antics. I'd put nothing past them, Box. Devious. That's what they are.'

Superintendent Mackharness suddenly rose from his chair, picked up the medal from his mantelpiece, and put it down in front of Box. He resumed his seat, and leaned back on the cushion, observing his subordinate with a rare glint of mischief in his eyes.

'There you are, Box,' he said. 'I've seen you

squinting at that thing over my shoulder for long enough! Well, there it is for you to see properly. That's my Crimea Medal. It was presented to me by Her Majesty at a great ceremony at the Horse Guards, on 18 May, 1855. I was only a young subaltern then — twenty-two or twenty-three. The Prince Consort was there, too.'

Box handled the medal reverently, noting the clasp, with the word 'Sebastopol' snaking across it. The medal showed a warrior, with sword and shield, receiving a laurel crown from some kind of angelic being. Beside the warrior was engraved the single word 'Crimea'.

'The four things I remember most, Box, were muddle, cold, disease and death. Sebastopol was a victory of sorts, but it was a sickening war. We lost nearly twenty thousand men — and nearly sixteen thousand of them perished of disease.'

Box turned the medal over, and looked at the image of a younger Queen Victoria.

'Yes,' said Mackharness, 'she was only in her thirties, then, but as regal, to my way of thinking, as she is today, in advanced years. The Turks were first-rate comrades, and General Omar Pasha was a very remarkable man. The Italians, too, were fiercely brave. Piedmontese, they were called. There was no

Italy, as such, in those days.'

'What about the Russians, sir? What were they like?'

'Oh, they fought as bravely as anyone amidst all that mud, water and filth, but they were led by heartless monsters, who sacrificed them as though they were sheep or cattle. By the end of the war, they'd lost a quarter of a million men. Nobody won in that war, truth to tell. And that's why I regret the way we fell out with the Turks, and followed Gladstone's dewy-eyed crusade into the Balkans. What have we gained by it? Nothing. And now, you see, the Russians are aching to plunge us all once again into the pit of destruction.'

Superintendent Mackharness picked up the medal, and put it back carefully on the mantelpiece. He looked slightly embarrassed, and shuffled a few papers around on his table. Then he spoke in his usual business-like booming tones.

'I'll make out an immediate warrant for this fellow, Box, under the name N. I. Karenin, on the charge of murdering Gabriel Oldfield. I'll get a general warrant from over the road later today, and they can both be signed by Mr Harrison at Bow Street. I think that's all, now, Box. Well done. What are you going to do for the rest of this morning?'

'Well, sir, I thought I'd take Sergeant Knollys with me and pay a visit to poor old John Martin, who got himself into trouble the other week. He's far gone in drink, I'm afraid, sir, and I feel a bit guilty at not calling on him.'

'Martin? Oh, yes. He was in Stables for years. I remember him well. Somebody mentioned him to me the other day. Yes, go by all means. If you find he's very bad, I should be able to get him a placing in the Holy Cross Almshouses, through the good offices of my friend Lord Maurice Vale Rose. Bear that in mind, will you, Box? Meanwhile — ' Mackharness struggled with one of his trouser pockets for a minute, and presented Box with half a sovereign. 'Give him that, will you, Box? And exhort him from me, if you will, to eschew the demon drink!'

* * *

'It don't half stink, sir,' said Sergeant Knollys, as he and Box threaded their way through a maze of twisting lanes south of Tooley Street, where old Mr Locke held court. 'Worse than breweries, it is, and that's saying a lot.'

Bermondsey was a centre of the leather trade, and the tanneries seemed to have been working overtime that morning, as had the local slaughterhouse. There were times — and this was one of them — when London's air seemed positively lethal.

'That's not a very elegant way of putting it, Sergeant Knollys,' said Box. 'This part of our great metropolis is famed for its tanneries, hence such names as Tanner Street and Morocco Street. Did you know that Bill Sikes fell to his death somewhere in these parts? In Jacob's Island, I think it was. So Charles Dickens says, anyway. A very famous borough, is Bermondsey. But you're right. It don't half stink.'

'Potter's Lane, that man in the market said, just beyond the railway ventilator — this looks like it, sir.'

Potter's Lane appeared to be a cul-de-sac of workmen's crumbling brick cottages, several of them shorn up with stout wooden beams. Some children were playing in the muddy roadway, and a few lean and hungry dogs sniffed hopefully around the outside middens. At the end of the dismal lane rose a three-storey public house. There was a long wooden board fastened to its frontage, bearing the legend 'Thwaite's Breweries. The Salutation.'

'That's the place, Sergeant,' said Box. 'John Martin lives on the top floor, so I was told by one of the ostlers at Whitehall Mews. We'd better have a civil word or two with the landlord before we visit poor old John.'

They found the landlord polishing a tray of glasses in his shabby bar. He was a seedy-looking man in shirt sleeves, who glanced at their warrant cards with a moist eye, and acknowledged their presence with a surly nod. Box began to make an enquiry.

'Mr Melon — '

'How do you know my name?' demanded the landlord wrathfully. 'Which thieving sneak told you that? I run a respectable house, here, mister. I've never had no truck with the police.'

'You're name's written over the door, Mr Melon. All I want to ask you is whether a man called John Martin lodges here? It's a civil enough question, so maybe I'll be favoured with a civil answer.'

'Well, no offence, guvnor, I'm sure. But there's people round here who tell lies for money. Cross their palms with silver, and they'll say anything. John Martin? Yes, poor old John lodges here. There's an outside staircase round to the left that'll take you up to his place. He's got a friend staying with him at the moment. Poor old John. He won't last the spring. He owes me ten and six in rent, but I'm minded to forget it.'

'So there's people who tell lies for money

round here, Mr Melon? You're not thinking of Barney Bernard, are you, or the likes of Twitcher Thomas?'

Mr Melon managed a kind of gnashing smile, which brought some animation to his unshaven, lantern-jawed face.

'So you know them, do you, Mr Box? Well, in that case, you'll know that a respectable man like me would never have anything to do with the likes of them!'

Box had been rummaging in one of the pockets of his overcoat. He brought out Superintendent Mackharness's half-sovereign, to which he added a silver threepenny bit and three copper pennies.

'I know you wouldn't, Mr Melon,' he said. 'I can see that you've got a beautiful nature behind all that delicate politeness. Here's the rent that John Martin owes. My sergeant and I will go up to see him now.'

Box and Knollys left the public house and walked round the side of the building, where an external wooden staircase rose to the third storey. It was a rickety affair, ending in a small landing. Box knocked on a stout unglazed door, which was almost immediately opened to him. He stared in surprise at the man standing on the threshold. He said to himself. So here you are at last, Malcolm Enright, mariner, aged forty-one: just a stone's throw away from Mr Locke's court in Tooley Street. He said aloud: 'Captain Edgar Adams, unless I'm very much mistaken? I am Detective Inspector Box of Scotland Yard.'

* * *

'It's a long and complex story, Mr Box,' said Adams, 'and this is neither the time nor the place to tell it. You've asked me how I came to know poor John Martin there. Well, I was evading a very determined gang of pursuers, men who had followed me from Germany to London. One way of escaping their clutches was to get myself locked up by the police, which I did. I had a confidant, a man who would give me sanctuary, but in case he couldn't locate me, I scribbled a note in my cell, and slipped it into poor old John's pocket, together with a couple of sovereigns.'

Arnold Box glanced at the bed in the cramped room, where John Martin was dozing fitfully. He saw that Adams had made a bed for himself on the floor, and that everything in the room was clean, tidy and shipshape. Royal Naval Officer or not, Captain Adams evidently believed in the value of scrubbing the decks.

'What did you write in the note, Captain Adams?' he asked. 'Incidentally, it's against regulations to pass notes to other prisoners. Likewise to give them money.'

'I'm sorry about that, Inspector, but the situation called for positive action. In that note I said who I was, mentioned the two sovereigns, and said that I would pay Martin that sum monthly if he would let me bed down in his place, always supposing that I turned up on his doorstep. When Oldfield — You know about Gabriel Oldfield, I expect?'

'I do, sir. It was I who investigated his murder. I knew that you'd been staying with him, and realized that you'd fled from Hatpin Man — that's what I call the killer, a man called Karenin.'

'Karenin . . . Yes, I've heard that name bandied about in certain quarters. I never slept during my stay in Falcon Street, and when I heard footsteps on the landing outside Oldfield's bedroom, I knew that the game was up. I was only just in time flinging myself out on to the roof, and making my escape. I came straight here, and I've been here ever since.'

'I expect you soon found out what had happened to poor Mr Oldfield?' asked Box.

'It was in all the papers by mid-afternoon. I sat here, in John's quarters, reading about it, and wondering whether I should have done something to prevent his murder. I still have qualms about that.'

Sergeant Knollys had sat down quietly by the bed, looking at the old groom who had worked so long for the police, and who was now clearly in a desperate state of decline. John Martin's eyes opened, and focused themselves on the three men in the room.

'Mr Box! It's good of you to come. And this big lad will be your sergeant, I expect. Have you met Captain Adams? Yes, of course you have. He's been so good to me, sending out for a doctor, and bringing me decent food. Like an angel, he's been, for all that he's a gentleman, and a naval officer . . . '

John Martin's eyes closed, and he was soon asleep. Box sat back on a spindly upright chair, his hands on his knees, looking at Captain Edgar Adams RN.

'You've nothing to reproach yourself with, Captain Adams. You had your duty to do. Now, what am I to do with you, sir? You can't stay here for ever.'

He's uneasy about confiding in me, thought Box. He's wondering how much I know. It'll save everybody's time if I told him.

'I know all about you, Captain Adams, and about your trip to Porthcurno. I think it's time that you banished your fear of being ambushed by villains, and presented yourself to Colonel Kershaw without delay.'

'And how am I to do that, Inspector? I don't know where he is — that's part of the way he works. And he doesn't know where *I* am. Poor Gabriel Oldfield was a man who worked for me directly. He wasn't one of Kershaw's 'nobodies'.'

'I wondered about that, sir, and about your connection with Mr Oldfield.'

'Our fathers were both chemists, Inspector, with thriving shops in Portsmouth. I knew Gabriel since we were both boys. When he decided to buy that shop in Falcon Street, he needed a bit of financial help, which I was able to give him. In return, I asked him to provide a safe haven for me in times of stress. He knew what kind of work I did. And now he's gone . . . '

'Yes, sir, he's gone, but he won't be forgotten. And one of these days, I've no doubt, he'll be avenged. When you're ready, I'll arrange for you to be taken to Colonel Kershaw.'

Adams threw Box a grateful glance, and then glanced at the old ostler's inert figure sprawled on the bed.

'And what am I to do about John Martin there?' he asked. 'I feel responsible for him, now. I can't just leave him to fend for himself — '

'There's no question of that, Captain Adams. Old John's not going to be left alone from now on, and very soon he'll be moving to a comfortable billet in the Holy Cross Almshouses, near Theobald's Road. Meanwhile, you need to see Colonel Kershaw.'

Box drew from his pocket the paper spill tied with twine that he had taken from Kershaw's cigar case in the churchyard of St Edward's, Coleman Street. He snapped the twine, and read the words written on the paper in a firm, upright hand.

Mr Boniface, East Lodge, The Crystal Palace, Sydenham

Sir Joseph Paxton's stupendous glass palace at Sydenham never failed to take Box's breath away. Composed entirely of glass and iron, it rose to a height of 175 feet above the 200 acres of beautiful landscaped gardens. He had been brought there as a boy, spent leisurely days there in his youth, and had twice gone out there to arrest a brace of rather genteel suburban poisoners.

The two detectives and Captain Adams made their way through the exuberant fountains and along the Upper Terrace until they came to a secluded square lodge surrounded by clipped privet hedges. It was clearly a much older building than the Crystal Palace, but it been dragooned by Paxton to serve as the East Lodge. Evidently they had been observed, for the door was opened by a genial, stooping man in tweeds, who was smoking a pipe, and holding what appeared to be a blueprint in his left hand.

'Come in, gentlemen,' he said. 'I suppose one could say that you're expected! My name's Boniface. The colonel will be able to speak to you in just a few moments.'

Boniface ushered them into the light and cheerful parlour of the lodge, where Colonel Sir Adrian Kershaw RA was standing at a table talking into a telephone. He smiled a delighted greeting to Adams, but held up his hand to prevent him speaking. He talked loudly and clearly into the instrument, which was of the new type, with a separate handset, and a cradle that could stand on a table.

' . . . And you are quite sure that she spoke to the Dean of Durham personally? It's very important to me . . . Yes, I see. Did your informant hear her mention my young lady by name . . . ? Yes, it sounds very much as though she's making a move at last . . . Yes, I agree, not before time! Thank you. I'll close the line now. Goodbye.'

Colonel Kershaw handed the instrument to Boniface, and shook Captain Adams heartily by the hand. He glanced at Box and Knollys, and motioned them to sit down at the round table, which was covered in maps and papers.

'Ah! Adams! Home at last! What does the poem say — *Home is the sailor, home from the sea, and the huntsman home from the chase*. Something like that. Thank you, Box, for rooting him out, and bringing him here. I knew you'd turn up trumps over this business. Adams, I want you to give me the gist of your recent adventures. The details can wait until later. You may speak quite freely before these two officers — they're seasoned colleagues of mine. Mr Boniface, would you please continue with your work on the model in the next room.'

The pleasant man with the pipe raised a hand in an informal salute, and left the little parlour. Adams began his tale.

'On 8 February, Kershaw, just a week after you and I returned from Porthcurno, I enlisted as an ordinary seaman, under the name Malcolm Enright, on board the *Lermontov*, which was then lying off Lowestoft. It was easy enough to arrange for someone to go sick, and to take his place. You know how it's done. The salient facts are these. The crew was part Russian, part Lascar, and part German. They spoke English among themselves, which is common enough on merchant vessels with mixed crews.'

'An interesting point, that. Pray continue.'

'They appeared to be operating exclusively as a cable repair ship, and all the cable-lifting equipment and specialized tools were properly greased and ready for use. We set sail for Königsberg on the ninth, which was a Thursday, sailed through the North Sea, and into the Baltic, holding a steady course some mile or so from the German coast.

'Nothing unusual happened until we neared Pillau, which, as you know, is the port of Königsberg. I assumed that we were going to sail into the Pillau channel, and tie up in the port. Instead, we continued several miles east, until the towers of Königsberg had disappeared. It wasn't my place to ask questions, but I wondered what we were doing venturing so far into the East Prussian wilderness.'

'Ah! Now we're getting somewhere!' said Kershaw. 'I expect you passed the inlet to the Rundstedt Channel, didn't you? You'd be fifteen miles east of Königsberg by then, and very near the Lithuanian coast of Russia.'

'Exactly. We dropped anchor there, started the winch engines, and turned the drums. We raised a single cable, which I could see travelled under the sea towards the Prussian coast, spliced into it, and transmitted a long message. Obviously, I've no idea what that message was, but I assumed that it was designed to end up in Berlin. The ship has its own advanced transmission equipment.'

'Could you see the Lithuanian coast from where you were anchored? Did you see — Excuse me, one moment. Boniface! Come back in here, will you?'

Still smoking his pipe and clutching his blueprints, the genial man in tweeds appeared at the door.

'You called me, Colonel Kershaw?'

'Yes. If you were anchored near the Rundstedt Channel, Boniface, within sight of the Lithuanian coast of Russia, what would you expect to see?'

'Well, sir, on a nice clear day I'd expect to see a vast, rolling tract of woodland, and a solitary onion-domed church at the land's edge. There'd be little or nothing visible on the Prussian coast, just scrubland and uncultivated wilderness.'

'Thank you, Boniface. Was that more or less what you saw, Captain Adams? And was the date 15 February?'

'Yes, it was. And I remember that church. The sun glinted off its gilded dome. I've no idea, as I said, what it was that they sent through that splice, because I was just an ordinary seaman. It wouldn't have done to show any special interest in what was going on.'

'It was on that day,' said Kershaw, 'that the German Foreign Office in Berlin received a message purporting to come from a German agent in Lithuania, telling them that a new and deadly weapon was being developed for use against Prussia. There was to be a 'grand strike', apparently, at Germany through its eastern territories, which would entail the destruction of the ancient Prussian capital of Königsberg. I think that's what you helped to transmit, Adams. I rather think, too, that it was the first serious attempt at disruption after those test-runs through the English cable complex at Porthcurno.'

9

Baroness Felssen Calls

Kershaw glanced at a sheet of paper which he had selected from the many spread out on the round table.

'The *Lermontov*, as you know, Adams, was originally a vessel of the Imperial Russian Marine, built in the 1870s, but it was sold off a few years ago, and now belongs to the Olafsson Steamship Company, of Stavanger. That company is in turn owned by a financial grouping called the Brandenburg Consortium, registered as a private company in Hesse-Darmstadt. It makes you think, doesn't it? It certainly makes *me* think.'

Very dimly, as though far off, Arnold Box began to glimpse an unpleasant possibility. At the same moment, he knew that Kershaw had done more than merely glimpse it.

'Sir,' he said to Kershaw, 'these names that you've mentioned — Brandenburg, and what was the other one? Hesse-Darmstadt. Do I begin to detect a German flavour to the proceedings?'

'You do, Box, you do indeed. And as usual

I must leave you in the dark until you yourself see the whole light. But there's something that I *will* tell you. The people at the German Embassy are not involved in whatever's going on.'

'There's something else I discovered about the *Lermontov*,' said Adams. 'It's armed. Two of its winch-houses on the forward deck are actually disguised gun emplacements. It was soon after I discovered that, Kershaw, that the ship's officers began to suspect me. It was then that I abandoned ship, as it were, and began my perilous return to Britain by land and sea. Do you want to hear about it?'

'No, not yet. That can keep till later. But your discovery of guns on board is very important. I imagine that it was the *Lermontov* that sank the German cargo-ship *Berlin Star*. The ship was seen to be flying the Russian ensign, but neither the victims nor the witnesses could identify the aggressor with any certainty. Yes, surely, it was the *Lermontov*. And that means . . . '

Colonel Kershaw gazed into space for what seemed like minutes. Then, with an effort, he brought himself back to the business in hand.

'When this meeting's over, Adams,' he said, 'I intend to spirit you away from harm to a place where we can talk at leisure. Meanwhile, there are other things waiting for me to do. The time for action against this growing threat to peace and stability is fast approaching, but there are two events that must take place before I begin to move. One is a meeting later this week, at Whitehall, which has been convened by Sir Charles Napier. It will be attended by various people from the German, Russian and French embassies. I shall be there, too.'

'And the second event?' asked Adams. Box noticed with amusement the edge of vexation in the captain's tone. Evidently, he'd resented being upstaged at this meeting by the annoyingly omniscient Kershaw, and to a lesser extent by Box himself.

'The second event, Adams, is a country-house weekend, where, among others, I hope to meet an old ally of mine, Count von und zu Thalberg. You know all about him, don't you, Mr Box? The count is a high-ranking officer in Prussian Military Intelligence. He is also a very decided Anglophile, and it's essential that I talk to him before I make a move.'

Colonel Kershaw got up from the table, and went to look out of one of the cottage-style windows of the little lodge. Box, watching the mild, sandy-haired man with the slight stoop, thought to himself, When this man 'makes a move', he will have the whole force of the Crown and its armed services behind him. It was an awesome thought.

'Well,' said Kershaw, 'the spring has decidedly taken hold, and the gardens here at the Crystal Palace are burgeoning into their many-coloured splendour. But if certain forces have their way, this year of 1893 will be one of unsettling strife among the nations, and when that happens, the common enemy will strike. There will be much work for us to do if we are to preserve the Queen's Peace.'

Kershaw turned from the window, and treated them all to his rather apologetic smile.

'Adams,' he said, 'will you go into the next room, where Boniface will arrange for you to be spirited away? I will be with you again without fail this evening.'

When Captain Adams had left the room, Colonel Kershaw turned to Box.

'What did you think of Mr Boniface, Box?' he asked.

'He seems a very agreeable man, sir.'

'He is. He's a naval architect by training, and for a number of years he was attached to the Admiralty as an intelligence interpreter. Then he came to work for me. He travels a lot, you know, and finds ways of surviving in hostile terrain. As you say, a very agreeable man. Perhaps you'll see more of Mr Boniface before this business is over.'

Kershaw looked around the little parlour of the lodge, as though to reassure himself that he was actually standing in it.

'This isn't one of my regular haunts, you know, Box. It's a bit out of the way for me, but it's very useful at the moment, and you'll find me here, or in the vicinity, for the near future. Somehow, I think that you and I are going to work even more closely on this Russian business than we have so far. Call whenever you wish.'

'Did you say Russian business or Prussian business, sir?' asked Box, impishly.

Colonel Kershaw subjected him to an impressively blank and forbidding stare.

'Why, what on earth do you mean? I said 'Russian', of course. You must listen more closely in future.'

Box smiled to himself, bowed, and turned to leave the room, followed by Knollys. However, Kershaw's voice checked them on the threshold.

'Sergeant Knollys,' he said, 'I'd be obliged if you'd stay behind. There's something very personal about this business which I need to discuss with you alone.'

As Box walked away from the East Lodge through the spectacular display of fountains, he wondered what the very personal business between Kershaw and Knollys could possibly be. Whatever it was, he was evidently not to be a party to it. It was no good sulking about it. The colonel had his little ways.

⋆ ⋆ ⋆

Sergeant Knollys stayed for half an hour. As soon as he had left the East Lodge, Colonel Kershaw went into the next room, where Mr Boniface was sitting at a plain trestle table, his unlit pipe clenched between his teeth. There was a strong smell of cardboard, fish glue and wood shavings in the air.

'Has Adams gone?' asked Kershaw.

'Yes, sir. Mrs Prout called for him, and has removed him from the premises in a four-wheeler. She had one of those hulking great porters with her.'

'Mrs Prout runs an excellent hotel, with excellent staff, Mr Boniface. Excellent from our point of view, you understand.'

Mr Boniface smiled, and pointed with his pipe to a model, meticulously constructed of wood and cardboard, standing on the table. It represented a long, cigar-shaped vessel, painted silver, and with a number of structures suspended from it by wires. It was quite unlike anything that Kershaw had ever seen.

'There it is, sir,' said Boniface. 'That's the

nearest I can get to what it must look like. I've based it on the twelve reports sent back to you, and the five documents furnished by Sir Charles Napier. The Russians, I gather, are convinced that we know nothing about it?'

'That's so. And for the time being I want them to continue in that belief. Germany, of course, knows all about it, and if it becomes necessary, I'll get Napier to show this model of yours to von Hagen at Prussia House. Just take me through the salient points, will you? I'm not a technical man, you know, apart from knowing all about heavy artillery.'

'Well, sir, this is the Russian aerial boat *Phoebus-Apollo*, currently under construction in the Lithuanian forest, and, to judge from its present state of building, due at any time for practical tests. Its length is two hundred and sixty-two feet, and its displacement three hundred and sixty thousand cubic feet.'

'And this thing is designed to rise into the air? Do you think that's feasible?'

'It may be, sir. In theory, it should be able to rise. I compute the total weight of the aerial boat to be eight tons, with an air displacement of twelve tons. That gives what you might call a surplus lift of four tons.

Oh, yes, it's feasible.'

'How is it powered?'

'They've developed a very fine single cylinder steam engine of twenty-five horse power, fuelled by pebbled coal. The engine will drive a propeller — you can see it there, emerging from the rear suspended carriage, which is twenty-four feet in length. There's room in there for an engineer, who is also the helmsman. From there, he can control the rudder. It's a boat, you see, but a boat of the air.'

'And the rest of the crew?'

'The captain, and one other, accommodated in that long forward carriage, which is fifty-two feet long. I estimate that it will do ten knots in still air, without too much turbulence. Ten knots — what's that? — eleven miles an hour. Its range could be between thirty and fifty miles. Always assuming, sir, that the thing gets off the ground in the first place.'

Colonel Kershaw sat back in his chair and sighed. He regarded the model with what looked like gloomy dislike.

'And this *Phoebus-Apollo*, Mr Boniface — is it designed to take wealthy Russians on thrilling trips across the Lithuanian countryside? Excursions, you know?'

'It is not, sir. If you look closely at the

forward carriage, you'll see a number of racks, pointing downwards — '

'I know, I know. I was only teasing you. I have a report from one of Napier's people at Moscow, which tells me that one of the smaller munitions factories there has been converted to the production of a special kind of shell or bombard, each three hundred pounds in weight. These bombards are filled with high explosive — picric acid, apparently. They will have been designed for those racks of yours, Boniface, and the purpose of the whole venture will be to drop the bombards on to unprotected towns, and sea-going vessels. Sir Charles Napier has been told something similar by von Hagen, who doesn't realize that I've been on to this devilish contraption for nearly a year. Armed attack from the air!'

'It may not come to that, sir. More humane counsels may prevail.'

'Oh, no they won't, Mr Boniface. Whenever mankind creates a new marvel, he will soon find ways of using it to destroy his fellow man. This *Phoebus-Apollo* may have nothing to do with the present unrest, but it must not go unobserved. Vigilance is all.'

* * *

Vanessa Drake lodged in a tall, gaunt building near Dean's Yard, in Westminster. It had once been the convent of an Anglican sisterhood, and the nuns' cells had been very sympathetically adapted to create a number of sets of rooms for single women. She had brought her work home on the Wednesday night, so that she could work quietly at her table in the morning, and report to Watts & Co. in the early afternoon. She had been stitching a fine and delicate gold braid to the edges of a bourse, and her fingers ached. She set the bourse down on the table.

Jack Knollys had taken her to the Alhambra again, and then to supper at a brilliantly lit restaurant in Regent Street, and next week, if the weather was decent, they were going to Hampstead Heath . . .

It would be nice to have a little villa out at Finchley, near to her friend Louise. She could easily make all her own curtains, and there were some marvellous new fabrics at Peter Robinson's, just come in. Was Finchley too far out for a man who worked at Scotland Yard? Still, they'd never be able to afford a place like that. Louise was paid a salary by London University, and her parents were very comfortably off. She wondered what Jack's parents did for a living. He'd never mentioned them yet . . .

Maurice was a nice name for a boy, and Louise for a girl, after Princess Louise. Or May, perhaps, like Princess May of Teck.

Someone was coming up the stairs. Vanessa frantically straightened the mess on the table, smoothed her dress, and sat down to wait for the knock. The door opened, and Colonel Kershaw came into the room. She was quite unable to suppress her cry of delight as she sprang up to greet him.

'So, there you are, missy!' Kershaw treated her to an amused smile, and sat down uninvited in a chair opposite hers. He was wearing the dark-blue undress uniform of a Royal Artillery officer, and was carrying his glazed peak cap in his hand.

'Well, Miss Drake, how are you?'

'I'm very well, thank you, sir.'

'Good, I'm glad to hear it. And you mustn't stand up to greet me in your own home. Young ladies don't need to do that. Now, if I tell you that something rather interesting is going forward, would you want to be associated with it?'

'Oh, yes, sir!'

Why conceal her delight? She *was* delighted. How smart he looked! She wondered where he could be going, in uniform, like that. The last time she'd seen him dressed as an officer, it had been in the full dress uniform of a colonel at poor Arthur's funeral.

'Very well. Now listen carefully. I think that very soon — within the next day or so — you will be approached by a German lady, Baroness Felssen, who will say that she admired your handiwork in some church or other. She may come here, or she may approach you at Watts & Company. I'm not quite sure what she'll say next, but I rather think that she'll invite you to stay at her house in Northumberland for a while, in order to carry out some commission. Now, I must say at once that there is more to this task than merely acting as one of my 'nobodies', because in this case it is the other side who have taken the initiative.'

'I don't quite understand, sir — '

'I mean that they know who you are. It's not as though I were to send you somewhere, incognito. They know that you're one of my people, and for some reason they want to see you. Now, I don't want to tell you too much about Baroness Felssen, but I'll warn you that some people consider her to be the most dangerous woman in Europe, at this moment. You're at perfect liberty to say, no, thank you, if she asks you to go with her. But if you *do* agree, I want you to go up there to Northumberland, do whatever she says, look, and listen.'

He smiled at her, and rather disconcertingly waited for her to make some kind of reply.

'Look and listen? You mean — '

'I mean you're to do nothing on your own initiative. No detective work. Just look, make a mental note of all you see, and listen. Try to remember what people say. There will be guests there. Watch them, listen to them. Engage them in conversation, if you like. But no snooping, no eavesdropping, no loitering about in odd corners trying to catch conversations. I'm very insistent on that point. Is all that understood, Miss Drake?'

'Yes, sir.'

'As soon as she makes contact with you, and if you agree to whatever she suggests, come and see me, and tell me what she said to you, so that I can take certain steps. Our friend in Coleman Street will be able to tell you where you can find me. When the time comes for the baroness to dispense with your services, say thank you, and come home.'

'And report directly to you, sir?'

'Yes, report directly to me, and tell me what you saw, and what you heard. There may be danger, and for that reason I will take certain measures to see that you come to no harm. In return, you must do as I tell you. No snooping, no taking foolish risks. For reasons that I must keep secret, this venture is one being undertaken by you and me alone. Other agencies will not be informed. I'll leave you now, missy. I've got a parade to inspect at Horse Guards. Goodbye. I knew you wouldn't let me down.'

⋆ ⋆ ⋆

On the morning of Friday, 24 March, Vanessa Drake looked up from her work as Mr Edwards, one of the managers at Watts & Company, came into the firm's sewing-room. He was accompanied by a very handsome middle-aged lady dressed in the height of fashion, a woman who spoke courteously enough, but with an air of restrained command.

'Miss Drake,' said the manager, 'I have the honour of introducing you to Baroness Felssen, who wishes to speak to you. Baroness Felssen has seen specimens of your work, and tells me she is profoundly impressed by it.'

Vanessa had felt compelled to rise in the presence of a titled lady, but the baroness hastily put out a restraining hand. Her rather forbidding face was suddenly transformed by a bewitching smile.

'Please don't get up, my dear,' she said, in perfect English, though with a slight foreign accent. 'I like to see you there, subduing all that damask, and all those brilliants, to your will!' She turned to the manager, and said, in a more distant tone, 'That is all, I think, Mr Edwards. You may leave Miss Drake and me alone.'

The manager bowed, and left the room, closing the door quietly behind him. Baroness Felssen sat down at the table, and subjected the girl to a silent but obvious appraisal, at the same time carefully removing her lilac gloves, and depositing them on the table. I hope you like what you see, Baroness, thought Vanessa. Meanwhile, a cat may look at a queen. This stately aristocrat is the kind of woman who'll be all smiles as long as you do what she wants. It would, though, be dangerous to cross her. What gorgeous clothes she had! That olive-green suit looks as though it was cut in Paris. And that necklace — surely those diamonds are real? They made her glass brilliants look tawdry!

What a pity that Colonel Kershaw had told her nothing at all about this woman, apart from the thrilling suggestion that she was dangerous. Her brief was simply to look, and listen. Perhaps she'd be able to do more than that, if the opportunity arose.

'Well, Miss Drake,' said the baroness, with a touch of amusement in her tone, 'we've sized each other up, and no doubt you've drawn a few conclusions about me. No, I won't ask you what they are, in case they're not very complimentary. And I'll not tell you my estimate of *you*, for similar reasons. Instead, I'll get down to business.'

'Business, madam?'

'Yes. I must tell you that I live at a place called Stonewick, on the Northumberland coast, some miles south of Her Majesty's Town of Berwick upon Tweed. My house is called Stonewick Hall, a fine, modern stone mansion built on the cliff top, with splendid views of the North Sea. I love that part of England — windswept, exhilarating, so different from this choking capital of yours!'

'You speak of London as though it's not *your* capital, too, madam.'

Vanessa's visitor laughed. It was a pleasant, good-humoured sound.

'That's a very nice way, my dear, of asking me to tell you my antecedents! Well, I'll interrupt my story for a while to tell you. My name is Baroness Felssen, and I am a Prussian noblewoman. My late husband was Keeper of the Armouries to the Emperor Friedrich, and I have a romantic, rambling estate in the eastern provinces of the German

Empire. I have always loved England, and some years ago, after my husband's death, I purchased Stonewick Hall. I spend much of the autumn and winter there, and it was in late February of this year that I visited Durham Cathedral for the first time — '

'Ah!'

'Yes, my dear, now you'll see where my rambling tale is leading. I was shown over the cathedral by the dean, and in one of the many chapels there I saw a beautiful set of altar furnishings, rendered in costly cloth of gold, with scenes from the New Testament finely embroidered in many coloured silks, and dotted with brilliants. I made enquiries, and found that the whole set was entirely your work.'

'Oh, yes, madam, I was very proud of that commission. So was Mr Watts, I'm glad to say.'

'And so he should be! Anyway, the dean, at my request, showed me the matching seasonal sets that you had made — the purple one, the glowing green, and the blazing red. And at once I said to myself, 'Amalie, you must get this girl to refurbish Stonewick Chapel'.'

Baroness Felssen opened her reticule, and took a small photograph from it. She handed the picture to Vanessa, who noted the many costly rings on the baroness's fingers. More diamonds. Really, on an Englishwoman they would seem vulgar, but not on this commanding Prussian aristocrat.

'That's Stonewick Chapel. It's actually the private chapel of the house, but for many years it's been used as a parish church. The previous owners of the house badly neglected the chapel, and I'm about to start a programme of restoration, with the assistance of Sir Giles Gilbert Scott. But I want you, Miss Drake, to recreate the set of frontals and other altar appointments, which will be my personal gift to the parish. Will you come up to Northumberland as my guest? Stay as long as you like. I've already spoken to Mr Watts, and he's very willing to let you go.'

Vanessa was silent for a while, thoughtfully turning over some of the rich materials laid out on the wide cutting-table. Northumberland . . . It would be an adventure, something to banish the fatal dullness that was beginning to overwhelm her. Why not go with this impressive woman, and live in a mansion at the edge of the sea, at her expense? It was what the colonel wanted her to do, and, who knows, something very interesting might come of it . . .

'I hope that you're not dissuaded by my being German, my dear,' said Baroness

Felssen, breaking in upon Vanessa's thoughts. 'I know that we are not popular here in England, just now, but one day, I hope, you will realize just how misunderstood we Prussians are. Come to Northumberland. I keep a full staff, and have one or two other guests staying with me, so you'll not lack for company.'

Vanessa had made up her mind before the older woman had begun speaking.

'Of course I'll come, Baroness Felssen,' she said. 'I'll need to know the kind of style and material that you want — '

'Of course, Miss Drake. We can discuss that later in the week. Or perhaps you can make your own choice, in consultation with Mr Watts? I want everything new, my dear. When you're ready, come to see me at the Savoy. Then we can travel up to Northumberland together. It will be a fresh young face to lighten up the house, and a welcome change for you from all this grime and gloom!'

Later that afternoon, Vanessa Drake climbed the four worn steps up into the churchyard of St Edward's, Coleman Street. The faded old man with the campaign medal, who was sweeping the path with an old-fashioned besom, stopped beside her, but still looked intently at the ground.

'What do you want?' he asked curtly.

'I want to see him.'

The old man sighed, and shook his head. These girls! What did the colonel want to be bothered with them for? Security was men's work. Well, it was none of his business. He leaned for a while on the handle of his besom, then treated Vanessa to an amused, toothless smile.

'All right. East Lodge at the Crystal Palace. This afternoon, at three.'

The old man moved slowly away towards the church, and Vanessa Drake made her way thoughtfully down the steps into Coleman Street.

10

Adventure at Stonewick Hall

'Hold quite still, Herr Bleibner. I've nearly finished.'

Sir David Blaine, an elegant man with a neatly trimmed beard, piercing grey eyes, and a tailor who knew how to flatter a middle-aged man's figure, concentrated his eagle gaze through the hand-lens, observing the area of his patient's left cheek, where it met the crease of the nose. He could see the tough, fish-like scales on the surface of the skin, but was interested to note that in this case the epidermis was not muddy brown, but of an almost leprous whiteness. Interesting! Here was yet another variant form of congenital hypertrophy.

'Well, Herr Bleibner,' he said, 'I'm happy to tell you that it's *not* leprosy. That was what you feared, wasn't it? It's a condition that we call ichthyosis, and it tends to be inherited. It's unsightly, but it's not contagious, and it can be treated to some extent. At present, though, there is no cure.'

He returned the lens to his travelling

instrument case, sat back in his chair, and looked at his patient.

'I suppose you were out in Africa?' he asked. 'That often gives sufferers from this complaint the fear that they've contracted leprosy.'

'Yes, I was out in German East Africa for a year or two. I was a civil servant attached to the prison system. I came back home with this condition ripening, if that's the word. I wasn't worried about the unsightliness. I'm not a vain man. But leprosy — well, you can imagine how I felt!'

Sir David stood up, and walked over to the drawing-room window. He looked out across the cheerful lawns towards the sea.

'It's a lovely morning, Herr Bleibner,' he said. 'Would you care for a stroll and a cigar before luncheon? The grounds are very well tended here, and I've never seen such a fine display of daffodils.'

'Baroness Felssen is very fond of gardens,' Bleibner replied. 'She brings our Germanic thoroughness to the subject, you see! Regimented ranks and files of flowerbeds; thoroughly drilled lawns . . . I've other friends who prefer something a little wilder! But come, by all means let us stroll in the grounds.'

Sir David Blaine admired Stonewick Hall.

It was a splendid modern mansion with spacious, airy rooms, and marvellous views from its cliff-top situation across the North Sea. It was a healthy house, in one of the healthiest parts of Northumberland, and it had been very civil of Baroness Felssen to invite him to stay. He could have travelled down from Edinburgh for the day in order to examine Herr Bleibner, but he'd no intention of declining an offer to dine and sleep.

The house party had assembled over the weekend — himself, a charming young lady vestment maker from London, and Herr Bleibner. A local couple, Major and Mrs Hotchkiss, had stayed until Monday morning. It was now Tuesday, the twenty-eighth.

The two men left the drawing-room through a wide French window, and strolled along the front terrace of the house. There was an invigorating sea breeze blowing, and the sun shone brightly in the open Northumbrian sky. They had lit their cigars, which were drawing nicely. Sir David felt inclined to gossip with his rather taciturn patient.

'Baroness Felssen strikes me as an intensely civilized lady,' he ventured. 'Until she invited me down here, I'd not had the pleasure of meeting her.'

'The baroness, Sir David, is only one example of the noble and *soignée* ladies who do so much to heighten the tone of German society. She is a renowned benefactor of deserving causes, a connoisseur of music, and a beautiful contralto singer. I sometimes think —'

The German stopped, evidently in some confusion.

'Think what, Herr Bleibner? Out with it, man!' Sir David Blaine was feeling very charitable towards his German patient. He was hoping that today's luncheon would be as satisfying as yesterday's. Decidedly, Baroness Felssen was an excellent hostess.

'Come down this path between the beeches, Sir David,' said Bleibner. 'It leads to the family chapel, a most interesting bijou Gothic church. Our fellow-guest, Miss Drake, is working in there on the new altar furnishings.'

They turned off from the main drive and on to the path leading to the chapel.

'What I was going to say, Sir David, was that I sometimes think that Britain's being an island works against her. Oh, I know that she's surrounded by a great moat, to keep us foreigners out — but, you know, insularity has its disadvantages.'

'And what are they?'

'Well, insularity prevents you from arriving at a true picture of the other countries and their inhabitants. I'll be quite frank, Sir David. What do you really know about Germans? Only what you read in the papers. Only what some of your more hidebound politicians choose to let you know. But there are thousands of Baroness Felssens. There are thousands of liberal-minded, talented German men in high positions of authority, who are quite unknown in this country. The only German popular with Englishmen was murdered by fanatics in January. Insularity . . .'

'You're referring to the late Dr Otto Seligmann, aren't you? He was blown to pieces by a factionalist's bomb at his house in Chelsea. But everyone knows that his murder had nothing to do with the vast body of the German nation. I take your point about insularity, Herr Bleibner. And just recently, I've been thinking how responsibly Germany has behaved over these Russian outrages. The sinking of the *Berlin Star* horrified the whole country, but the Kaiser has made no move of revenge — '

'The Kaiser is a man of peace! He is horrified at the thought of a coming European conflict. Russia, Sir David, is waking up from the sleep of centuries. It has cast its envious eye on your Indian Empire, it has threatened the integrity of Canada. We know that it is contemplating an armed incursion down the Baltic coast and into Eastern Germany — it's all in the German papers! But then, you English can't read German, so you cannot grasp the magnitude of the Russian menace, which threatens both our countries. But there, I have said enough. You are, no doubt, offended.'

For the last ten minutes they had been standing in the porch of the little chapel, the door of which stood open. Sir David Blaine wondered whether the young lady guest from London had heard their rather unusual conversation.

'I'm not in the least offended, Mr Bleibner. In fact, I'm very interested in what you're saying. I'm dining with our Member of Parliament next week. I think I'll ask him what steps the government is going to take in order to check this Russian menace. Perhaps this country is showing too much hostility to Germany — '

'It's true. And we Germans are confused and bewildered. Surely, there are strong bonds of kinship between our two nations? Or, if you deny that, surely there are strong bonds of self-interest?'

Herr Bleibner lowered his voice, and glanced along the path, as though to make certain that there was no one who could possibly overhear what he was about to say. He still remained apparently rooted to the spot where he had stopped on their walk, immediately in front of the open door of Stonewick Chapel.

'I have friends in Berlin, Sir David, who have entrée to the German Foreign Office. These friends very much fear that a monstrous Russian attack on an English coastal town is contemplated, prior to open invasion of Germany, in the region of the Brandenburg Marshes. A number of cable messages to that effect have recently been intercepted by the Prussian State Telegraph Office.'

'But that's abominable, my dear Bleibner! Surely Her Majesty's Government — '

'The British Government, Sir David, will exercise its usual caution, fearful of offending the great British public by telling it unpalatable truths. Meanwhile, the Russian aggression grows unchecked. People die. Ships are sunk. Sovereign territories are threatened . . . But what is that to us? Come, I have said too much. You and I are mere pawns in a great game. Let us change the subject. Isn't that the luncheon gong being sounded? Let us go back to the house.'

In the quiet interior of the chapel, Vanessa Drake sat at a long trestle table set up near the altar. She had brought a rich selection of materials and embellishments from Watts & Company, and for the last three days she had worked on the replacement of the fading vestments and altar furnishings.

Her stay at Stonewick had been very pleasant. Her hostess had sparkled in conversation, and had shown great skill in drawing others out by sympathetic questions. The Scots surgeon, Sir David Blaine, had waxed lyrical about the various foul diseases that fascinated him, and it had been amusing for Vanessa to watch his unconvincing attempts at modesty.

The local couple — she had not been able to remember their name — had been decidedly down-to-earth and uncomplicated. Poor Mr Bleibner had been rather shy, because of his alarming complexion. He really did look like most people's idea of a ghost. They had lunched and dined well, and spent the evenings in conversation and reminiscence. She, too, had fallen for Baroness Felssen's charm, and had given the assembled company a little lecture on the arts of church embroidery.

Yes, everything had been natural and normal. But she remembered what Colonel Kershaw had said to her when she had visited him just before setting off for

Northumberland. 'They will strive to make everything seem quite ordinary and harmless, Miss Drake. Let me assure you that you are venturing into the lion's den. If anyone there claims to be a friend, treat him as you would a phial of deadly poison!'

And now, the ghostly-pale Herr Bleibner had revealed yet another dastardly Russian plot, bellowing it through the chapel door for her to hear, and carry back to Colonel Kershaw! Did that man think she was stupid and gullible, simply because she was so very young?

* * *

Sir David Blaine left for Edinburgh soon after luncheon. The afternoon was uneventful. Baroness Felssen came out with Vanessa to the chapel for a while, and was genuinely appreciative of the work that she had done. She sat in one of the pews, talking about her life in England.

'One can never entirely leave one's native country behind, my dear,' she said. 'That is why I have been so pleased to receive poor Herr Bleibner here when Sir David Blaine offered to look at his skin condition. Hans Bleibner trained as a surgeon in his youth, but abandoned that for a career in the

German Colonial Service. He's all but retired now, and lives on a modest government pension.'

'Does he live here, Baroness? He seems very familiar with the house and grounds.'

'Live here? Oh, no. He visits often, at my invitation, partly because he knew my late husband so well. They were both at Heidelberg. He'll be returning to Germany next week.'

At dinner that night Herr Bleibner seemed more at ease. He spoke passionately of the treasures of German science, and the need for co-operation between England and Germany. The baroness agreed, and gently encouraged Vanessa to ask questions.

'What do you think of these dreadful Russian threats, Herr Bleibner?' she asked, hoping that her wide blue eyes conveyed a sufficiently convincing air of innocence.

'My dear young lady, what am I to say? A poor old German's no longer listened to in England! We're the bogey-men, used to affright your children when they are naughty. Russia takes advantage of that groundless prejudice. Always, you English revert to 1870, nearly a quarter of a century ago, when there was a different Kaiser and another government. Why not go back further than that, to Waterloo? Who was it who assisted Wellington to achieve his great victory over the tyrant Napoleon?'

'Well,' said Vanessa, glancing desperately around the room as though it would furnish a clue to the right answer, 'I suppose he was helped by . . . by — '

'By the Prussian Marshal Blücher, as you should have been told at school. Why are you not taught these things? Why — ?'

'My dear Herr Bleibner,' said the baroness soothingly, 'Miss Drake cannot be expected to know the answer to your questions. But I'm sure she'll take your point, as I do. Britain must discover anew where her true friends lie. Together, Britain and Germany would be invincible.'

'True, true,' said Bleibner, nodding a vigorous agreement. 'An alliance between England and Prussia, Miss Drake, would mean that the Russian threat would vanish overnight.'

'And that,' declared Baroness Felssen with a smile, 'is enough of politics for one evening. Let us go into the music-room. It's a beautiful moonlit night, and we shall leave the curtains open. At this time of year, the moon hangs over the North Sea like a great lantern, shining across the water.'

A fine Bechstein grand piano stood on a Chinese carpet in the wide bow window.

Coffee had been set out on a long, low table, and for a while the three of them sat in armchairs facing the window. The grounds of the house were in darkness, but the sea beyond glimmered in the strong silver light of the moon.

After coffee, Baroness Felssen seated herself at the piano, and sang a number of rather sad but sweet German songs. The music was unfamiliar to Vanessa, but she enjoyed its pleasant harmonies, and was delighted at the baroness's contralto voice. When Baroness Felssen stopped singing, Vanessa clapped appreciatively. Baroness Felssen smiled.

'Those songs were by Robert Schumann, and were written for the soprano voice. I had to transpose them to a lower key, but I'm glad you liked them. Do you sing or play, Miss Drake?'

Vanessa bit her lip in vexation. She had never got the hang of the pianoforte, and her attempts at singing usually made people wince. It wouldn't be very ladylike to tell the baroness that she was quite good at whistling, but that tennis and cycling were more to her taste.

'I'm afraid not, Baroness.'

'Well, it doesn't matter, my dear. Your skills are in your fingers, and your cunning needle.

That golden frontal you are working on is one of the finest things I've seen! Come now, Herr Bleibner. See! The moon is beckoning to you — she expects a tribute in sound. What will it be? Schumann's *Mondnacht*?'

Herr Bleibner uttered a violent kind of hoot, that may have been an attempt at a laugh. He rose from his chair, and seated himself at the Bechstein.

'Like Miss Drake, I will not venture to sing, lest the servants come to see what is amiss. So here is my tribute to the moon, Baroness. Beethoven's Piano Sonata Number 14, the 'Moonlight'.'

As soon as Herr Bleibner began to play, Vanessa realized that he was a very talented amateur. His hands were strong and sinuous, with long, white fingers from which some of the nails were missing, a misfortune that had made Vanessa shudder when she had first become aware of it. Those maimed hands, though, had total control over the keyboard, and over the challenging subtleties of Beethoven's music.

As he played, Herr Bleibner seemed to become enrapt, closed in upon himself, noticing neither his audience nor the great silver moon hung in the sky over the North Sea. He played without music, and his lips moved silently from time to time, as though mouthing some incantation. The moonlight fell upon his chalk-white face, making it even more menacing than it had been in the full glare of gaslight. At one moment, near the plaintive final bars of the sonata, a single tear rolled down Herr Bleibner's cheek. When he finished playing, and lifted his hands from the keys, both women remained silent, for silence was the tribute that his performance merited.

* * *

In the chapel next morning, Vanessa plied her needle, and thought of this visit of hers to Baroness Felssen, at her fine modern house in Northumberland. It was Wednesday now, and she had been at Stonewick Hall since Saturday. The work had proved to be interesting and challenging, and the days were passing agreeably enough. Her hostess was charming and unaffected, a truly cultured woman with a mind of her own, and a talent for managing people. Colonel Kershaw had described her as dangerous, but to Vanessa she was simply a gracious and welcoming hostess.

And Herr Bleibner? What was she to make of a man scarred by disfigurement, a man with tortured hands which spoke of some terrible past? His chief failing seemed to be an overmastering patriotism, which turned him into a fearless advocate of his native land, its culture, and its achievements. Was that a fault? He was also fearless in exposing the wickedness of the present governing powers in Russia.

Last night, he had allowed the two women to glimpse something of his private inner torments in his performance of the 'Moonlight' Sonata. Was music his special refuge?

Vanessa had been outlining some lilies embroidered on a pulpit-fall with a delicate green thread. She had reached the end of the first bobbin, and rummaged through her workbox for the second. It wasn't there. She uttered a little sound of impatience, and rose from her chair. She would have to go back to her room and open her large sewing-case. She was settled comfortably in the chapel, where it was warm, light and quiet. Still, she couldn't sit there all day without the means of completing her work.

It was very pleasant outside in the grounds, and she loitered a little as she made her way through the trees towards the main path. She had almost reached the end of the little plantation surrounding the chapel when she heard a crashing of feet among the trees. She spun round, startled, and was just in time to see the figure of a heavy man in a grey coat plunge away into the shrubbery behind the chapel.

Her heart beating rapidly, she hurried out of the trees on to the path. The house loomed up reassuringly above her, the French windows of the drawing-room opened invitingly. She scrambled up the sloping grass to the terrace, and turned round to face the way she had come. She fancied that she saw the flitting shapes of other men among the trees for a second or two, then all was silent. A nervous fancy? She stepped over the sill into the house.

Her room was on the first floor, at the rear of the mansion. The ground floor appeared to be deserted, and she recalled how the servants at Stonewick Hall seemed trained to remain quite invisible until they were summoned by their mistress. She mounted the wide staircase, and came to the first floor.

Colonel Kershaw had warned her not to poke or pry. She was simply to see and hear, and report to him on her return to London. But ahead of her, at the end of the white-panelled corridor, the door of Baroness Felssen's bedroom stood invitingly open . . . It would do no harm, surely, to take just a little peep inside? She tiptoed along the red and blue Turkey carpet, and crossed the threshold of the baroness's room.

It was a large, sunny chamber, with quietly tasteful furniture in light oak, apart from the bed, which was a voluptuous fantasy in William Morris style. A wide dressing table stood in the window. What expensive fittings the baroness had! Those silver-backed brushes would cost a fortune.

Vanessa caught sight of her reflection in the dressing-table mirror, and shuddered. Somehow, her own image suggested an interloper, which, of course, was what she was. There was a fireplace in the room, hidden behind two beautiful Japanese screens. She stepped behind them, and stood in silence for a while. A marble clock ticked slowly on the mantelpiece, somehow emphasizing the quietness of the spacious room.

On either side of the clock stood a photograph in a black ebony frame, with a crucifix rising from the top. One showed a pretty woman in court dress, a woman with frank and fearless eyes. A small plaque beneath the picture read: *In Memoriam. Adelheid, Gräfin Czerny*. The companion photograph was of a handsome man with a short, trimmed beard. He was wearing uniform, and sported the sash of a foreign order. His inscription read: *Engelbert, Graf Czerny. Resurgam*.

Count and Countess Czemy . . . Vanessa

suddenly felt a nauseous fear hold her in thrall. She had no idea who Baroness Felssen was, but she was evidently an intimate of the woman whom Vanessa had known as Ottilie Seligmann, and of her husband, Count Czerny, who had met their deaths only months before in a frightful marine explosion off the coast of Scotland. Both of them had been closely involved in the complex secret affair known as the Hansa Protocol.

As Vanessa stood motionless behind the screens, she became aware of the low murmur of voices. It came from somewhere beyond the room, but near enough to be heard from where she was standing. By a great effort of will she overcame her fear, and ventured out from behind the screens.

A door on the far side of the room was open. It led into a small, high dressing-room, filled almost completely with a large mahogany wardrobe. Scarcely daring to breathe, Vanessa slipped quietly into the room. Directly to her right was the arched entrance to a long, narrow chamber, a sort of gallery filled with books. She could see the Baroness and Herr Bleibner sitting at a desk, with their backs towards her. A man she did not know was standing beside them, consulting a watch. She crouched against the lintel of the door, and listened to their conversation.

'I assure you, Cathcart,' Herr Bleibner was saying, 'that there is plenty of time. I've given you the messages, and their translations into English and French. You have only to slip away and return to Newcastle, where your beloved engines await you. Send those cables at the times I've indicated, and that debt of yours will be cancelled within the week.'

'Be sure to keep your side of the bargain, Mr Cathcart,' said the Baroness. 'If you fail us, you will find that we are fatal people to cross.'

Vanessa had managed to position herself in such a way that she could see through the crack in the hinge side of the door. Cathcart was a nondescript fellow, a clerk, perhaps. He stood nervously, evidently waiting for orders of some kind.

'By the end of this week,' Herr Bleibner was saying, 'the series of canards against the Russians will be complete. English public opinion will be so inflamed against them that when the little bombardment of Whitby takes place, the public here will be ready to do away with all the Russians in London.'

'And as soon as the shelling is over,' said Baroness Felssen, 'the assault on Eastern Prussia will begin. Those joint atrocities will drive the British and the Prussians into each other's arms.'

‘Whose side are you on, then?’ asked the man called Cathcart. There was a genuine bewilderment in his voice that cancelled out the offensive abruptness of his question.

Baroness Felssen laughed.

‘Let us say, Cathcart, that we are on the side of the gods. Now go. And don’t fail us, if you value your own life.’

Vanessa heard Cathcart walk away. Mercifully, his route did not take him back through the dressing-room. Baroness Felssen and Herr Bleibner had begun to talk to each other in rapid German. Vanessa saw Bleibner glance back towards the open door of the dressing-room, and felt another surge of fear. She began very gently to make her way back the way she had come. It would take her only a minute to reach the landing, and then she could hurry along to her own room, retrieve the bobbin of silk that she needed, and make her way quite boldly back to the chapel. She left the dressing-room, and re-entered Baroness Felssen’s bedroom.

Herr Bleibner, his back pressed firmly against the outer door, his face transfixed by a ghastly smile, was waiting for her.

‘So, my pretty little spy,’ he said, ‘you thought that no one could see you as you crouched behind the door. But I have eyes that see everything, and I saw you clearly enough: you were reflected in my glasses.'

'Colonel Kershaw — '

'Colonel Kershaw is not here, my dear, so whatever he told you has no validity. We thought to send you back to him crammed full of pro-German sentiments. It was worth a try, and it showed him, in any case, that his flabby array of 'secret servants' and 'nobodies' is entirely known to us. Goodbye, Miss Drake. Poor, foolish child!'

As he said these words, Vanessa saw a tear roll down his flaking cheek. At the same time, he drew what appeared to be a woman's hatpin from behind the lapel of his morning coat.

Vanessa Drake screamed, and not for the first time she was astonished at the volume of the noise that she made. Last time that she had screamed in that way, a door had been carried off its hinges, and she had been rescued from injury or worse. This time, though, nothing was going to happen . . .

With an explosive rending of timber, the door behind Bleibner's back was carried off its hinges, sending him sprawling into the room, and the raging figure of Jack Knollys hurled itself directly at the German. Vanessa had the sense to leap away from the struggling men, and to dart out on to the landing. She found it seemingly full of blue-uniformed soldiers.

'It's all right, miss,' one of them said in rough accents, 'you're safe with the Northumberland Fusiliers.'

Still trembling with fright, Vanessa looked back into the room. Bleibner was making a desperate effort to free himself from Jack Knollys' furious grip. He was wasting his strength! Jack had saved her yet again. He was as strong as a lion, as fierce as a tiger, he was —

Vanessa watched in horror as Knollys suddenly uttered a choking cry, dropped to his knees, and then collapsed with a sickening crash to the floor. She was just in time to see that Bleibner had escaped through the inner room, and that two soldiers were bending over Jack Knollys' inert form, before she fainted.

11

War of Words

Sir Charles Napier sat back in his chair at the head of the long polished table, listening to the clipped tones of Colonel von Hagen. He was alert not only to what the Prussian military attaché was saying, but also to the controlled anger behind his voice. Beside him, in a chair placed a little apart from the table, sat Colonel Kershaw.

The military attachés and their secretaries had assembled only half an hour earlier, and after they had agreed on English as the language for this pourparler, Napier had called upon Colonel von Hagen to open the conversation. It was eight o'clock on the evening of 3 April, the earliest time that these three men and their regular secretaries had been able to attend.

The Foreign Secretary's meeting room, a grander place than his own office on the floor above, was illuminated by silk-shaded oil lamps, which created a soothing atmosphere, casting long shadows upward towards the dark oil-paintings on the panelled walls.

'I have assured you, gentlemen,' von Hagen was saying, 'that the Kaiser and his government are anxious that peace should prevail. But peace at what price? We Germans are a patient people, but there are limits to that patience. I have made no secret of my priorities, which are centred on the health and progress of the German Reich. Well, now I see an approaching military threat, so bold and arrogant in its designs on German territory that it must be countered immediately.'

Colonel von Hagen looked sufficiently arrogant himself, thought Napier. His moustache bristled with indignation, and the lamplight glinted off his monocle. He looked petulant and uncooperative, as though he was there under duress. His secretary, a bullet-headed young man with an unsmiling countenance, appeared as surly as his master.

Monsieur Laplace, sitting opposite the German attaché, asked a question in the lazy, insolent way that he affected. Napier wondered about Laplace, the French attaché. He had the air of an artist rather than a diplomat, and had been a friend of Rimbaud. He'd gained his military expertise in North Africa. The French President didn't like him much. Was Laplace aware of the secret treaty of non-intervention between France and Russia?

‘A masterly exposition, von Hagen,’ said the Frenchman, ‘but when are you coming to the point? What is this arrogant military threat? Surely you are not allowing yourself to be swayed by journalistic rumours? Your own country has often been seen — and felt — as a military threat.’

Colonel von Hagen flushed red with anger.

‘You can sneer as much as you like, M. Laplace. You can choose, if that is your wish, to live your life permanently in 1870. I am not the only person here who suspects that your country has assured itself of a peaceful life during the next decade at the expense of other nations — ’

That’s torn, it, thought Napier. Now Laplace will stand on his dignity, such as it is. He could, if he wished, sit there silently, thinking his cynical republican thoughts, but Laplace would never be able to disguise his rooted dislike of the Germans. Von Hagen wouldn’t get away with it.

‘What are you implying, Colonel von Hagen? I can categorically deny that there has been any secret treaty between France and another power.’

(Ah! So he *does* know about the secret treaty. That’s why he looked so damned complacent when he came in here tonight.)

Colonel von Hagen smiled, and treated the

Frenchman to a mock bow.

'Deny what you like, *monsieur*,' he said. 'Pretence is part of our diplomatic art. Deny, by all means, that France did not enter into a secret negotiation with Russia on the eighth of May last, at Cannes. Let us lie to each other, by all means.'

Von Hagen sat down, but not before glancing at Napier, whose face bore an incipient smile. Von Hagen's secretary was gazing at his master adoringly. Laplace, white-faced, had seemingly forgotten all about the Prussian diplomat. He sat talking in low tones to his secretary.

At the other end of the table, the Russian attaché, Major Count Menschikov, an elderly, balding man with a scarred face, slowly rose to his feet. He, too, was white with rage.

'You, sir,' he bellowed, in a voice that was disconcertingly young and powerful for a man of his years, 'what are you implying about Russia? Russia is tired of German slanders, tired of German stories, and tired of German duplicity. You choose to insult M. Laplace, and he meets your arrogance with becoming silence. But you will not insult *me*, sir! Who is your secret ally here? Or needn't I ask? What is this threat that forms the basis for your lie?'

Von Hagen sprang to his feet, knocking

over a water-glass in the process. His face had turned puce with anger.

'A lie?' he shrieked. 'Why, if you wish to play with fire, Major Menschikov, be careful that you are not burnt! As for Prussia, her only ally, as always, is the Austrian Empire. But you, sir: deny your aggression if you will. Yes, let me hear you deny that Russia is creeping like a venomous snake down the shores of the Baltic, through the land of the Lithuanian people — the land that you have stolen from them — ready to strike at the northern coasts of Germany. Go on, deny it!'

He'll have a fit if he doesn't stop, thought Napier, watching von Hagen, whose rant was developing into a scream. Let's hope not. We can't afford to lose him at this juncture.

'I *do* deny it! I tell you, von Hagen, there is no truth whatever in these rumours. We have all heard them. They are not true. We have no troops moving down the Baltic. We have no engineers in Meshed. We have no designs on India. We have no designs on Canada. We have sunk no German ship. These things are canards. You are free tonight with accusations of lying, Colonel von Hagen. But I do not lie, and here is an interesting truth for you to ponder. If you Germans venture to set foot aggressively on Russian soil, you will be utterly annihilated.'

Colonel Kershaw, who had been studying the carpet for the last few minutes, looked up sharply. Sir Charles Napier leaned forward in his chair. He'd learnt a great deal from this meeting. Von Hagen was a firebrand, a real Junker, quite happy to go to war if he had to. But he had heroically resisted revealing his knowledge of Russia's secret weapon, knowledge which he had chosen to share earlier with Napier. Von Hagen, it seemed, was grudgingly convinced of England's good faith.

Laplace had been invited merely for form's sake, but it had been he who had ignited the spark. Poor Count Menschikov, Napier knew, thought that the Germans and the English had long been plotting together against Russia. Menschikov had sensed the air of sympathy emanating from the French attaché; von Hagen had picked that up, with the odd sixth sense that was characteristic of him, thus adding fuel to his suspicions of both Russia and France.

Why had Menschikov suddenly thrown diplomacy to the winds, and threatened Germany with annihilation? Because he wanted to shut von Hagen up, in case he started to blurt out a few inconvenient truths about the secret aerial boat *Phoebus-Apollo*. He would have known that both England and

Germany knew about the project, but that France didn't, even though there was a secret treaty between France and Russia.

An altogether delightful diplomatic impasse.

'Gentlemen,' said Napier, 'my purpose' in asking you to this pourparler was to take soundings, and to see where we should go from here. I want to thank you for speaking so fearlessly and frankly this evening. I wish now to make a proposal. It is clear that a very dangerous situation is developing. Relations between Russia and the German Empire are rapidly deteriorating. There is, too, much ill feeling against Russia in Britain since the assassination of Sir John Courteline. The matter has gone beyond the ambassadorial level. I therefore suggest that a conference be convened by the Great Powers, where all prevailing treaties can be examined, and misunderstandings cleared up.'

'Excellent!' said von Hagen. 'The voice of reason has been heard. I would suggest that such a conference should be held in Vienna, at the invitation of the Austrian Emperor.'

'I applaud the suggestion,' said Major Count Menschikov. 'But I would expect a date to be fixed as soon as possible. We cannot wait for months and months. Today is the third of April. The heads of government must assemble this month, and the Austrian

Imperial Chancellor must be invited to arbitrate between us.'

Napier listened to the murmurs of agreement, and watched as the meeting broke up. In the way of pourparlers, there had been no formal closure. There was a lot of stiff bowing, and frigid *politesse*.

As von Hagen and his secretary left the room, Colonel Kershaw sprang to his feet. 'Excuse me, Napier,' he whispered, 'but I must go after that man.' Before Napier could reply, Kershaw had hurried out into the vestibule.

* * *

In an empty, echoing room on the ground floor of the Foreign Office, Colonel Kershaw talked earnestly to Colonel von Hagen. He had caught the Prussian diplomat as he was nearing the exit into Whitehall, and persuaded him to send his secretary away.

'Von Hagen,' Kershaw was saying earnestly, 'while I applaud the idea of a conference at Vienna, I'm convinced that it would be an irrelevance. I want you to get a massive grip on your temper, and listen calmly to what I'm about to say. Russia is quite guiltless of any designs on Eastern Prussia — '

'But I tell you I have seen their intercepted

cables! Their intentions were made abundantly clear. I read them myself.'

'You can read Russian?'

'No. They were in German.'

'Why? Why should Russians communicate with each other in German? You were meant to read those cables, and the people who sent them out were not Russians. They were Germans. Have you ever heard of a man called Bleibner?'

'Hans Bleibner? Yes. He was a colonial servant, dismissed for cruelty to the natives in the African prison where he worked. He was one of those romantic fanatics that grew up in Germany after our victories over France and Denmark. He was a misfit, attracted to secret societies like the *Eidgenossenschaft*, the Red Hand Brethren, and all the rest of the riff-raff.'

'Well, Colonel, Bleibner has been very successful in England, creating hatred of the Russians. It was he, under the name of Karenin, who arranged for the murder of Sir John Courteline. He has since been quite successful in killing various agents of the Crown. I believe that Scotland Yard has issued a general warrant for his arrest.'

'Karenin! Naturally, I believe what you tell me, Colonel Kershaw. But are you saying that Russia is as innocent as the babe newborn?'

'Oh, no. Of course not. They have that monstrous machine under construction in the Lithuanian forests. Have you heard about it? What purpose lies behind that? Germany is right to fear Russia in the Baltic. You would be mad to do otherwise. But the danger to peace is not coming from Russia: it's coming from within Germany itself. It's coming, Colonel, from the remnants of the *Eidgenossenschaft*, and its financial outlet, the Brandenburg Consortium, which owns the rogue cable-ship *Lermontov*.'

Colonel von Hagen looked at the mild, sandy-haired man sitting opposite him. This man was one of the powers behind the British Throne. Only two months previously, in the events surrounding the secret of the Hansa Protocol, he had destroyed the leading lights of one of Germany's notorious semi-secret societies which had almost brought Britain and Germany to the brink of war. Now he was saying that the *Eidgenossenschaft* — the 'Linked Ring', as the English had called it — was still operating. It would be imprudent to trust this man absolutely: it would be foolish not to listen calmly to what he had to say.

'Please tell me the whole story, Colonel Kershaw,' said the German military attaché. 'I have already spoken confidentially to Sir

Charles Napier. If I am persuaded of the truth of what you tell me, I will place all my expertise at your service.'

They talked together for over an hour. It was nearing ten o'clock when they stood up, shook hands, and parted. Kershaw enquired about Sir Charles Napier at the reception desk, and was told that the Under-Secretary had already left for St John's Wood. He refused the porter's offer to summon a cab, and stood on the Foreign Office steps, looking out at the stream of evening traffic in Whitehall. A thin rain had begun, and the pavements gleamed wet in the gaslight.

Diplomats! They spoke their own language, and imprisoned themselves in the gaol of arid form and protocol. It had been stifling back there, listening to Laplace rehearsing his latest experiment in sarcasm, and watching poor Menschikov dropping the mask of political etiquette, and threatening Germany with annihilation. Napier was no different. He actually enjoyed that kind of scene, and he's got his own way in the end. A conference at Vienna, with which he'd be associated. Napier had never had a conference.

Colonel von Hagen was a different matter. Proud, arrogant and a firebrand, he was at the same time an utterly honest man, who could recognize and respond to honesty in others. For an hour they had discussed, among other things, the nature of the East Prussian terrain, especially the wide and wild tract of land on either side of the Rundstedt Channel. The area, von Hagen had told him, lay in the section of Brandenburg-Prussia protected by Military Field District 7, the headquarters of which were at Lindstedt-Schwanefeld, twelve miles south-west of Königsberg. There was a militia barracks at Gehrendorf, not three miles from the harbour at Rundstedt . . .

He would have to drop some very strong hints to Count von und zu Thalberg when he met him at Minster Priory at the weekend. Thalberg would know what strings to pull in Berlin. If this venture came off well, someone had better put in a discreet word for von Hagen with the German Chancellor . . .

Damn! It was starting to rain heavily, and he couldn't stand here for ever on the Foreign Office steps. How odd it was to be so alone at a time like this! The man he'd really like to talk to was — Surely that was him, now, standing at the entrance to Downing Street, talking to a couple of constables? Yes, it was Inspector Box. The constables have saluted, and Box has raised his hat. Now they're walking off towards King Charles Street. If Box is going back to King James's Rents, he'll have to cross the road . . . Yes, here he is.

'Good evening, Mr Box. Are you, by any chance, free at the moment? I'd like a word with you, if that's convenient.'

'Good evening, Colonel Kershaw. Yes, I'm free, sir, and I'd very much like a word with you. Are you going my way?'

Kershaw hurried down the steps, and joined Box in the street. It was wet, but not cold, and somehow the presence of the perky young police inspector lifted the colonel's spirits. They walked along in silence for a minute or two until they reached the rather gloomy entrance to Whitehall Place. Kershaw stopped, and took Box by the sleeve.

'Mr Box,' he said, 'do you know somewhere private where you and I can speak undisturbed? I don't want to go with you to King James's Rents, because someone there may recognize me, and start to draw unwelcome conclusions.'

Arnold Box glanced round rather helplessly. What would the colonel consider to be 'somewhere private'? Well, better to be hanged for a sheep as a lamb. He'd take him to Pat Nolan's place in Sussex Lane.

'If you'll follow me, sir,' said Box, 'I know just the place. It's only two minutes from here.'

Kershaw followed Box down a very dark cobbled alley which seemed to have no pavements. After a hundred yards or so they turned abruptly right, and came into a dimly lit road, lined with small commercial premises, all firmly closed and shuttered. At one end of the road a blaze of light spilled out of a public house, from which came the noise of cheerfully raucous singing, accompanied on a very loud piano.

'This is Sussex Lane, sir,' said Box, 'and that's the Duke of Sussex. We'll be able to have a quiet talk there.'

Box pushed open a door at the side of the public house, and the two men entered a pitch dark passage. The noise of singing, and the fortissimo crashing of the piano, came to them loudly through a glazed door to their right, upon which Kershaw could read the reversed letters 'Private'.

Really, thought Kershaw, what extraordinary places Box knows! There's a man with pretensions to a tenor voice singing something now, and the pianist seems to be in a thumping frenzy about it. What *is* the fellow singing?

Martha, (thump, thump)
What've you done to my Arthur? (thump, thump)

My Arthur was a good boy, till now!
(thump, thump, thump, thump)

Box suddenly pushed open the door, and poked his head into the public bar. A miasma of beer fumes and tobacco smoke hit them, and the noise of the singer and his accompanist increased fourfold. Kershaw watched Box semaphore some request or other to a stout, cheerful man in shirt sleeves who was standing behind the bar. The man nodded, smiled, and jerked a thumb towards the ceiling.

He's only seventeen, and a soldier of the Queen,
Too young for walking out with girls like you — Oh!
Martha (thump, thump) . . .

Box closed the door on the deafening scene, and began to mount a flight of stairs that Kershaw could now see in the gloom of the passage. They came to a small landing, and Box opened a door which took them into a long room overlooking the cobbled street. The inspector struck a match, went over to the fireplace, and lit the gas bracket over the mantelpiece. The light sprang to life with a little plop.

'We won't be disturbed here, sir,' said Box. 'This is the meeting room of the Ancient Order of Jebusites, a kind of benevolent club. It's not much of a place, but it'll serve the purpose.'

The room was furnished with a number of tables and many chairs, and smelt of stale beer. There were pictures of racehorses on the walls, and the words 'Ancient Order of Jebusites' had been written neatly in whiting on the mirror. The two men sat down at one of the tables. They could still hear the frantic singing in the public bar below, but it had a muted sound, now. Evidently, thought Kershaw, the floors at the Duke of Sussex were made of stout stuff.

'How can I help you, sir?' There was a very slight hint of restraint in Box's voice which Kershaw was quick to notice, because he had expected it.

'You can help me, at once, Mr Box, by clearing the air. You're annoyed about what happened to Sergeant Knollys, so you'd better say what you have to say about that before we proceed.'

'It's six days now, sir,' Box replied, 'since the man called Bleibner tried to kill my sergeant. I've visited him in University College Hospital, and he told me that you had called in to see him. That was very much appreciated by both of us. I spoke to the doctor who's looking after him, and he told me that the hatpin missed the right lung by the merest fraction of an inch, snapping when it came into contact with one of the ribs. Knollys survived by sheer accident. Naturally, sir, I'm annoyed.'

'Bleibner once trained as a surgeon,' said Kershaw. 'Somebody told me that, the other day. That's why he was successful in despatching poor Mr Oldfield in his sleep. Can you guess *why* I sent Mr Knollys to Northumberland — accompanied, I may say, by a platoon of soldiers from the Northumberland Fusiliers?'

Box smiled to himself, and sat back in his chair. What was the use of being annoyed with a man who had to juggle at times with the destiny of the nation? There was neither the space nor the time for the luxury of annoyance when you were involved with Colonel Kershaw.

'Oh, yes, sir, I know well enough why you sent him up there. I spent a long evening in Westminster with Miss Drake, who told me everything about her visit to Stonewick Hall. She was angry with herself for fainting, and very relieved to hear that Sergeant Knollys will be out of hospital by the weekend.'

'So all's well between you and me? Good.

Speaking of Miss Drake, I'll be calling on her tomorrow. I expect you can imagine what I am going to say to her. But now, Box, I want to hear what you think all this Russian business is about. I promise you I'll not interrupt you while you tell me your ideas.'

'Sir, I believe this whole business has been engineered to turn Britain and Germany against Russia. There has been serious interference with the cable system at Porthcurno, where false messages have been fed into the cables from a rogue ship, the *Lermontov*, posing as a Russian vessel, but in reality nothing of the sort. We've seen the results of that mischief in the newspapers: threatened invasions of India and Canada, and the atrocity of the sinking of the *Berlin Star* by an armed vessel flying the Russian ensign. I could go on, sir, but I'm beginning to think that time is precious in this business.'

'I'm convinced that you're right, Box. In fact, I *know* you're right. What else?'

'One of the active agents in this scheme to blacken Russia's reputation is the man I call the Hatpin Man — Dr N.I. Karenin. That is the man who arranged for the assassination of Sir John Courteline, brought about the death of a man called Joseph Kitely, and then murdered Mr Gabriel Oldfield with one of his lethal hatpins.'

'Go on.'

'It was Karenin who silenced a young man called William Pascoe, who had come to suspect the truth of the whole matter. And now, as a result of the events in Northumberland, I know that this Karenin is, in fact, a German called Bleibner, the man who attempted to murder Sergeant Knollys. They are clearly the same person. The fact that both are suffering from some kind of leprous skin complaint can't be sheer coincidence.'

'And so you've drawn a conclusion, haven't you? Don't be shy of telling me, Box, because your conclusion is true.'

'The people behind this spate of outrages is the Linked Ring, the gang of terrorists to which the late but unlamented Count and Countess Czerny belonged. Miss Drake saw their memorial portraits in Baroness Felssen's house. It's the Linked Ring.'

'It is, Mr Box. The *Eidgenossenschaft*. The idea, of course, is to drive Britain and Germany into each other's arms, and to send them eastward, united against Russia. They failed by force last time; this time, they hope to succeed by cunning. In the next few weeks, I intend to send the whole lot of them to perdition.'

Both men sat in silence for a minute, listening to the hissing of the gas bracket over the mantelpiece. In the bar below, the piano still made itself heard, as a man with a deep voice began a mournful song which began with the line:

Peggy, come back o'er the briny to me.

'Well done, Mr Box,' said Kershaw quietly. 'You've arrived at those conclusions with precious little help from me. What do you propose to do next?'

'Sir, I have obtained warrants of arrest for the man Hans Bleibner, alias N.I. Karenin, on separate charges of murder. I intend to go after him, and arrest him. I gather that he was able to escape from Stonewick Hall.'

'He was. I imagine that he has already made his way back to Germany. He has an apartment in Berlin, so I'm told.'

'And this Baroness Felssen, sir — how did *she* manage to escape? All those gallant soldier-boys weren't much use, were they? If I'd been in charge up there, the good baroness wouldn't have escaped. Not half she wouldn't!'

'Well, Box, these things do happen. Things don't always go exactly according to plan. But to return to your arrest-warrants. If you're going after Bleibner personally, your path would be very much smoothed if you came with me. Wait a little while until I'm ready, and then you and I — and a few others — can cross France and into Germany with no impediments placed in our way. That I can guarantee.'

Box stood up. It was nearing midnight, and the denizens of the Duke of Sussex would soon be pouring out on to the wet cobbles of Sussex Lane.

'Thank you, sir,' said Box. 'I accept your invitation. I'd very much like to be of assistance to you when you send the remnants of the Linked Ring to perdition.'

⋆ ⋆ ⋆

Vanessa Drake opened the door of her sitting-room, stood aside for Colonel Kershaw to enter, then resumed her seat at the table. As usual, he sat down opposite her without being invited. She watched him as he peeled off his black suede gloves, and dropped them into his tall silk hat. He retained his long dark coat with its astrakhan collar, thus maintaining the fiction that he had just dropped in while passing.

'Well, missy,' he said quietly, after looking at her inscrutably for a minute or more, 'it looks as though you and I have come to the parting of the ways.'

She felt the tears sting her eyes, and dashed them away angrily. That was a sure way to arouse his contempt. He'd think that she was trying to appeal to his fatherly concern for her welfare. Best to say nothing. Just listen.

'When you agreed to join my crowd, Miss Drake, I explained to you what being a 'nobody' entailed. It meant carrying out a simple but vital task, then retiring from the scene. I warned you this time that your identity was known at Stonewick Hall, and I told you to look and listen. You were not to pry. You chose to disobey me.'

Vanessa's mind leapt back to the snow-pocked cemetery at Highgate, where this modest, respectful artillery officer had approached her as she left the grave of Arthur Fenlake, her murdered fiancé. His offer of work with the secret intelligence service had given her new life, and with the passing of the weeks she had realized the enormous power exerted in the state by her newfound friend and mentor. And now it was all to end.

'You chose to disobey me,' Kershaw repeated. 'You chose to be a 'somebody' instead of a 'nobody', and the result was that Sergeant Knollys was stabbed in the chest by a hatpin, wielded by one of the most dangerous men in England. What do you say to that?'

Stay quiet. Don't contradict, don't try to

excuse yourself. Just listen.

Colonel Kershaw gave vent to an exasperated laugh.

'I *knew* you would! Disobey me, I mean. I knew you'd start endangering yourself, and our enterprise, by looking for adventure. You've been reading too many magazine stories — *Marion Forster, the Girl Detective* and so forth. That's why I sent Sergeant Knollys up there to look after you, together with a whole platoon of soldiers. What do you say to that?'

'Sir, if you'll give me a second chance, I promise most solemnly to behave myself. I'll open the gates at Coleman Street to let Mr Box in, sweep the paths, so that you don't slip on the leaves — '

'Enough! Very well, Miss Drake. I'll give you a second chance. As a matter of fact, I'd no intention of letting you go. You're far too valuable. In any case, missy, there's unfinished work for you to do.'

'Oh, thank you, sir! I swear I'll do exactly as you say in future. But what unfinished work is there for me to do?'

'Well,' said Colonel Kershaw, treating her to an enigmatic smile, 'there's all that costly embroidery left unfinished at Stonewick Hall. I think, when the time comes, that you'd better go up there and finish the job.'

12

In the Prussian Wilderness

Minster Priory, a fine old half-timbered house dating from the latter years of the seventeenth century, lay in a remote Wiltshire valley, several miles east of Corsham. Beside it stood an immense sandstone ruin, all that was left of the Benedictine priory that gave the house its name.

Colonel Kershaw stood on the terrace at the rear of the house, talking to a very distinguished man in faultless evening dress, who was smoking a cigar. It was early evening, and the sky was darkening above the old oaks that surrounded Minister Priory.

'One feels safe here,' observed Colonel Kershaw to his companion, 'at least for a while. Wiltshire's never been too keen on railways — or roads, for that matter. It's very kind of Archie Campbell to invite us here for these musical weekends.'

'It was clever of him to lure Madame Alice Gomez down here from London,' observed the distinguished man. 'She really is a fine concert singer. Her renditions of those songs by Brahms were quite delightful. I suppose we must go back in, soon.'

Kershaw, who had also been smoking, dropped the butt of his cigar, and ground it into the pavement with his heel. If he made no move soon, Count von und zu Thalberg would continue to tease him with trivialities for the rest of the evening. He was evidently determined to make Kershaw take the initiative.

'Don't the Talbots live in this part of the world?' asked the Head of Prussian Military Intelligence innocently.

'Yes, Count, they do, over at Lacock Abbey. Very well, I surrender! Your relentless small-talk has defeated my determination to say nothing until you began to talk sense. So please tell me what you think I should know about the rogue cable station on the Rundstedt Channel.'

Von und zu Thalberg glanced down the terrace, as though to ensure that the two men were not being overheard. Then he lowered his voice.

'This former cable relay station stands at the edge of the land at Rundstedt, which is quite a small place, little more than a dock and some repair sheds. The station was originally part of the Prussian State Telegraph Service, but it was closed when a new line was opened from Königsberg to Berlin in 1889. The relay was resited south of Königsberg, at a place called Halsdorf.'

'And I suppose it's assumed that this former relay station has been put to other uses?' asked Kershaw.

'I believe so. Once the station closed, that whole remote area was sold to the Brandenburg Consortium. That was in 1890. The consortium owns the private harbour of Rundstedt, where the *Lermontov* is currently moored. The consortium said that it wanted to develop the area as agricultural land. The relay station buildings were to be used for the storage of farming machinery. That's what I've heard, anyway.'

Count von und zu Thalberg glanced towards the lighted windows of Minster Priory, where the guests were assembling for the second half of the evening's concert.

'You'd better come in with me now, Kershaw,' he said. 'I know what a dreadful Philistine you are, but you must listen to Madame Alice Gomez singing Clara Schumann, if only for form's sake. I'm very anxious to hear her, because I must be on my travels again early tomorrow. It's time I visited my estate. So come, Colonel, bear me company while *la diva* sings. After that, well — Archie Campbell tells me there's a very snug little gunroom just beyond the garden passage. You might find things more to your liking there.'

They stepped into the house through the open French window. The parlour was a long, low Tudor gallery panelled in black oak, with many twinkling candle sconces on the walls. Madame Gomez, in an elegant white evening dress, stood beside the grand piano, talking in low tones to her pianist.

Kershaw cast his eye over the other weekend guests, who had arranged themselves around the room on the tapestry-covered chairs and sofas. They were all old school and army friends of Archie's, accompanied by their wives. If they wondered why two army officers, one English, the other German, were also guests, they were too well bred to enquire. Archie Campbell, the self-effacing connoisseur of music, landowner and former artilleryman, was one of Kershaw's secret servants.

The second half of the concert began. Kershaw sat down with Von und zu Thalberg on an upholstered window seat. Madame Gomez sang sweetly, and her accompanist was very obviously an expert partner in the musical enterprise. Kershaw listened, and for a while shared the evident rapture of the other guests.

And then, from somewhere in his memory, another song began to clamour for remembrance. It was not as sweetly harmonious as Clara Schumann's compositions, but it had its own validity. It represented another part of the threatened world of civilized peace that both Kershaw and Von und zu Thalberg were dedicated to preserve.

Martha,
What've you done to my Arthur?
My Arthur was a good boy, till now!

Bleibner . . . He had been a different kettle of fish entirely from Baroness Felssen. It was an outrage that he had been allowed to escape from that house in Northumberland. Perhaps there had been collusion somewhere? One of his people had seen a man of his description boarding a ferry at Harwich, bound for the Hook of Holland.

Kershaw had sent the kindly Mr Boniface to hear poor, penitent Miss Drake's account of her stay at Stonewick Hall. She'd offered to write it all down, forgetting the golden rule of the organization: never write down anything . . . Missy's tale had allowed them to pick up one misfit, a wretched clerk called Cathcart, employed at the Post Office Relay in Newcastle. By the end of this business, they would have collected other small fry. That would be one of the lesser spoils of victory.

Really, this lady was a superb singer. No wonder she was a favourite of the London concert halls. It was a pity that so many of the Schumanns' subjects were pining away for love, or the lack of it. That was because they were given to setting sentimental poets like Heine to music. Everything ended up soaked in tears. That man Bleibner, according to Missy, had shed a tear while playing Beethoven, and had shown a similar kind of sentiment when he was about to take the hatpin to her.

It was positively embarrassing to have the anonymous singer of the Duke of Sussex taking up residence like this in his mind. What would this genteel company think? It was all Box's fault.

He's only seventeen, and a soldier of the Queen,
Too young for walking out with girls like you.

A burst of clapping brought Kershaw back to the present. Madame Gomez curtsied, the pianist bowed, and the whole company began to move towards the dining-room, where they had been promised a hot and cold buffet. Count von und zu Thalberg attached himself to a quite young lady in green, ignoring his erstwhile companion. Colonel Kershaw left the company, and made his way towards the garden passage.

He found the gun-room without difficulty, and knocked on the solid door. There was the sound of a key turning, and the door was opened, first cautiously, and then fully, to reveal a stocky man dressed in a long greatcoat. He had a wide, wooden countenance, adorned with an old-fashioned German moustache. He clicked his heels in salute, ushered Kershaw into the room, and closed the door.

The room was warmed by an oil stove, and lit by a number of candles in china holders. The walls contained racks of sporting guns, and smelt strongly of oil and metal filings. The man with the moustache sat down at a table, upon which were a number of files, notebooks, and folding maps.

'Lieutenant-Colonel Kershaw,' said the man, 'I am Oberfeldwebel Schmidt. His Excellency Count von und zu Thalberg has detailed me to guide you and your party as soon as you arrive on the territory of the Reich. I am also to give you an intelligence briefing, which I will do now.'

'Thank you, Sergeant Major,' said Kershaw. 'I will look forward to meeting you again in Germany. For the moment, though, I am anxious to hear the latest intelligence on the *Eidgenossenschaft*.'

'Yes, *Herr Oberst*. The *Eidgenossenschaft*, which owns the Brandenburg Consortium, has secretly re-established the relay station at Rundstedt. Over the past year, it has run subterranean cables to join the Prussian State Cable System at Halsdorf — '

'One moment, *Oberfeldwebel*. How long has that fact been known?'

'Sir, it has been known to Prussian Military Intelligence only for a week. The State Intelligence Office as yet knows nothing about it.'

The German soldier smiled under his moustache. He added, 'We are a superior service, sir. The Military Intelligence, you understand.'

'Oh, of course. I share your sentiment, Sergeant Major. And so these people have joined up with the Prussian State Cable System? I wondered about that.'

'They have, sir. And it is from that rogue station near the Rundstedt Channel that various dangerous and false messages have originated. I am permitted to tell you that cables ostensibly sent by three of the esteemed Sir Charles Napier's agents, Abu Daria, Piotr Casimir, and Jacob Kroll, all originated from Rundstedt, and not from Petrovosk and Vilna.'

'I've long believed something of the sort,' said Kershaw. 'Those agents of Sir Charles Napier's — Daria, Casimir and Kroll — were first killed, and then impersonated over the cables, retailing stories that were not true. And they were killed not by the Russians, but by the *Eidgenossenschaft*.'

'Yes, sir.' Oberfeldwebel Schmidt suddenly treated Kershaw to an alarmingly wolfish smile. 'Sir Charles Napier's cables are supposed to be secret, but, you'll appreciate that we have ways of reading them! A precaution, nothing else.'

The sergeant major rummaged through the papers laid out on the table.

'And so, our mission, Colonel Kershaw, is to seize and destroy these traitors. They have identified themselves with the State. They are mistaken. They will be punished. The area which they occupy is privately policed, and virtually derelict. To subdue them will be no schoolboy's adventure. It would be foolish to approach them from the sea. We must creep up towards them from inland' — he stabbed an area on one of the open maps — 'here, across this wide and wild tract of land to the south of the Rundstedt Channel.'

'I have been told that the area falls under the protection of the Germany Army?'

'It does, *Herr Oberst*. It is part of the territory of Military Field District 7, the headquarters of which is at Lindstedt-Schwanefeld, twelve miles south-west of Königsberg. But His Excellency is not anxious to involve our regular forces. It could create a wrong impression among those whose business it is to watch for troop movements. I mean the foreign spies, you understand.'

'So what will we do?'

'There is a militia barracks at Gehrendorf, which is only three miles from the Rundstedt Channel. The officer commanding that barracks has been ordered to place himself at our disposal when the moment comes to strike. I have been attached to him on a temporary basis for the duration of this exercise. I know him well, sir, and he knows me. We're both true Prussians!'

The sergeant major smiled, looked up from his maps, and sat back in his chair.

'The commanding officer — his name is Major Kerner — knows me well, as I say, but as a field strategist. He knows nothing of my secret work for Count von und zu Thalberg.'

This man, thought Kershaw, is a pearl

without price. It would be a privilege to work with him. This was the kind of man who would know how to exceed orders to some purpose.

'And now, sir, for the date. The military assault on the cable station has been scheduled for Thursday, 20 April. This would entail you and your party setting foot in France on Monday, the seventeenth. Is that possible?'

'It is.'

'And can you tell me how many men will constitute your party, *Herr Oberst*? You will all be travelling as civilian visitors to Germany, of course. That, at least, is what the documents will say.'

'That is so, and we shall come with all the correct papers, passports and *visés*. Once in Germany, we will place ourselves under the orders of the military authority. There will be five of us — myself, Captain Edgar Adams RN, Mr Boniface, who is a naval architect, a man called Robert Jones, who's a specialist telegraphist, and Detective Inspector Box, of Scotland Yard.'

'Box? Ah, yes. I have heard of him. Finally, as regards languages, sir — '

'Adams and I both speak German well. Adams is fluent in Russian. Mr Boniface is a true polyglot. I should think that the others speak only English.'

'A true polyglot?'

'I mean that he's one of those men who seem able to speak any language you care to mention.'

Sergeant Major Schmidt muttered a word that sounded like '*vielsprachig*', scribbled a note, and then closed the book.

'I will leave you now, Colonel Kershaw,' he said. 'When next we meet, it will be in Germany. And there, we will capture the illegal telegraph station, take its operators captive, and use your men to signal the truth of the whole matter to the Chancelleries of Europe.'

Sergeant Major Schmidt rose from his chair, and stood stiffly for a moment in salute. When Kershaw left him, he had returned to his work, poring over his maps and plans in the candle-lit gun-room.

* * *

The long railway carriage juddered over a set of points, and Arnold Box woke up. At first, he wondered where he was, and then memories flooded back. England seemed a lifetime away. It was Wednesday today, 19 April. The five men constituting Kershaw's party had crossed the Channel on Monday afternoon. It had taken them twelve hours to cross France, their train passing through beautiful countryside, skirting vast towns and stopping once or twice at what seemed to be country halts before reaching the German border towards three o'clock on Tuesday morning.

Various uniformed officials had boarded the train, and Colonel Kershaw had dealt with them all, speaking rapidly in German. There had been a certain amount of heel-clicking, and the officials had departed. Then, in pitch blackness, they had clanked and hissed across a vast railway bridge, and found themselves in Germany.

To Box's relief, they had soon left the train at a village called Klagenfurt, where they had been met by a pugnacious-looking man with close-cropped hair and a moustache, who had greeted Colonel Kershaw apparently as an old friend. He was introduced to the Englishmen as Sergeant Major Schmidt, and there had been another outbreak of heel-clicking.

They had stayed the night in a kind of hostel belonging to a monastery, and next morning had travelled in what looked suspiciously like a police van to a section of railway track a mile or so from Klagenfurt, where a train, made up of two long grey coaches pulled by a massive steam-locomotive, was waiting to receive them. Sergeant Major Schmidt told them that they were now transferring to the Prussian Military Railway.

That had been on Wednesday morning. They were still on the military train, travelling at a relentless fifty miles an hour into the easternmost recesses of the land of Prussia. The scenery became wilder as the day advanced, and the landscape began to take on the appearance of a wilderness.

As dusk fell on Wednesday afternoon, they had crossed another vast iron bridge, and Box had seen a solitary railway guard standing on the footway, holding up a white wooden disc on a stick, evidently some kind of signal to the engine driver. The train had stopped briefly, the great engine still hissing, and Box had seen Captain Adams climb down on to the narrow footway, accompanied by another man, who was carrying Adams's valise. The railway guard had lowered the disc, and the military train had continued on its way.

Box sat up in his seat, and looked about him. It was after eight o'clock in the evening, and the little oil-lamps set into the ceilings of the two coaches had been kindled. It was warm and soporific, and quite pleasantly gloomy. The temptation to fall asleep all the time was strong.

He looked down the swaying carriage. Colonel Kershaw sat opposite him, reading a book. He was clad in a warm greatcoat, and wore a close-fitting cap with cheek guards, which buttoned under the chin. From time to time he exchanged a few words in German with a smart Prussian officer sitting to his left across the wide gangway.

Between Kershaw and the Prussian officer lay the door to the next carriage. As the train twisted and turned along the sinuous line, the door would slide open and shut of its own volition. Box could see through to the other carriage, which was filled with German officers in field grey. Isolated from them in a seat near the communicating door sat Sergeant Major Schmidt, poring over endless maps and papers.

Sitting beside Box across the gangway was Bob Jones, a quiet, level-headed man in his forties, an experienced telegraphist from Porthcurno, and a friend of poor young William Pascoe. Behind Bob Jones sat the cheerful Mr Boniface, whom Box had encountered in the East Lodge at the Crystal Palace.

Captain Adams had sat apart from the others, towards the rear of the carriage. From the start of their venture, he had seemed preoccupied, and it had come as no surprise to Box to see Adams suddenly leave the train when it had paused on the bridge. He had asked Colonel Kershaw what Adams was doing, and had received the cryptic reply, 'Well, Mr Box, I expect there's somewhere he wants to go, so he's gone.'

The military train kept a steady pace, its wheels clacking and clattering over the track, and Box found his eyes closing again. The trouble was, there was nothing to do. Not everyone could read a book, like Colonel Kershaw, or look steadily out at the dark landscape, like the Prussian officer.

The Hatpin Man . . . He was going to get the Hatpin Man. Here he was, now nodding and smiling, his clown's face painted white, each finger ending in a gleaming hatpin. 'Which would you like, Mr Box? Take your choice.' Perhaps he'd have to speak to him in German? No, because here was Martha, and Arthur, and — '

Box woke again with a start. The train was coming to a halt. He peered out of the window beside his seat and saw a dimly lit platform, upon which stood a man in a black uniform with gleaming silver epaulets, and wearing a braided pill-box hat. He was clutching a leather briefcase to his chest. The train stopped, and the man climbed up the iron ladder into the carriage. Sergeant Major Schmidt had jumped up from his seat in the next carriage and opened the door for the visitor.

The man with the briefcase came into Colonel Kershaw's carriage. He had a fat, wide face, and little eyes that peered around through tiny round steel spectacles.

He spoke briefly in German to Colonel Kershaw, then turned to face the other passengers.

'Herr Box?'

'What? Yes. That's me. But I never — '

Box saw Colonel Kershaw smile in evident amusement. The man sat down next to Box, and opened his briefcase.

'This will not take long, Herr Box. I am Inspector Langendorf of the Königsberg District Police Headquarters. You have warrants for the arrest of a German citizen, one Hans Bleibner, of 5 Königstrasse, in Berlin, otherwise known as Johannes Bleibner, and wanted in London on charges of murder. You can produce these warrants?'

Wasn't it lucky that these foreigners could speak English? He wouldn't have to beg the colonel to hold his hand. English must be a very easy language to learn.

'Yes, Inspector, I've got them here.'

Box brought the warrants out of his inside pocket, and presented them to the German policeman. Everybody in the other carriage seemed fascinated by what was going on. A group of officers had congregated in the little vestibule between the carriages, and were listening avidly.

Inspector Langendorf muttered his way through the two warrants, occasionally glancing quizzically at Box through his little steel glasses. Finally, he placed the documents flat on his briefcase, and produced a rubber stamp and ink pad from his pocket.

'All is in order, Herr Box. Now I will stamp these warrants with my dated consent — so! And now, with this special pen, which has a fountain of ink already contained inside it, I sign across the stamped consent — so. Bleibner is now yours, if you find him here in Ost-Preussen. Find him, and you may take him to England. Good night, Inspector.'

Langendorf turned towards Colonel Kershaw, and delivered a smart bow.

'*Herr Oberst*, your servant.' Catching sight of the curious gaggle of officers, Langendorf saluted stiffly, which provoked an outburst of clicking heels.

In a moment the policeman had left the train, and they could see him hurrying along the platform of the little unnamed station. Everyone returned to his seat, the engine roared back to life, and the train continued its journey along the Prussian Military Railway.

13

The Fight at the Rundstedt Channel

The military train left the main track just after dawn on the Thursday, and turned on to a branch line that took them through a stunted, overgrown wood. In minutes they had emerged into a small railway yard, where the train stopped. All around them were wooden huts, and two long barrack blocks built in stone. As they lowered their cramped limbs down from the train to the track, a group of officers, dressed in the rather drab uniforms of Prussian militia, came forward to greet them. There was a lot of saluting and raising of hats.

One officer came forward from the group, a man of forty or so, who looked more like a country schoolmaster than a warrior. The Iron Cross pinned on his uniform jacket belied his appearance.

'Lieutenant-Colonel Kershaw?' said the officer. 'I am Major Kerner, of the German Militia Field Intelligence. You will have already met my Clerk Strategist, Oberfeldwebel Schmidt, who has been temporarily attached to us from Number 7 Military District. Welcome to Gehrendorf Militia Barracks. Orderlies will be here presently to show you to your quarters. Breakfast will be available at seven o'clock. After that — well, we have a lot to do today. There is a nest of traitors to be taken!'

Later, as they were being escorted to one of the long wooden huts, Box said to Kershaw, 'Do I detect a hint of ozone in the air, sir? I keep thinking of Southend.'

'You think correctly, Mr Box. Gehrendorf is only three miles from the Rundstedt Channel, where the *Eidgenossenschaft* have their lair. That hint of ozone is wafting to you from the waters of the Baltic Sea.'

⋆ ⋆ ⋆

Major Kerner unrolled a map, and spread it out on the table. The four Englishmen stood with the Prussian soldiers, allies in a common enterprise. They had all assembled after breakfast in one of the stone-built barrack blocks of the militia headquarters at Gehrendorf.

'Here, gentlemen,' said Kerner, 'is a sketch-map of the area where our mission today will be carried out. At the bottom of the map, you can see this barracks, and the arms park adjacent. The public road to Klagenfurt crosses the area diagonally from south-east to north-west. Minimal but sufficient cover is provided by thin lines of trees on either side of the road.'

'What is the scale in miles, Major?' asked Kershaw. 'Between us and the target, I mean.'

'It is three miles from Gehrendorf — here — to the cable station, which you can see at the top of the map.' He smiled at Kershaw, and added, ''Target' is a true artilleryman's word. I'd prefer to call it our rendezvous. The cable station, as you see, stands on the edge of the land at Rundstedt, which is little more than a hamlet. On the right here you can see the Rundstedt Channel, coming in from the sea, with the dock belonging to the Brandenburg Consortium facing the cable station on the opposite bank.'

Major Kerner turned towards Sergeant Major Schmidt.

'*Oberfeldwebel*,' he said, 'you will please outline the general strategy for today's exercise, for the benefit of the English observers.'

'Gentlemen,' said Schmidt, 'the land slopes gently down from Gehrendorf to the coast, which gives us a certain advantage. Our object is to seize a number of civilians who are manning the station. They may or may not be armed, but we will take no chances. We propose to take a platoon of twenty-five men, armed with rifles, and four officers with pistols. We will move on foot along this line, here, over the rough terrain, until we can cross the Klagenfurt road in the shelter of the trees. That covers one and a half miles.'

'Do you propose to provide artillery cover?' asked Kershaw.

'Most certainly, *Herr Oberst*. Once we have left the belt of trees above the road, we will be more or less exposed to enemy view. It's not likely that eight civilian telegraph operators — we believe there are eight men in there — will make an attempt to engage with a platoon of armed soldiers, but why take a chance? So we will attach a light field-gun to a pair of horses, and have it follow the attacking party at a sensible distance. A warning shot or two from that would soon bring those civilians tumbling out into out hands.'

'Do you have a late intelligence report?'

'We do. At this moment there are thought to be eight men in the cable station. There is no one living in the immediate area, so other civilians are not threatened.'

'There were armed civilian guards down there until last week,' said Major Kerner, 'but they seem to have gone. The dock is deserted at the moment, but we know that the *Lermontov* is at anchor in the bay lying beyond the headland, and to the rear of the dock promontory. The whole area has been closed to transport since three o'clock this morning.'

Major Kerner nodded briefly to Schmidt, who rolled up the map, and slid it neatly into a cylindrical leather case. Major Kerner cleared his throat.

'It is now eight-fifteen,' he said. 'The exercise will commence at nine o'clock. Let us show the authorities that the militia is equal to any regular army unit in a crisis. I want those men taken without loss of life if possible, and with minimal damage to the cable station. Once the building is cleared, the English party will enter, and carry out their own assignment. The sun has risen, it will be a clear day, and victory will be ours. Long live the Kaiser and the Fatherland.'

As they walked away from the barrack block, Box thought of the civilian guards who had conveniently disappeared from the scene, and of the deserted dock. An empty wilderness. Or was it? He saw Colonel Kershaw looking at him quizzically, and asked, 'What do you think, sir?'

'I'm not sure, Mr Box, but I'm recalling the old adage, or proverb, or whatever it is:

‘There’s many a slip ’twixt cup and lip’. Let’s wait and see.’

⋆ ⋆ ⋆

At nine o’clock the raiding party set off from the barracks on foot. The men marched slowly in the heavy German infantry fashion, so that Box, Bob Jones and Mr Boniface had little difficulty in keeping up with them. Colonel Kershaw seemed quite used to exercise of this type. After a mile’s walk they came to an isolated clump of gnarled beeches, where Kerner insisted that the Englishmen should take up their position as observers.

‘You must stay here, gentlemen, until the cable station has been subdued and secured, which will be within the hour. Once that has been accomplished, you may break cover, and carry out your mission.’

The Englishmen stood among the trees, from where they could see down the sloping terrain to the Baltic, which shimmered in the bright morning sun.

‘There’s the tree-lined road that we saw in the map,’ said Kershaw. ‘On the face of it, those two ranks of trees will provide sufficient cover, but once on the other side of the Klagenfurt road, as Kerner admits, our troops will be exposed on the right flank.'

The platoon, comprising twenty-five well-disciplined and well-armed young men, was led by four older officers. Major Kerner brought up the rear. The troops broke formation as they moved down the slope towards the road. Behind them, two horses, with soldiers in the saddles, pulled an eighteen-pound field-gun on its carriage.

Box looked beyond the soldiers to the cable station, a long white building comprising a central block with a short wing on either side. It stood exposed on the headland, less than a mile away. The morning sun glinted on the waters of the Rundstedt Channel, and gilded the few derricks and cranes of the private dock.

'Sir,' said Box, 'none of this seems real to me. It's as though we've gone on a day excursion to Eastbourne. It's hard to believe that anything's going to happen.'

'Battles are like that, Mr Box. They don't seem real at all until the carnage begins. Things may look peaceful, but I can assure you that appearances in this case are deceptive. You'd be far more comfortable at Eastbourne.'

'What would you have done, sir, if this had been your task?'

'Well, Box, I would have brought up that

eight-inch howitzer I saw back there in the arms park, and blown the cable station to smithereens. Howitzers have a high trajectory, and throw a forty-five pound shell. They're lighter than field-pieces, but deadly in their own special way. Then I'd have sent the troops in to mop up. But look! They've reached the road. It's time we all moved closer down the slope, whatever Major Kerner said to the contrary.'

Keeping close behind Colonel Kershaw, the English contingent left the clump of beeches, and crossed the Klagenfurt road.

The militiamen had already burst out from the further line of trees, and had begun to run down the grassy slope towards the cable station. They crouched as they ran, their rifles trailing low, and Box could see how they fanned out into three groups, each led by an officer. It was clear that they intended to surround the cable station in one swift, co-ordinated manoeuvre. The field-piece clattered off the road and on to the stunted grass behind them.

At a signal from Kershaw, the Englishmen crouched down in the shelter of a shallow embankment. The Rundstedt Channel was very near now, its waters glassy and undisturbed. Mr Boniface passed his field-glasses to Bob Jones, who surveyed the cable station in silence for more than a minute.

'They've channelled their land lines underground,' he said, handing the glasses back to Mr Boniface. 'They've dismantled the original system of telegraph poles, but have left the old dispatch frame on the roof. It'll be interesting to see what engines they're using — '

Suddenly, a volley of shots rang out from the building. Box could see the stabs of flame at half a dozen windows, and was reminded of Killer Kitely's desperate fusillade from the house in East Dock Street. The soldiers immediately fell to the ground, and soon the crackle of rifle-fire filled the air.

'They were expecting us,' said Kershaw quietly.

The men in the cable station were now returning fire fiercely. Sergeant Major Schmidt passed near them, breathing heavily as he made his way back up the slope, to where the field-piece stood, its gunner lying beside it. Evidently Kerner and Schmidt thought the time had come for a warning artillery shot.

The section of men moving towards the left of the cable station suddenly rose to their feet and charged, firing all the time. Box saw a number of windows shatter, and at the same time two of the soldiers screamed and fell on the grass. The sun shone bright, and a pleasant breeze was blowing.

'Gentlemen,' said Kershaw, 'there's something wrong up at the gun emplacement. Schmidt is shouting something, but the wind's carrying his voice away. He may need a specialist gunner. I'm going back up to see what's amiss.'

'Sir, be careful — '

'We're out of range here, Box. I'm quite safe. We've lost two men at least, despite Kerner's optimism. They were only waiting for us to get within their sights.'

Colonel Kershaw hurried away. The troops on the centre and right flanks were slowly advancing, slithering across the ground like so many grass-snakes. They were keeping up a continuous volley of rifle fire, and more of the windows in the cable station buildings had been smashed.

Suddenly there came the deafening report of the field-gun. The sound seemed to run around the sky, and glance off the waters of the channel with an echoing roar. At the same time they heard the whistling of the shell overhead. In a moment it had hit the ground in front of the cable station, where it exploded with what sounded like a scream of rage. Clods of turf were torn from the ground and splattered across the front of the building.

It was the signal for a charge. The soldiers sprang up from the ground and stormed the building, shooting the door off its hinges. In minutes a deadly calm had settled on the scene. The men crouching under the embankment sat up, and looked across the field. Box could see three men lying dead on patches of bloodstained grass.

Colonel Kershaw came down the slope to where his companions were sheltering. His face was uncharacteristically pale, and his voice tremulous with controlled anger.

'Box,' he said, 'when I arrived up there, I found Schmidt beside himself with rage, and the gunner dead. His comrade — there should be two men to a field-piece — had run back to base on an errand — '

'Killed, sir? Killed by a shot? I thought you said they would be out of range up there?'

'They were, and so was I. The gunner had been killed by a hatpin driven through the base of his skull. Box, your fugitive Bleibner is here, and he's not yet finished his murderous work.'

Angry voices came to them across the grass as the soldiers emerged from the vanquished building with their captives. The prisoners came out with their hands above their heads, seven — no, eight — surly men in everyday civilian clothes. They were made to kneel, and their hands were tied behind their backs with rope.

'Why did they hold out like that, sir?' asked Box. 'Surely they knew that they couldn't win?'

'They knew that they were all traitors, Box, whatever fancy language they may have chosen in which to cloak their treachery. So they decided to make a last stand. There's nothing particularly heroic about that kind of desperate bravery. They'll all hang, every one of them.'

Major Kerner emerged from the cable station, looking pardonably pleased with himself.

'Victory is ours, Colonel Kershaw!' he cried. 'You see, we were right about using a field-gun to flush them out. I've lost three men; but without that gun I might have lost many more. The cable station is now made safe, so you and your party can enter it.'

Without waiting for a reply, he hurried away to talk to one of his officers.

'Sir,' asked Box, as they walked across the grass towards the cable station, 'if the gunner was dead, who fired that shot?'

'I did, Box. I'm a gunner too, you know. Sergeant Major Schmidt helped me. I knew that man would be able to go against convention if he saw the wisdom of doing so. But here we are at the cable station.'

They followed Bob Jones and Mr Boniface as they picked their way through the broken glass and fallen plaster of the entrance passage. They looked into the four rooms on the ground floor, three of which were clearly living quarters, with truckle beds and rough wooden tables still covered with plates and cutlery. The fourth room was the transmission room, a long chamber at the back of the building. Bob Jones stood on the threshold, and looked critically at the row of eight telegraph machines standing near the long window.

'No problems here, Mr Boniface,' he said. 'These are all old friends. I'll use three of them simultaneously to open communication with Berlin, St Petersburg and Paris. They're all equipped with Morse keys. Then it's up to you to send news of the truth in the necessary languages.'

Kershaw signalled to Box to leave the two men to their task. They picked their way through the broken glass and went into one of the mess-rooms at the front of the building.

'Sir,' said Box, 'are these people really part of the *Eidgenossenschaft*? Bleibner's little more than a deranged murderer, and those men in the cable station — they seemed nonentities to me. They're a lifetime away from the likes of Count and Countess Czerny.'

'Bleibner and the others, Box, are the leavings from a very unpleasant meal, but they are lethal, none the less, because they know there will be nowhere for them to hide. German public opinion has shifted away from the secret gangs. That's why those men made a last hopeless stand here before they were taken. And that's why — '

There came a sudden shout of alarm from the telegraph room. In a moment Mr Boniface had burst in upon them from the passage.

'Sir!' he cried. 'The *Lermontov* — she's suddenly appeared off the point. Perhaps she's trying to make her escape.'

'The *Lermontov*,' muttered Kershaw. 'I'd rather hoped that that particular nest of rats had deserted the sinking ship. But evidently she's not sunk yet. Escape? I think not.'

From the wide window of the transmission room they could all see the rogue ship steaming rapidly along the Baltic shore, little more than a hundred yards from where they were standing. Black hulled and with a dark red funnel belching black smoke, the old iron ship had tall masts fore and aft, with tightly-furled sails on the spars. There appeared to be no signs of life on deck.

Crash! Something hit the upper floor of the cable station with resounding force, followed immediately by a deafening explosion. Part of the ceiling near the door collapsed, destroying the first of the telegraph engines.

Box had glimpsed the angry flare of red from the fore deck of the *Lermontov*, and had flung himself to the floor before the shell had hit the building. He got to his feet, and saw that Mr Boniface and Bob Jones had returned to one of the two remaining engines. Jones busied himself with various terminals and dials while Boniface's fingers worked frantically on the Morse key.

Box moved cautiously to the window, and peered out. The *Lermontov* still lay menacingly offshore, with no sign of life on the decks. She seemed to be waiting for the right moment to resume her attack on the station. To the right, and beyond the headland, Box could see a long strip of coast, clad to the shoreline in thick pine forest. Right on the water's edge stood a solitary church tower, its gilded onion dome catching the morning sun. It was the very scene that Mr Boniface had described to Kershaw in the lodge at the Crystal Palace.

Box turned away from the window.

'Sir,' he said, 'couldn't we send those messages later? We'll be pulverized if we stay here.'

'Well, you see, Mr Box,' said Kershaw, who was crouching on the floor near the further door, 'those rotten remnants aboard the *Lermontov* have got their own telegraph system aboard. I'm quite sure that before they sailed out of hiding on the other side of the Rundstedt Channel, they would have spliced into the land line and started feeding false information into the Prussian State Telegraph system. They'll report this battle and its aftermath as the expected Russian invasion of Prussia. Before the day's done, Germany will have declared war.'

Crash! The rear window exploded in a thousand shards of glass and timber, and a gaping hole appeared in the far wall of the room. At the same time, the upper storey of the cable station began to collapse inward with a deafening roar. It took them less than a minute to scramble through the wreckage and out on to the grass.

'Did you manage to send anything?' asked Kershaw curtly.

'I sent the agreed message to Paris — '

'Paris, Paris! Why didn't you make Berlin your priority?'

'There was static on the Berlin line, sir,' said Boniface. 'I think the enemy had made certain that communication with Berlin would be closed until they chose to open it.'

A further tremendous report shattered the calm, as the *Lermontov* continued its work of destruction and retribution. The echoes reverberated across the inlet, and were thrown back by the hills to the west. The wing of the station to the left burst into flame.

14

A Gift from the Gods

'We must do something!' cried Kershaw. 'Mr Jones, make your way as quickly as you can up to Major Kerner. Tell him to cable immediately to the naval base at Königsberg to send an armed vessel to stop this damned juggernaut — '

Even as Kershaw was speaking, a new and frightening sound came to their ears. It seemed to hang in the sky, a vibrating whine with a terrifying pulse behind it, like the beating of a heart. They stood petrified, and looked as one man towards the far coast of Russian Lithuania, from which the spectral sound seemed to emanate.

The pine trees of the forest rising behind the solitary church were shaking and trembling, even though there was no wind to stir them. The vibrating whine became louder, causing the militiamen halfway up the slope to freeze in their tracks, shading their eyes to look across the waters of the Baltic.

Then, above the trees, there rose into sight an enormous aerial ship, the like of which no man there had ever seen. Cigar-shaped, and covered in some material that had been painted a shining metallic silver, it moved slowly but with seemingly malign purpose up over the forest and across the sky, towards the Prussian coast. Each side of the great craft was blazoned with elegant Cyrillic letters, followed by a stencil of the Imperial Russian eagle.

'My God!' Kershaw whispered. 'The *Phoebus-Apollo*.'

'Yes, sir.' Mr Boniface's voice held a mixture of awe and delight 'Just look at it . . . Two hundred and sixty-two feet long, air displacement twelve tons. In a minute, you'll see the suspended carriages. The long one's for the navigator and the bombardier. There! You can see it now. And behind it is the smaller carriage, with the three-bladed propeller, driven by a specially built single-cylinder steam engine. Look through your binoculars, sir, and you'll see the racks where the bombards are stored.'

It suddenly came to Box like a revelation that Mr Boniface could only have known these details if he had been actually invited to inspect the aerial boat by the Russian authorities. That could only have been as the result of one of Colonel Kershaw's secret and subtle wiles.

'What is it doing here, Boniface?' asked Kershaw quietly.

'Perhaps it's come to finish the *Lermontov*'s work for it, sir.'

'You're not thinking clearly, Boniface. The people on that cable ship are no friends of Russia.'

The great aerial vessel had what appeared to be a ship's rudder, and they saw the device move eerily as the *Phoebus-Apollo*, shimmering in the bright sun, turned towards the shore. Box watched, enthralled. He'd heard of hot air balloons, though he'd never seen one, but this awesome machine was no mere balloon. One part of his consciousness wondered what it was going to do. Another part already knew the answer.

The *Phoebus-Apollo* hovered menacingly over the *Lermontov*. Then Kershaw spoke. 'The bombardier is out on the racks.' They could see the man, now, a small figure in uniform with his hands on a lever, which he suddenly pushed forward.

Three massive silver shells plunged silently downward through the still air, their metal casings glinting in the sunlight. They fell simultaneously on to the decks of the *Lermontov*, where they exploded with an almost unendurable roar of destructive power. The stricken ship erupted into flames, and through the dense pall of smoke Box could see the tall funnel crinkle and shrivel to nothing, like a ball of newspaper tossed into a fire. The shattered masts and spars were flung about on the churning water, and through the thick black cloud of smoke they could all discern the red-hot glow of the iron decks. A further violent explosion told them that the ship's hidden magazine had yielded to the fierce blaze.

In another quarter of an hour, during which Box and the others had stood in awed silence, the blazing wreck began to capsize with an almost animal groan of protest. What was left of its structure was torn apart by the force of the water, and the *Lermontov* sank from view beneath the waters of the Baltic.

'There will be no survivors, sir,' said Box, his voice subdued with awe.

'There were no survivors of the *Berlin Star*, Box,' said Kershaw. 'This evens things up a little.'

Mr Boniface had felt in his pocket for his unlit pipe, which he placed between his teeth. He was still gazing upward at the great aerial boat.

'Those were three hundred-pound high-explosive bombards, Colonel Kershaw,' he said. 'Perhaps we have witnessed here this morning the dawn of modern warfare.'

‘Perhaps,’ Kershaw replied. ‘And if so, then I’m glad that I’ll not be alive to see its sunset. It’s a remarkable invention, I’ve no doubt, but I can see no future for it in warfare. It’s time for you and Mr Jones to inspect what’s left of the cable station. Are any of the engines useable? There’s work still to be done.’

Without a word, the two experts turned their backs on the scene of triumph, and hurried across the grass towards the wrecked building.

Softly at first, and then louder, the cheers of the German soldiers came to Box and Kershaw as they stood on the grass sward, gazing up into the sky. Box looked up the slope, and saw the men throwing their hats into the air, and waving their arms in greeting to the stupendous Russian aerial boat, which was slowly turning in the sky for its journey back to its Lithuanian forest base. Two of the German officers had raised their swords in salute.

‘Do you know what I think, sir?’

‘What’s that, Box?’

‘I think Captain Adams had something to so with that show.’

Kershaw looked with appreciation at Arnold Box.

‘I wouldn’t be surprised, Box, if you’re

right. That kind of thing is Adams's cup of tea. Look — the aerial boat has finished its cruise, and reached the Lithuanian forest again. That's what eleven miles an hour can achieve. See how the trees are writhing in protest! There, it's sunk out of sight.'

Kershaw turned as Mr Boniface and Bob Jones came up to them from the wrecked building. Both men were smiling.

'Sir,' said Mr Boniface, 'the telegraph engines in the main transmission room have all been destroyed, but the right wing of the station's undamaged, and in it we found a brand-new Muirhead Siphon Recorder, complete with all the necessary transmission apparatus — '

'Another gift from the gods, in fact! Well, gentlemen, now is the time for you to send those vital messages to Berlin and St Petersburg, announcing the completely changed political situation in Europe. Give full praise where it's due, particularly to the bravery of the Russian authorities, who sent up that frightening craft at the risk of who knows how many lives. Be sure to demand acknowledgements. Don't leave the engines until you've received them.'

Box and Kershaw walked a little way beyond the cable station, and sat on a low stone wall near the bank of the Rundstedt

Channel. The April sun shone warm and bright, and the waters of the Baltic seemed as smooth as glass.

'This scene today, sir — this cheering of the Russians by the German troops — once that gets into the papers, ordinary people will realize that what the diplomats are saying is true.'

Colonel Kershaw did not reply. He was looking through his field-glasses across the sea towards the wooded shore of Russian Lithuania, then pointed across the water.

'See, Box,' he said, 'There's an open steam launch approaching. I expect this will be a Russian delegation, coming over to tell the Germans what their intentions were.'

'Sir,' said Box, who had been gazing intently at the rapidly approaching launch, 'one of the three men in that vessel is Captain Adams. I knew he had something to do with what happened this morning.'

As the steam launch neared the little dock across the Rundstedt Channel, the whole unit of militiamen swarmed down the slopes to greet the visitors. The cheering was renewed, and then the men fell into line, their officers standing to attention in front of them.

'Box,' said Kershaw, 'the time has come for the likes of you and me to make ourselves scarce. Let's join the others in that undamaged section of the cable station. Once the fraternization down there is completed, Captain Adams will come up here, I have no doubt, to seek us out.'

⋆ ⋆ ⋆

As Kershaw had predicted, Captain Adams came to them in the cable station once the initial civilities between the Russians and the Germans had been completed. Major Kerner and his militia had conducted the Russian delegation back to the barracks at Gehrendorf. Without waiting to be asked, Adams told them his story.

'It was my own decision to leave the military train when we reached the bridge at Frankenberg,' said Adams. 'I felt that it was vital to let the Russians know what was afoot, and, as you see, I made the right decision. I used the regular train service from Königsberg into Lithuania, travelling on my civilian passport, and with the necessary *visé*. I made my way directly to the restricted area in the Grosny Forest, and by a combination of bullying and wheedling had myself taken to the commandant. I told him who I was, mentioned both you and Boniface as colleagues, and then I told him the whole saga of the *Eidgenossenschaft* and its nefarious aims. He believed me.'

'That doesn't surprise me, you know,' said Kershaw. 'You are not entirely unknown to the Russian intelligence authorities.'

Box glanced at Kershaw, and recognized a particular expression of inscrutability that he had seen once or twice before. It told him that Kershaw, in some devious way known only to himself, had alerted the Russian commander in Lithuania to Adams's impending visit. He wondered if Adams himself realized what Kershaw must have done.

'The *Phoebus-Apollo* was undergoing tests to the steam engine,' Adams continued, 'and when the *Lermontov* began its assault on the cable station, the officer in charge immediately ordered the aerial boat into action. It had not been tested in the air, and it was a very brave thing to do. Fortunately, its mission — the sinking of the rogue ship — was entirely successful.'

'Well, Adams, with the destruction of the *Lermontov*, our work here is done. What do you propose to do now?'

For answer, Captain Adams turned to look at Arnold Box.

'You say our work here is done, Colonel Kershaw. I wonder whether Inspector Box here agrees?'

'Well, Captain Adams,' said Box, 'I must

confess that *my* work isn't done! I came all this way to arrest Bleibner for murder and attempted murder. Once again, he's been too quick for me — '

Captain Adams held up a hand to stop the indignant Box in mid-flow.

'Let me reassure you, Mr Box, that with patience you will get your man. I am setting out immediately to stalk Bleibner, or Karenin, as he called himself, and expose him in his lair. It was he who followed me across Northern Europe from this very place, putting me in fear of my life, and eventually tracking me down to poor Gabriel Oldfield's shop in Falcon Street. Well, he's going to earth, now; but I know the path he'll take, and I'll be only a few steps behind him. We'll get him, Box, never fear.'

They emerged from the devastated cable station, and stood on the trampled and bloodstained grass, debating how best to return to the militia barracks at Gehrendorf. As they talked together, they became aware of something curious happening a mile to the west of where they were standing. On the rim of the western horizon a disturbance in the air was taking place, as though immense clouds of dust were rising, and then resettling, and then the desolate scene was redefined as a landscape with figures.

'Gentlemen,' said Kershaw, 'I rather think that we are being approached by a regular unit of the German Army. They'll be on their way to Gehrendorf, I expect. Perhaps we can persuade them to let us accompany them.'

What they had heard as a dim drumming now turned into a veritable thunder of hooves. Soon, they could distinguish the grey and scarlet uniforms of the mounted soldiers, and see the lances and pennons carried by the flanking outriders. The dust continued to rise in clouds from the dry, unmetalled road, and now, in the midst of what Kershaw declared to be a company of the Prussian Lancers, they saw a single closed coach, with a civilian driver up on the box.

When it seemed that the smart troop of men would be upon them, the Lancers veered away to the left, cantering steadily up the sloping field of the recent battle towards the wooded Klagenfurt road. The dusty coach came to a halt just feet away from them, the coachman climbed down on to the grass, opened the door, and pulled down the steps. A man in a long black cape emerged from the coach, and raised his tall silk hat in greeting.

'I thought it would be an idea to come in person, Kershaw,' he said. 'From what I hear, you and your colleagues would benefit from a complete change of surroundings.'

'Count von und zu Thalberg! This is an unexpected pleasure. What on earth are you doing in this God-forsaken wilderness?'

'This,' said Count von und zu Thalberg, waving an embracing arm in a vague circle around him, 'is Thalberg. Oh, didn't you know that? I told you in Wiltshire that I was going back home to visit my estate. Well, this is it. And that's the reason why I'm here so opportunely. Or at least, it could be the reason, always supposing that I had to give one.'

Colonel Kershaw shook his head in rueful amusement.

'Upon my word, Thalberg,' he said, 'I'm not often caught napping, but I must confess you've won this particular little battle of wits! So this is Thalberg. It's not — well, it's not very prepossessing, is it?'

'It serves its purpose, Kershaw. I'm not often here, preferring my two houses in Berlin, where I'm of more use to Germany. But come, let me gather you all up and take you away from this graveyard of the *Eidgenossenschaft*, to Petershalle, my manor house a mile from here across the heath.'

'You were escorted here in style, Thalberg. A whole company of mounted soldiers!'

'Oh, that? A purely fortuitous circumstance. The authorities in Berlin received your cable, and decided to flood this area with units of the regular army. The 4th Brandenburg Lancers are the first on the scene, and they agreed to let me travel with them. Their quartermaster had been ordered to bring your things across to Petershalle from the militia barracks.'

* * *

Arnold Box walked through the apple orchard, savouring the peace and beauty of Count von und zu Thalberg's remote country estate. He had met the intensely Anglophile Prussian aristocrat earlier in the year, when he had been involved in the affair of the Hansa Protocol, but had never imagined that he would stay as a guest in his house.

Petershalle had proved to be a high, five-storey mansion, painted a gleaming white, but with bright green woodwork. To Arnold Box it was luxurious, fascinating, and irredeemably foreign. Its lawns looked as though they had been closely shaven, its surrounding beech trees were carefully clipped and pruned. And here he was, having benefited from a good night's sleep in a proper bed, and an English breakfast into the bargain, walking in the orchard, while Colonel Kershaw and the others withdrew for a private conference.

Some yards ahead of him Box saw a man in a rusty old frock coat sitting with his back to him on a camp stool drawn up to a card table set out on the grass. He seemed to be absorbed in a pile of documents spread out in front of him, which he was consulting with the aid of little round gold-wire spectacles. As Box approached, the man turned round, and smiled a greeting.

'Inspector Box,' said Sergeant Major Schmidt, 'come and join me. Draw up one of those stools. I've something I want to tell you.'

Box sat down on a stool, and studied the man sitting opposite him. Schmidt was wearing civilian clothes, which made him look rather like a weather-beaten old farmer.

'Mr Schmidt,' said Box, 'I thought we'd left you behind at the militia barracks. I'm glad to have found you again. What are you doing here?'

'I'm here, Mr Box, because His Excellency is here. True, I know Major Kerner, and he knows me, but I work only for Count von und zu Thalberg. You know he is head of Prussian Military Intelligence? Well, I arrange things for him. Like that exercise yesterday. I served him once, years ago, when he was in the army, and I stayed with him when he moved on to other things. He and I are both good Prussians. Yes, I arrange things.'

'Will you be going back to Berlin?'

'I will. The plan is for us to return as soon as is convenient. His Excellency is needed urgently in the capital, and I believe there is a plan to send you English folk back to London by regular express train from Königsberg. You will all return in style — no more military trains, with their wooden seats!'

Sergeant Major Schmidt leaned across the little table and lowered his voice.

'Now, Inspector, let me talk to you about Bleibner. You know he was there, yesterday, at the Rundstedt Channel? He murdered one of the two gunners in the midst of battle, and once again made good his escape. But he's a creature of habit, and he'll act according to pattern. Captain Adams knows that, and has gone after him. When he comes to the end of the trail, Herr Box, make sure that you are there as well.'

'You mean — '

'I mean that he will retreat as far as he dares, and that will be to England. Watch where Captain Adams goes, and be sure that you don't lose sight of him. Bah! You don't need a poor soldierman to tell you your business. What is the name of that rocky, rainy county of yours, lashed by the Atlantic at the end of the civilized world? Cornwall. That is where Bleibner will seek refuge. Go there, my friend, when the time is ripe, and arrest the ravening beast. When he is under lock and key, this whole dangerous and devilish business will be at an end.'

15

Revelations

Sir Charles Napier glanced briefly at the front page of the previous Saturday's *Sketch*, and then turned to a short column on page 3, entitled 'Impressions of the Week. By 'The Limner'.'

> Last week (*he read*), the whole world rang with the news of the great battle in the Prussian wilderness, and of the miraculous appearance in the sky of the fearsome aerial craft which will put an end to war. The Russians, it seems, were not, after all, as black as they had been painted. And the Prussians? Well, they had employed more rant than rancour.
>
> And so all Europe rang with the news. Peace had been assured not just for now, but into the next century. In St Petersburg and Moscow, the bells rang as though for a great victory, and sublime services were sung in Church Slavonic by robed and bearded hierarchs in the many cathedrals. The Tsar contrived to think

kindly of his tetchy royal cousin Wilhelm in Berlin, then turned his mind once more to the lure of China, and the problem of Japan.

In Berlin, crowds milled around the royal palace, singing and cheering. In the Friedrichstrasse fresh wreaths were laid at the foot of the Column of Peace. A large portrait of the Tsar was displayed in the foyer of the Reichstag.

In Paris, the boulevards were crowded with fashionable ladies and gentlemen, offering themselves to view as part of a celebration which did not directly concern them, while on the Left Bank, earnest intellectuals debated the merits of peace and war, the theory of monarchy, and the ideal of a republic.

Napier laughed, and threw the paper down. He glanced across to the window, where Colonel Kershaw was standing thoughtfully with a coffee cup and saucer in his hands, looking out on to the spring glories of St James's Park.

'Fiske of the *Graphic*,' Napier observed, 'having wielded the big stick in the direction of St Petersburg, has now taken refuge in what he imagines to be satire. 'The Limner', he calls himself, when he wants to hide from public scrutiny.'

'Fiske's a good fellow in his own way,' said Kershaw. 'There's more than a grain of truth in what he's written there. But 'all Europe', as he calls the interested public in the various capitals, seems to have forgotten that the evil genius behind this whole business is still at large. Perhaps they don't care.'

'You mean Hans Bleibner,' said Sir Charles Napier. 'Well, from my point of view, it would be convenient if Bleibner could be forgotten. He's a subject for the civil authority — by which I mean your friend Detective Inspector Box — and if he's brought to justice, then there'll be a trial.'

Napier drained his own coffee cup, and placed it on the desk. Kershaw said nothing.

'A trial here, Kershaw, in London, probably at the Old Bailey. All the old wounds will be opened, all the old recriminations remembered. Yes, I hope devoutly that Bleibner disappears from public memory.'

'There speaks the born diplomat.'

'Diplomacy is my business.'

'Speaking of diplomats,' said Kershaw, still holding his cup and saucer and gazing thoughtfully across the park, 'that fellow Andropov, the Russian military attaché who took liberties with your shirt front, was returned to his regiment and sent out to

Karkhov. He'd been there no more than a week when he was severely beaten by unidentified thugs. Foreigners of some sort. I thought you'd like to know.'

Napier looked across at the quietly spoken man in the sober frock coat, and thought: He must have arranged for that to happen. He's done things like that before. Perhaps he's hinting at a similar fate for Bleibner, when he's found.

'Very unpleasant for Andropov, I've no doubt,' Napier replied. 'But he's another fellow who can be quietly forgotten, Kershaw. In thinking of the present, we can make some attempt to ensure a peaceful future.'

A certain portentousness crept into the Permanent Under-Secretary's voice that Kershaw recognized. Whenever he spoke like that, Napier the man disappeared beneath the mask of Napier the Civil Servant.

'The Foreign Secretary has decided that the new understanding between the Powers should be known as the Grand Rapprochement. On Friday, the twelfth of May, there is to be a Grand Rapprochement Banquet, held at the Goldsmiths' Hall, when every opportunity will be seized to bring home to the public the renewed stability of existing relations between the Powers.'

In St James's Park a phalanx of nannies,

wheeling basinets, had appeared in the neighbourhood of the great lake. Kershaw turned away from the window, and put his empty cup and saucer down on the edge of Napier's desk. Napier the Civil Servant was still talking.

'The banquet will be graced by the presence of Their Royal Highnesses the Duke and Duchess of Connaught. Mr Gladstone will be there, and, of course, Lord Salisbury. The banquet is essentially being given for the Diplomatic Corps, and I should think there will be several hundred guests. I've not yet seen the guest lists, but I expect you'll be there.'

'Oh, yes, I'll be there. I'll have to go now, Napier. I'm due to see Admiral Holland at eleven o'clock. So you don't want Bleibner to steal your thunder?'

'What? Really, Kershaw, you dart about like a gnat, sometimes. I'd be happy if Bleibner disappeared from the public consciousness completely. This rapprochement is real enough, and I can see how it could be consolidated by a conference at Vienna in the autumn — '

Colonel Kershaw laughed. He had struggled into his long astrakhan overcoat, and had picked up his tall silk hat.

'I wondered whether you'd get your

conference, Napier. I wish you joy of it. Meanwhile, Bleibner is retreating as discreetly as he can from Europe, closely pursued by Captain Edgar Adams RN. Both Adams and I know where he's going, and when he gets there, he'll find someone waiting for him — someone whom he won't like one bit.'

'That's very reassuring, Kershaw. But it will mean a trial — '

'It will, indeed, mean a trial, but not necessarily at the Old Bailey. There is a way round your difficulty, Napier, and if you'll leave the matter with me, I'll see what I can do.'

* * *

Stonewick Hall seemed to have mounted a festal display to welcome Vanessa Drake as she walked through the ornamental gates from the Berwick road. Two gardeners were at work on the crisp green lawns, and the well-tilled flower beds were a riot of colour. Could this be the house where she had been within seconds of a violent death? And how was it possible for Baroness Felssen to be still living there?

She glanced at the reassuringly nondescript man walking beside her. She remembered

Major Hotchkiss as one of the guests at the house party in March. He and his wife had left on the Monday morning, returning to their home nearby. It was Major Hotchkiss who had called upon her at her lodgings in Westminster, to announce that the time had come for her to finish her work at Stonewick Hall. She knew then that the major was another of Colonel Kershaw's people.

The door was opened to them by a young woman in a grey dress with the keys of a housekeeper at her waist. Vanessa had not seen her before, but evidently she was well known to Major Hotchkiss.

'Helga,' he said, 'I've brought Miss Drake up from the station. Her luggage will be arriving in a few minutes' time. Goodbye, Miss Drake. Nice to have met you again.'

He was gone before Vanessa could recover from her surprise. The woman called Helga curtsied slightly, and beckoned Vanessa to follow her. She threw open the door of the musicroom, where Hans Bleibner had played Beethoven, the tears running down his awful blanched face.

'Miss Drake, *Frau Baronin*,' said Helga, and when Vanessa had entered the room, she closed the door behind her.

Poised and elegant as ever, Baroness Felssen was standing in the wide bow window. Vanessa looked at her in awe, at the same time admiring her emerald-green silk morning dress, enlivened at the throat by a scintillating diamond brooch. Baroness Felssen smiled, and held out her hands.

'My dear! I'm so glad you've come back to Stonewick. Very soon, we'll have luncheon, and I'll discuss what else needs to be done in the chapel. All your beautiful work is still there, waiting for you.'

'I don't understand,' Vanessa stammered. 'You harboured that terrible man here. You were plotting a raid on Whitby with him! I thought you'd be in goal — '

Baroness Felssen gave vent to a peal of laughter. She sat down on a sofa near the fireplace, and patted the cushion beside her.

'Come and sit here, Miss Drake, while I tell you why I'm not in gaol. That's it. For goodness' sake, girl, relax! Compose yourself like a sensible young woman, and listen. Since late January of this year, Stonewick Hall has been a trap, waiting for Hans Bleibner. It was a baited trap, and the bait was security. My late husband had been at Heidelberg with Bleibner, and I knew him quite well. He was a dangerous, unstable man, with a love of music as his only redeeming feature. He was fluent in English, a persuasive speaker, and an effortless liar.'

Baroness Felssen sighed, and unconsciously patted the girl's hand.

'My part in all this was to play the accomplice. It was not a role that I relished, my dear, but it had to be done. And all the time, the trap was being refined, and the right moment chosen to remove Bleibner from the scene. Someone was sent to suggest to him that Sir David Blaine, the Scottish dermatologist, might be able to cure his skin disease. I invited Sir David here, and watched while Bleibner worked his spell upon him.'

'His spell? What do you mean, Baroness?'

'Bleibner used all his rhetorical tricks to send Sir David Blaine away from here a total convert to his way of thinking. The great specialist was like putty in his hands! Russia was the bogey, Germany was all innocence — you heard him yourself! That, of course, had been part of his mission all along.'

'You say this house was a trap. If so, who set it up? I don't understand — '

'It was set up by my good friend and neighbour in East Prussia, Count von und zu Thalberg, in co-operation with Colonel Sir Adrian Kershaw. It was their joint venture from the start. I was the *femme fatale* — the wicked lady of the plot!'

Baroness Felssen laughed.

‘Colonel Kershaw — then you were on our side, all the time!’

‘No, Miss Drake, I wasn’t on ‘your side’. That’s all very well in stories, but real life is more subtle than that. I played my part in the affair out of patriotism. I have no time for criminal gangs masquerading as political saviours. I believe only in legitimate government, as you do. My loyalties lie with the Kaiser, and the German Fatherland. In this matter, though, Germany’s interests, and those of England, coincided.’

‘I think I understand, Baroness,’ said Vanessa. ‘But surely Bleibner was doing Germany a service by turning the other countries against Russia?’

‘He was doing nothing of the sort!’ cried Baroness Felssen, sharply. ‘He sowed only lies about Russia, lies compounded by murder and treachery. The German military attaché here in Britain was misled, but when he knew the truth, he proclaimed it immediately. Germany and its rulers have no place for liars and perjurers.’

Vanessa Drake had grown very quiet while the baroness spoke. She was recalling Colonel Kershaw’s gently chilling words to her when he had visited her at Westminster. ‘I told you to look and listen. You were not to pry. You chose to disobey me.’

'It was my fault, wasn't it, Baroness, that the trap didn't work?'

'Yes, my dear, it was. You see, Bleibner suddenly wanted one of Colonel Kershaw's agents to be present in the house when he posed as the innocent German liberal surrounded by Russian monsters. I think he had some idea of distancing the 'honest' Bleibner from the murderous Karenin. I told him I could help, and travelled down to London to see Colonel Kershaw. He told me about you, and about your great skills in embroidery. He also told me where I could see samples of your work — Colonel Kershaw is nothing if not thorough. I went to Durham, accompanied by my neighbour, Major Hotchkiss. I saw the dean, who showed me your work in the cathedral, and then Major Hotchkiss used the electric telephone to let the colonel know that you were to be engaged.'

'That's why he kept warning me not to exceed my orders,' said Vanessa mournfully. 'I was a fly in the ointment. He knew I wouldn't be content without taking some kind of initiative myself. All I had to do was ply my needle and be quiet.'

'Instead of which, Miss Drake, you chose to exceed your orders, and you did so at the very moment that the trap was to be sprung!

Bleibner and I were interviewing a wretched English traitor, a man called Cathcart — '

'I heard that bit. You sounded really wicked, talking about shells and things.'

'Yes, and all the time, Miss Drake, there was a platoon of soldiers silently infiltrating the grounds, ready to storm the house. Only they didn't get the chance, did they? Because you gave yourself away, and Bleibner threw caution to the winds, and turned into a murderous lunatic. If Colonel Kershaw hadn't sent your young man after you as a shadow, you would have been killed.

'And now, perhaps, you'll appreciate what your actions forced *me* to do? Sergeant Knollys was unconscious, and you had fainted. The soldiers would have handed the whole business over to the civil authorities, because they would have no truck with covering up attempted murder. So I was obliged to hide Bleibner and myself in a secret chamber we had had constructed in the attics in case of any possible difficulties. And then, after all the excitement had died down, I personally supervised Bleibner's escape to the Continent — *I* did it, young lady, because I dared not communicate with any of our people.'

'You helped him to escape?' asked Vanessa faintly.

'Yes, I took him, disguised, to Newcastle, and he crossed incognito to Holland. I've since learned that when that glorious battle was fought at the Rundstedt Channel, he murdered one of our soldiers, by the simple expedient of thrusting a hatpin into the base of his skull.'

Vanessa Drake burst into tears, covering her face in her hands. Baroness Felssen stroked her blonde hair, and made some attempt at soothing noises.

'Come, now, my dear, somehow I don't see you as the tearful type. Let's go to luncheon. The moral of our story is this: always obey orders. It's much the best way.'

* * *

After luncheon, the housekeeper Helga brought their coffee on a tray upstairs to Baroness Felssen's spacious and sunny bedroom on the first floor. She moved the two Japanese screens, placed the tray on a small carved table near the fireplace, and then withdrew.

The baroness poured coffee for them both, and then glanced at the two ebony-framed memorial photographs on the mantelpiece. She took up the picture of the pretty young woman in court dress, and handed it to Vanessa.

'Countess Czerny — Adelheid von Braun before her marriage — was my niece, the only daughter of the youngest of my three sisters. The von Brauns are fanatical Pan-Germanists, and my sister's child inherited her father's passions. You will remember her by a different name, a name that she borrowed from a dead friend. You know how she set out to secure the death of Dr Otto Seligmann, and how her mission proved successful. But she paid for her success with her life.'

They listened to the marble clock ticking on the mantelpiece. Vanessa looked down at the photograph, and at the frank and fearless eyes of Adelheid von Braun. This woman had belonged to a criminal conspiracy that had come close to plunging Europe into war.

'But you have never shared Countless Czerny's beliefs, Baroness Felssen. So why do you keep her photograph here, in your private room?'

'Because she was my niece, Miss Drake. I played with her, when she was a tiny little thing. She is part of my family. You can see, can't you, how complex loyalties can be? One can't always simply be 'on someone's side'.'

She took the photograph from Vanessa, placed it back on the mantelpiece, next to that of Count Czerny, and sat down again at the coffee table.

'Adelheid's husband, Count Czerny, was an unfailingly courteous and cultured man, a man who showed me many kindnesses at difficult times in my life. He was very popular in England, having been educated at a private school near Stowe, and many English people still speak of him with affection. And there he stands, beside my niece. I loathed his politics, but I loved the man. Loyalties again, you see! He was a true aristocrat, a nobleman of the Roman-German Empire. You know what happened to him. He lies in an obscure grave on a lonely Scottish island. The body of my niece was never found.'

They finished their coffee, and Baroness Felssen stood up. She smiled, and offered a hand to her young companion.

'Enough of the past, Miss Drake. You are my guest here for a week, and there is work to be done in the chapel. This really *is* my home, you know, and my desire to see the chapel refurbished is quite genuine! So come, my dear, let us leave the past alone, and get on with our lives.'

As they left the quiet, sunlit bedroom in which she had almost met her death at the hands of the frantic Hans Bleibner, Vanessa glanced once more at the photographs, and saw the frank and fearless eyes of Countess Czerny following her.

* * *

The grey Atlantic waves hurled themselves angrily against the rocks of Spanish Beach, but Andrew Sedden, sitting in the back room of The Cormorant, was used to the noise that they made, and scarcely heard it. He was giving all his attention to the corpse-pale man on the chair opposite him. Sedden had made some attempt to shave that morning, but he still looked unkempt and slovenly.

Hans Bleibner opened a chamois leather bag gathered at the neck with a leather thong, and unleashed a shower of gold sovereigns on to the table. Sedden licked his lips, but said nothing. It was always better to wait for Herr Bleibner to speak.

'Here is a hundred pounds, Mr Sedden,' said Bleibner, 'in payment for past favours. You were my gateway to England, and my fortress in times of trouble. Well, my star in Europe is set, and the time has come for me to start a new life elsewhere.'

The surly landlord began to gather up his golden hoard, carefully counting the coins as he slipped them back in the chamois leather bag. Yes, he'd made it his business to usher this man in and out of England, hiding him when that was necessary, and denying all knowledge of him when snoopers began to ask questions.

Damn them all! This German outcast and he were brothers under the skin. They cared for nobody but themselves, and they both knew the freedom that money could bring. Bleibner had traded in ideas, with a profitable sideline in murder. He, Andrew Sedden, was too craven at heart to risk his neck, but if he could have got away with murder, he would have done it — if money was to be had. As it was, he was content to trade not in ideas but identities.

'You say you'll start a new life, Mr Bleibner. What kind of a life do you have in mind?'

'I'm thinking very seriously of making my way to America, Mr Sedden. I've already salted away a good bit of money in Chicago, and that's where I intend to settle. A man of my talents could very soon be in demand over there.'

Andrew Sedden indulged in a throaty laugh. He reached for an open bottle of gin, and poured them each a measure in small, bleared glasses.

'America . . . Do you want me to get you the necessary papers? I can get you all that,

Mr Bleibner, and I can book you a passage on any of the Atlantic liners in any name you choose — No! I don't want any more money, you've just given me a fortune. But if I was to turn up myself over there in Chicago, would you give me a billet?'

'A billet? Ah! You mean employment. Yes, assuredly. In fact, Mr Sedden, I find the idea very appealing. The days of ideology are over for me, alas! and I must make do with enterprise. Yes, I would very soon find work for you.'

Both men finished their gin, and Sedden began to make a few cryptic notes in pencil on a greasy scrap of paper.

'It's the fourth of May, Mr Bleibner, and I'll need about ten days to get all that you need together . . . How about the sixteenth? I'll have all your papers ready by then, and a berth booked on a decent liner. It's folk in London and Liverpool who make these arrangements for me, the folk who brought you here in the first place. So let's meet down here again on Tuesday, the sixteenth.'

Sedden returned to his notes, and Bleibner sat back in his chair, looking at him. Really, this nondescript, overweight man had been a blessing ever since the venture of the substitute cables had begun. His obscure alehouse at the foot of a dangerous cliff had proved to be an infallible means of entering England unseen and unsuspected.

Immediately after the débâcle at the Rundstedt Channel he had set out by certain devious routes through Germany and northern France to England, slipping unseen into Harwich early on the morning of the 25 April. At one time, he'd fancied that someone was stalking him, but it must have been nerves. A man working on the quay at the Hook of Holland had looked rather like the British Naval Intelligence agent Captain Adams, but he had remained there, working stolidly among the crates and bales, as the ferry had pulled away from the land . . . What was Sedden telling him?

'You'll be stuck up there at St Columb's Manor for a fortnight or more, Mr Bleibner. Keep a cool eye on Squire Trevannion. He's been seeing visions, and hearing voices, and the doctors sent him to the asylum at Helston for a while. He's released, now, and staying with a cousin in Penzance. But he'll be back, I've no doubt.'

Sedden caught Bleibner's eye for a moment, and the German saw the unspoken warning in the Cornishman's glance.

'Men like that — turned in their wits — are likely to blab, Mr Bleibner. So watch him, if he comes back. I've victualled the Manor for you, so you'll be snug up there until such time as friends of mine take you up to Liverpool to catch the Atlantic boat.'

Hans Bleibner shook hands with his accomplice, and left The Cormorant. It was a chill, blustery day for May, but the weather exhilarated him. A new life was beckoning. He made his way up the steep path to the headland, walking carefully through the stunted shrubs and the weathered rocky outcrops. Soon, he would be back in the shelter of St Columb's Manor.

So Squire Trevannion had frightened himself out of his wits? Well, such men could certainly not be trusted to keep their own counsel. Trevannion was a little difficulty asking to be surmounted.

In the back room of The Cormorant, Andrew Sedden tied the leather thong of the chamois leather bag tightly, and got up from the table. As he did so, the door opened.

'Hello, Mr Sedden,' said Detective Inspector Box. 'Remember me?'

As he spoke, three uniformed policemen came into the room.

* * *

In the long, low parlour of St Columb's Manor, Hans Bleibner sat beside the fireplace, lost in thought. Yes, Europe, its powers and its passions, would become — *must* become — dim memories. There were many possibilities in the New World for two enterprising gentlemen from Cornwall.

But Squire Trevannion was a danger, and he would have to be silenced. He'd already been confined to an asylum. What had he said to the doctors there? He knew too much. It would be as well to be prepared.

Leaving the parlour, Bleibner climbed the old twisted staircase which led to the second storey. The house seemed to be full of alarming creaks and imagined footsteps, and it was easy to understand why Trevannion, his mind turning, fancied that he had heard the voice of his dead sister.

Here he was at his bedroom, a room that had once been occupied by Margaret Trevannion. Today it was full of quiet sunlight, which glanced off the mirror above the vanity-table. It was from this room that he had seen the interfering William Pascoe walking on the cliff top, and had gone out to send him to his death. Curiosity killed the cat . . . It was time to make preparations for the demise of Squire Trevannion. There, on Meg's vanity-table, was the little box of hatpins, all of them long and thin, like needles, and capped with a charming little diamanté globe. He opened the box.

It was empty.

'I'm sorry, Herr Bleibner,' said Detective Inspector Box, 'but I've got your precious hatpins here. I thought it'd be better if I took charge of them. You know Sergeant Knollys, I think? This other officer is Inspector Tregennis, of the Cornwall Constabulary.'

'Hans Bleibner,' said Tregennis, 'I arrest you for the wilful and felonious murder of William Pascoe, at Porthcurno, in this county, on the fourteenth of March in this current year . . . '

As Tregennis read out the charge, Sergeant Knollys secured Hans Bleibner, alias Dr. N. I. Karenin, at the wrists and ankles. The prisoner said nothing, and his glazed eyes showed that he had withdrawn into himself as a kind of desperate defence against reality. His corpse-white face had mutated to a sickly shade of oatmeal grey.

16

New Beginnings

'I'm not given to bestowing lavish praise on my officers, Box,' said Superintendent Mackharness. 'Too much commendation goes to a man's head, and while he basks in his new-found self-satisfaction, his work suffers.'

'Yes, sir.'

Box had been thankful that the new week had not brought the dreaded Assignments, and when he heard the familiar sound of the limping tread filtering through the stained ceiling of his office, he had been waiting in the vestibule for the ritual summons upstairs.

'Nevertheless, Box,' Mackharness continued, 'in this particular instance, I feel that some kind of recognition would be — er — fitting. Requisite. So, well done, Box! You'll be aware, I expect, that Colonel Sir Adrian Kershaw KB approached the Commissioner, asking particularly for your services. The Commissioner came across here in person, and asked me whether I would release you. Naturally enough, I agreed.'

'It was very kind of you, sir. I'm sure the

Commissioner was very grateful.'

Inspector Box had contrived to glance at the mantelpiece. The Crimea Medal was still there, and beside it a slim, morocco-bound book with gilt edges. That was new . . .

Superintendent Mackharness smiled. It was something he rarely did, and the gesture wiped away at least ten years from his appearance.

'I don't know about that, Box, but it was gratifying to be consulted in the matter. And so you experienced the rigours and dangers of military conflict, and acquitted yourself well. And then, on your return, you arrested the villain Karenin, or rather Bleibner. Well done, again! I see he's to stand trial for the murder of William Pascoe, and that the trial will be held at Exeter. Much the best way. We've had enough of Bleibner in London.'

The superintendent paused for a moment, and seemed to be gazing into space. Box was content to wait. All this praise pouring from Old Growler's lips was like balm to an injured man.

'You know, Box,' said Mackharness, 'your passing near Sir John Courteline's house just after he'd been murdered — that was almost providential, don't you think? A most unusual concatenation of circumstances.'

'Concatenation — '

'Yes, Box. It means a chain of circumstances.'

Mackharness rose from his chair, and took the slim leather-bound volume off the mantelpiece. He blushed as he handed the book to Box.

'I want you to have this little token of my — er — approbation for all that you've done in this case to confound the Queen's enemies. You're like me, now, Box: a veteran of the battlefield. Read it. You may find it not only interesting but — er — profitable.'

Box opened the book, and read the title page.

Leaves from an Officer's Diary
Some Recollections of Life in the Crimea.
By Lieutenant P.A. Mackharness of the
Royal Irish Rangers
London: Privately Printed. 1868

'A book? By you? Well, thank you, sir. I consider that very handsome — '

'Not at all, Not at all.'

Superintendent Mackharness waved the matter away, cleared his throat, and rummaged round on his desk for a few moments.

'Now, on the twelfth of this month, Box, there is to be a grand celebratory dinner at Goldsmiths' Hall. It's to be called the

Rapprochement Banquet, and it will be graced by the presence of His Royal Highness the Duke of Connaught, accompanied by Princess Louise. It will be a glittering occasion, attended by all the Heads of Mission.'

'Oh! And have I been invited, sir?'

'Invited? Well, hardly that, I think. But I expect you meant that as a joke. Ha! Ha! Now, obviously, the City Police will be there, but the Commissioner thinks that the presence of a Scotland Yard man would convey the right impression to the distinguished company. It will give them reassurance, you know. Who better than yourself? Go there, will you, Box? It's this coming Friday.'

'Guard duty, then, sir?'

'What? Yes, I suppose you could call it that. But then, one can't always hobnob with the captains and the kings. Duty calls. I think that's all. Good morning. And once again, Box, well done!'

* * *

As Inspector Box walked through St Paul's Churchyard early on Friday evening, he was suddenly overcome with a feeling of profound gratefulness that he was once again back in

London, walking in the shadow of Sir Christopher Wren's great cathedral, which represented for him the centre of the Empire. Throngs of people were hurrying through the narrow thoroughfare, intent on their own concerns. Had he really known a wise old German sergeant major called Schmidt? Had he really ducked to avoid the murderous shells of the *Lermontov*?

'Hello, Mr Box. How are you, today? I don't suppose you remember me.'

Box looked at the boy in the Norfolk jacket, knickerbockers, and stiff Eton collar, who had just given him this perky greeting. He was carrying a brown-paper parcel under his arm.

'Of course I remember you: Thomas Slater, aged fourteen, Number 7, Beaufort Lane, Monument. I'm very well, Tom. How are you? Fixed up with a billet, yet?'

'Yes, thank you, sir. Mr Palmer, the photographer, he's taken me on for a month's trial. He's a very nice man, and I think he and I will get on very well. I must be off now. I've got to deliver this box of lenses to a man in Warwick Square. Goodbye, Mr Box. Oh, and well done for nabbing the man who murdered my old guvnor. Nice to have met you.'

The boy disappeared in the crowds streaming up towards Ludgate Hill. Box smiled to himself. 'Well done', indeed! Cheeky young sprig. Still, he'd played a vital part in the whole business. He'd do well with old Palmer.

The approach to Goldsmiths' Hall in Foster Lane was crowded with people and vehicles, but the City Police were there in force. Box made his way to a stone-flagged tradesmen's entrance at the side of the building, and established himself on a tall stool near the door. There was nothing much for him to do, and he'd be stuck there for at least three hours, twiddling his thumbs. Well, never mind. As Old Growler said, duty calls.

The glittering panoply of titled guests arrived, and were ushered into the splendours of the banqueting room. After half an hour or so, various officers of the City Police joined Box in the tradesmen's vestibule. While the great ones dined and listened to speeches, the assembled policemen chatted about the various trials and tribulations of the City and Metropolitan forces. Crumpled newspapers were produced, and there was talk of someone making a brew of tea.

Towards half past nine, a uniformed porter came into the room, carrying a massive ring of keys.

'Which of you gents is Inspector Box?' he asked. 'You're to come with me, if you please, sir. There's someone wants to see you in the assay office.'

Box followed the porter, who conducted him along a narrow corridor, which was filled with the aromas of recently cooked food. The man selected a key from the ring, and unlocked a glazed door set in a tall arch. He and Box entered a long, white-painted room lit by electricity. It was filled with benches, arrays of tools, and tall anvils, upon which reposed sets of stamping-dies in wooden trays.

'This is the assay office, Inspector Box. If you'll wait in here, the gentleman will come to you presently.'

The porter walked slowly away, leaving Box to his own devices. He sat down gingerly on a tall stool near one of the benches. The room exuded a chilly, almost clinical atmosphere, an impression enhanced, no doubt, by the fact that there was nobody in it. It was here, Box knew, that the officials of the Goldsmiths' Company assayed and hallmarked a never-ending panoply of valuable objects, both useful and ornamental. If they passed muster, then they received the coveted leopard's head mark. But everyone had gone home, and the treasures were locked away securely from prying eyes and light fingers.

There was a noise of footsteps from the

passage, and Colonel Kershaw came into the deserted room. He was wearing evening dress, and the collar, sash and star of the Most Honourable Order of the Bath. His face was flushed, but it still carried that almost apologetic air that he reserved for Arnold Box. He perched himself on another of the office stools.

'I knew you were here, Mr Box,' he said, 'and I just had to come out and find you. Have you ever been in the Goldsmiths' banqueting room? It's an awesome place, eighty feet long, I'm told, and forty feet broad. We're sitting at a huge horseshoe of tables, groaning with gold and silver plate, and lit by candelabra, and there are massive chandeliers, burning hundreds of candles — if one of them fell, a dozen people would be crushed to death.'

Box felt a sudden surge of excitement and pride. How many other ordinary men like him would be sought out at such a time by such an eminent man?

'It sounds very impressive, sir,' he said. 'Are they feeding you properly?'

'They are. It's all in French, but it boils down to very good food when you get it. And very good wines to match. But it's hot in there, Box, with all those candles! Still, when the wine flows, the tongues wag more mellifluously. Sir Charles Napier's just made the most insincere and glutinously sickening speech I've ever heard. It was all about the enduring trust between the peoples of Europe, a trust that had triumphed over feud and faction. Everybody cheered, and thumped the tables.'

'How are the Russians taking it, sir? Prince Orloff and his suite.'

'He's rather like Mr Pickwick tonight, twinkling, you know. He's arm-in-arm with the German ambassador, who's due to entertain us next. Mercifully, no one dare ask me to say anything. I'm billed merely as Extra Equerry to Her Majesty — ah! Here he comes, at last.'

The door opened to admit a liveried footman, who was carrying a silver tray containing an ice bucket, in which reposed a dusty and venerable bottle. Two tall fluted wine glasses stood beside it. The footman placed the tray on the bench, bowed to Kershaw, and left the room.

'Box,' said Colonel Kershaw, 'I've had this very decent champagne brought here because I think it's time that you and I drank a special toast, which I'll propose just as soon as I've poured us out a glass each. This dinner will go on for another hour or two, and when 'the captains and the kings depart', people like you will be left behind, still on duty, and their deeds unsung. Although not officially one of my folk, you were — are — a bona fide member of our gang in Secret Intelligence, and so this toast is really to you — '

'Sir — '

'But as you can't very well toast yourself, we'll drink to 'Ourselves'. There you are, Box — to Ourselves.'

'To Ourselves.'

The two men followed the mutual tribute with another glass or two of champagne. 'I've received intelligence from Count von und zu Thalberg, Box, to the effect that the *Eidgenossenschaft* is now completely destroyed. The headquarters of the Brandenburg Consortium in Hesse-Darmstadt were raided, and the company's records and assets seized. That was all done very effectively by the security police in Berlin. I'm afraid that a goodly number of heads will roll.'

'Didn't you say that the *Lermontov* was owned by a Norwegian company, sir?'

'Yes, that's right. The Olafsson Steamship Company was merely an outlet of the Brandenburg Consortium. The Norwegian Government has obligingly frozen its assets until it can be formally liquidated.'

Kershaw got to his feet.

'I must get back to the banquet, Mr Box,'

he said. 'Congratulations, by the way, on securing the arrest of Bleibner, and thank you for agreeing to my request to let him be charged and tried in Cornwall, away from the limelight. I promised Napier that something like that could be arranged. I knew that you'd agree to my request. We have very different minds, you and I, but we work together very well indeed. Goodbye, Box.'

'Goodbye, sir. Perhaps we'll work together again, some time.'

'Perhaps. We'll have to wait and see how the world wags. Goodbye.'

The two men shook hands, and Colonel Sir Adrian Kershaw KB walked thoughtfully out of the Goldsmiths' assay office.

⋆ ⋆ ⋆

A pale sunlight, more silver than gold, bathed the gilded domes of St Isaac's Monastery a mile or two outside Odessa, bringing with it a firm promise of warmth in the unfolding Russian spring. In his ornate study, sitting at a desk placed below a great icon of the Holy Trinity, Archimandrite Seraphim gravely listened to his visitor.

'I have come, you see, as arranged, despite the griefs and sorrows that have burdened me in recent months. I have buried my good husband, and listened to the plaudits of the thousands who revered him. Let him rest in peace, and rise in glory! I have buried my English years with him in his tomb. I come now, Father, to reclaim the past.'

She still speaks Russian fluently, thought Archimandrite Seraphim, but she speaks it with a decidedly foreign accent. Those English years of hers will not remain buried for long. She spoke to me earlier of her love for Odessa. Well, time will tell whether an unacknowledged love for London will ultimately prove stronger.

'You have known great sorrows, Lady Courteline,' he said aloud, 'and they cannot be quickly assuaged. You must accept them as part of your personal heritage. Remember, too, Maria Alexeievna, that my monastery is not a place that holds, as though preserved by miracle, the images of youth. He is much changed.'

Lady Courteline caught the note of compassion in the Orthodox prelate's voice, and turned pale. She suddenly recalled the chilling description of Charles Dickens's Dr Manette in *A Tale of Two Cities*, a creature reduced from vibrant humanity to a vacant mind imprisoned in a withered, parchment-like body, and preserved in torn rags. She shuddered. Seraphim, reading her thoughts, stood up.

'Come,' he said, 'I will take you to him.'

They walked along one side of a white cloister, and into a quiet passageway containing a number of rooms. Seraphim opened the door of one of them, and motioned Lady Courteline to enter.

The man she had come to see sat in a tall chair beside an open window, a bent and aged figure with gnarled hands like the exposed roots of dead trees. His thin face was almost completely hidden by a long and fulsome white beard. She saw that his right eye was blind, and that the left could focus only with difficulty. She crossed the room, and placed her fingers on one of the gnarled, unmoving hands.

'Nikolai Ivanovich Karenin,' said Fr Seraphim, 'you have a visitor today. I will leave you together.' Turning to Lady Courteline, he added in a low voice, 'He is frail, and older than his years, but his health is quite sound. Come to see me before you return to Odessa.'

* * *

'I thought, you see, that you had avenged yourself on John by shooting him. I have never in my life experienced such desolation and despair when I saw your calling-card beside my husband's hand.'

Dr Karenin permitted himself a slight smile. He moved in the tall chair, and looked at the woman who had been talking to him for the last half-hour. It had been twenty-five years since he had seen her, but it seemed more like a century. He was glad of the visit, moved, even; but Maria Alexeievna was as one with the many faded daguerreotypes of his long-dead family that the good fathers had shown him when they had begun their task of dragging him, body and soul, from the living death of the Imperial Russian prison system.

'No, I would not have done such a wicked thing. My quarrel was with a dying social system, not with poor fellow-victims and their foreign friends. That quarrel is over for me, though others, no doubt, will continue it. Look at me, Maria: could such a human wreck have embarked on a venture of that nature? You say that my simulacrum, this second Dr Karenin, hired a professional assassin to do the deed. How would a man, imprisoned in the labour colonies of Siberia for a quarter of a century, know how to do that? When we are finally expelled from those places, Maria, we are like the dead.'

'But you hated him, I expect?'

'No! That is your woman's vanity speaking. After my arrest, I was as good as dead. John Courteline was alive, a man with great prospects. You did right to marry him.'

Dr Karenin stopped speaking, and his eyelids began to close. A table stood beside him, on which reposed a great open Russian Bible, and an anthology of prayers. Lady Courteline glanced round the room. It was not a monk's cell, but a well-furnished guest room. Nikolai Ivanovich belonged here.

She looked at him, old before his years, his revolutionary zeal silenced, and suddenly felt great pity and anger for his situation. And with that pity came a realization that her consuming love for this man had in reality perished in the '60s, leaving only a romantic illusion behind. It was with John Courteline that her true life had been lived out.

'Nikolai,' she said, laying a hand once more on his sleeve, and watching his tired eyes open and focus once more, 'there is something that I must know about those vanished times. It has been said that John Courteline betrayed you to the authorities so that he could marry me. Was that true?'

'No! I have heard of that false calumny. Courteline did nothing of the sort. I was betrayed by my 'faithful' friend and fellow dissident, Zinoviev, who was in the pay of the secret police. It was they who circulated that rumour in order to protect their informer. They made a point of telling me so, soon after I was taken to the Peter-Paul Fortress! It is all folly, and all past. My life will be lived out here, at the Monastery of the Holy Trinity, in the tender care of the holy Archimandrite Seraphim and his brethren.'

'I will say goodbye, then, Nikolai Ivanovich. By seeing you, some of the ghosts of my troubled past have been laid.'

'Goodbye, Maria Alexeievna,' said Dr Karenin. 'Remember, that I am a guest here, not a monk. You can visit when you will, and I will enjoy talking to you about the olden times.'

'No, my friend,' said Lady Courteline. 'It is all folly, and all past. If I call — *when* I call — we will talk about the present, and about the many steps that must be taken on the road to your complete restoration. In the meantime, I will return to London, and throw my energies into continuing the many saving works instituted by my late husband. My work shall be his memorial.'

She gently kissed the ruined man on the brow, and saw his pleased but passionless smile of contentment.

* * *

Arnold Box stood on the sandy beach at Porthcurno, looking out to sea. A few hundred yards offshore a ship lay at anchor, smoke drifting lazily from its single funnel. A crowd of men had assembled at the sea's edge to help as a new imperial cable was floated into Porthcurno Bay on a long line of bobbing buoys.

'It's an amazing business, Bob,' said Box, shading his eyes against the bright sunlight of the May afternoon. 'That ship out there — it makes me think of the *Lermontov*, lying in wait for us off the Rundstedt Channel.'

Bob Jones laughed, and removed his pipe from his mouth.

'That's the old *Venturer*, Mr Box. No hidden shells in her. She's a good old British cable-layer. Come on, let's leave them to it.'

He turned away from the beach, and Box followed him up the steep path that would take them both back to Porthcurno Cable Station. The way was bright with early summer flowers, and a warm breeze blew.

'Porthcurno's an amazing place altogether, Mr Box,' said Bob Jones, 'but it's only the tip of the iceberg where the Eastern Telegraph Company's concerned. We've got twenty-three thousand miles of submarine cable altogether, and sixty-four cable stations. You'll find us in France and Spain, in Portugal and Egypt, in — But there, you didn't come down to Cornwall to hear me advertising the company.'

They came at last to the impressive cable station, and stopped on the grass bordering the tennis court. The company's flag blew proudly in the breeze.

'So it's all over, Mr Box?' asked Bob Jones.

'It is. Captain Adams was as good as his word, trailing Bleibner back here to Cornwall, and then alerting Scotland Yard to the fact. We arranged a trap for him, and he walked right in to it. I've spent the morning with my colleague Inspector Tregennis, assembling our evidence, including the signed deposition of Caleb Strange, who witnessed the murder of your friend William Pascoe. Hans Bleibner will pay the ultimate price for the murder of that young man.'

'He was a clever lad, you know,' said Jones, 'and a brave one, too. He's sadly and sorely missed down here at Porthcurno. He was a native Cornishman, and very friendly with Squire Trevannion. I wonder what'll happen to him?'

'In my book, Bob, he was an accessory after the fact, but the powers-that-be think otherwise. They've got the doctors to say that he wasn't responsible for his actions when he harboured Bleibner in his house. I think he'll be back at St Columb's Manor, miraculously restored to sanity, before the month's out.

'But we got our surly friend Sedden, landlord of The Cormorant at Spanish Beach. There's no way that he'll be able to wriggle out of a long spell in gaol. Quite a revelation, he was — a one-man immigration business. They'll be sweeping out a cell for him at Dartmoor before long.'

'Does Captain Adams work for Colonel Kershaw?' asked Bob Jones. 'I feel entitled to ask, seeing that Kershaw, you, and I, were all 'stormed at with shot and shell' together in Prussia.'

'Captain Adams was working *with* Colonel Kershaw, Bob, but he's actually employed by Admiral Sir James Holland, of Naval Intelligence — the man who saved the day last January up in Caithness. In the end the whole lot of us work for the same person. I'm referring, of course, to the Widow Lady who lives in a castle at Windsor.'

Bob Jones laughed good-humouredly, and shook hands with Box.

'You'll find a pony and trap waiting in the stable yard, Mr Box, to take you back to Inspector Tregennis at Truro. I wish you well. Maybe we'll meet again. It's a small world.'

The two men parted, and Bob Jones, recently promoted to chief cipher clerk in place of his dead friend, returned to the main office of the cable station. He was greeted by the busy clicking and clattering of the telegraph engines receiving cables from the farther reaches of the Empire, and transmitting messages in diverse languages to the four corners of the earth.

We do hope that you have enjoyed reading this large print book.

Did you know that all of our titles are available for purchase?

We publish a wide range of high quality large print books including:
Romances, Mysteries, Classics
General Fiction
Non Fiction and Westerns

Special interest titles available in large print are:
The Little Oxford Dictionary
Music Book
Song Book
Hymn Book
Service Book

Also available from us courtesy of Oxford University Press:
Young Readers' Dictionary
(large print edition)
Young Readers' Thesaurus
(large print edition)

For further information or a free brochure, please contact us at:
Ulverscroft Large Print Books Ltd.,
The Green, Bradgate Road, Anstey,
Leicester, LE7 7FU, England.
Tel: (00 44) **0116 236 4325**
Fax: (00 44) **0116 234 0205**